List of Characters

The Gang

Ruth Dillon

Nathan Render

Gwendoline De Montford

Rory Renshaw

Ana Novikov

Luke Chapman

Vanessa Mayfield

Maryam Suncliffe

Renshaw's

Amelia Renshaw - Rory Renshaw's wife and business partner

Corinne – Renshaw's front of house mana~~r

Leia – chef

Lucy and Rowan – Rory and Amelia's twi

GW00481858

Beaudesert

Sylvia Dillon – Ruth's Mum and CEO of the family crane hire business

Steven Dillon – Ruth's Dad and COO of the family crane hire business

Alastair – butler at Beaudesert

Valerie – chef at Beaudesert

Anthony – driver at Beaudesert

The Hartley's– next door neighbours

Anthony – driver

Frank – back up/weekend driver

Heronsfield

Penelope – chef

Mike – butler/estate manager

Adie – nanny

Sunita – maintenance

Sarah – driver

Adam – maintenance

Lydia – cleaner

Mark – gardener and maintenance

Rupert – Gwen's husband

Mr and Mrs Pinecastle – Gwen's Mum and Dad

Linkertons

Lois and Edmund Teedale – Retired history teacher and lab technician and Linkertons

Mrs Francis– Retired science teacher at Linkertons

Beverley Kingsley – Old school friend

The others

Dominic – Nathan Render's personal assistant and tech expert.

Ryan Francis – Mrs Francis' son

Keith – Maryam's Dad

Joshua Hartlepool– Yoga instructor

Chapter 1

Hands under her armpits were frantically tugging, maybe up, or across, she didn't know which way she was moving.

"Babe, babe, open your eyes, look at me, how much have you taken?"

She used all of her remaining strength to flutter open her eyelids to see a familiar face looking at her, anxious. No words came out of her open mouth as she tried to talk and she drifted back unconscious, wondering whose that face was.

She struggled to move. Why couldn't she move?! Strapped down, swaying side to side. Was it in her head? No, a train, she was on a train. No, more likely an ambulance to take her to hospital...." wait no, no I don't want to be save......"

Bright lights above her head. Lots of noises, sensory overload, an overwhelming feeling of wanting to give up.

Voices. Two familiar voices sounding panicked.

"Steven, it's happening again, she needs to be with us".

"No sweetheart, she needs professional help, we need to section her again".

"She needs to be around her family and friends who love and understand her".

The room faded back into silence.

More faces, smiling, looking down at her, this time, less panic, more concern.

She didn't want to be here. Not just here...she didn't want to be anywhere...she just didn't want to be.

"Hey furball".   The husky voice sounded familiar, but who? There were lots of familiar sounds and faces, but nothing seemed to make sense in her head yet. Opening her eyes slowly, she saw,

"Oh, you guuuys. I'm so sor..."

"Please don't apologise, ", Maryam interjected. "You've got nothing to apologise for. Let's just focus on getting you better. I'll call Sylvia to let her know you've come round"

"The whole gang's here you know darling, well, I mean they're on their way. Rory, Amelia and the twins are driving down this evening after school, it breaks up soon I think, Luke will be here this evening too, he's in court today working on some big case, Ana closed the art gallery early and jumped on the first train here and Vanessa doesn't have any gigs this weekend so is driving up as we speak. Nathan will be here, but he's jetting in from Silicon Valley, private jet of course." When Ruth was feeling mean, she would describe Gwen as a gossip monger, but when she was feeling more amenable, she'd describe her as the loquacious friend at the heart of the group. Right now, Ruth just wanted to know what was going on.

"But why are you here, I don't understand"

"Darling, Sylvia sent out an SOS this morning to myself and Ana, after doctors started reducing your sedation, and we, of course got in touch with everyone." Gwen and Ana had always remained in Ruth's Mum's good books as an "approved" friend and Sylvia had stayed in touch with them along with a few others after they finished school and left Coventry.

"Ohhh shit..." It was coming back to Ruth, not flooding, but trickling back, each sad detail.

"Let's leave you to sleep and we'll come back soon. It's a lot to process right?" Maryam always had a knack of reading other people's emotions, probably better than she understood her own and was great at intuitively knowing what they needed emotionally.

"Guys, my work, I was due to present to a new client....erm.....today maybe, I don't know what day it is...I just....."

"They've been contacted, you are officially on sick leave and don't need to think about work, just get better, ok?" Soothed Maryam

"We'll see you soon darling"

Ruth fell into a deep, fitful sleep.

Chapter 2

Amelia looked at her husband, his eyes fixated on the road. He'd got the call from Gwen just after 10 this morning. One of his oldest school friends needed him and he was going to be there for her. He'd spent the rest of the day planning their trip to the Midlands, which was coming a little earlier than they had planned, but it all seemed to be fitting together. Amelia had just left her job for good two days ago and had been getting everything packed up, so she thankfully didn't need to negotiate additional time off. The kids were due to break up from school next week, but they wouldn't miss much on the last few days of term and they were starting a new school in January anyway, so the headteacher gave a special allowance for them to break up early. Rory's own work was mainly focused on a case that was in the research stages at the moment, so he just needed an internet connection and a phone line to work. But that was all going to change soon hopefully.

Amelia was so proud of her husband; he was the kindest, most hardworking guy she had ever met and she loved how loyal he was to his family and friends. The kids were lucky to have him as a dad and she felt so happy to still be in love with him.

"Well, it's only like a week early isn't it, so not the end of the world right? The kids won't miss too much school will they? Do you mind coming early? It's the right thing to do right?" Rory was a successful corporate lawyer and represented large FTSE listed companies in court with such confidence and gravitas, yet in his personal life, he always needed reassurance.

"Of course, Ror, you've done a great job getting this all organised. I'm just sorry I haven't been around much to help out, works just been so…"

"I know, I understand, I've been there too. Remember why we're doing this right?"

"For our family"

"Yes, for our family"

"I'm so excited for our new beginning."

"Me too" Rory sighed a satisfied sigh, knowing everything was well planned and under control.

They pulled up to the gates of Beaudesert house and rang the intercom, immediately getting buzzed in.

"I never cease to be amazed by this place" said Amelia in awe, looking down the beautifully lit driveway until the house came into view, which took her breath away. The lights this year were something else. The porch, which was big enough to drive a land rover through, was home to a huge Christmas tree, probably sourced, like they always did, from a local Warwickshire farm. The front doors had a giant bow tied around them, to make it look like a present, wonderfully over the top fairy lights, lining the exterior of the house and one wall of the stables. The six-car garage looked like it had been extended since they were last here, but wasn't lit up, unsurprisingly as they probably didn't want attention drawn to this building that housed many millions of pounds worth of cars.

Sylvia came to the door before they'd even stopped the car, holding a tray of drinks. Emma and Rowan jumped out of the car,

"Auntie Sylvia!!" they chorused happily.

"Two hot chocolates with extra cream and marshmallows for my two favourite twins! And, mulled wine for you two beautiful people! Welcome welcome!"

"Thanks for having us at such short notice, Sylvia. It should only be a week; we close on the new place next Friday"

"Nonsense! You know you're always welcome here and thank YOU for coming down so quickly, Ruth is so lucky to have such good friend like you. Emma and Rowan are a bundle of joy and we love having you all here. It injects some life into this huge, place. Sometimes, despite all the people here, it feels a little lifeless. And such exciting news that you're coming back to the area! For good, hopefully? Now before you get settled, can I get you some supper? I asked Valerie to stay on to whip you something up."

"I think the kids might appreciate something, thanks Sylvia. Maybe Valerie could just shove some pizzas in and we can sort it from there?" Amelia always felt a little uncomfortable having so many staff to wait on you around Beaudesert, despite knowing that Sylvia made sure each and every one of her staff was treated with the respect they deserved.

"Rightio, I'll let her know. You're in your usual rooms. Are you ok taking your luggage up yourselves, Alastair is off for the weekend." The twins shot off upstairs, leaving Rory and Amelia to bring their suitcases in.

"Before you go Rory," Sylvia continued, "I thought I'd let you know, you're booked in to see her tomorrow morning at 10. They suggested only staying for about 10 minutes and it's just you, no-one else."

"Oh, thank you for sorting that out Sylvia. Is there anything she has asked for, magazines, chocolate?"

"No, she's not asked for anything. Physically she's quite tired still, but mentally she seems quite strong, she's talking about plans she's making for the future, it's as if this latest visit to hospital has been her final straw and she is resolved to not let it happen again. I think she'll be out in a day or so"

"That is the best news." Rory gave a tired smile

"OK, I'll give you 20 minutes, then see you in the kitchen for supper?" Chop chop ordered Sylvia.

Rory picked up the last suitcase and followed Amelia who was already carrying three suitcases upstairs. They'd packed light, knowing that the removal company would be packing the rest of their things and bringing it to their new house in a week, so if they'd forgotten something, it would only be a week they'd have to do without. Rory and Amelia had always been made to feel welcome at Ruth's parent's house. They generally stayed at Beaudesert three or four times a year for a couple of days when they came back to see friends and family. Rory no longer had family in the Midlands, his parents having retired to Bournemouth 7 years ago so, Sylvia always insisted that him and his family stayed there whenever they needed to; having known the place since he was at school, it felt like a second home to him. Amelia's family lived in Coventry, but their tiny flat couldn't comfortably accommodate the family of four descending on them, it would be completely taken over by the Renshaw family, so Beaudesert was a good base for them.

They met in the kitchen 20 minutes later for pizza, and mince pies. This was the second kitchen, not where Valerie worked and cooked up her mouth-watering creations, but the one for informal entertaining and dining with a breakfast bar the size of some people's entire kitchen.

"Stevens on a call with a client in the US, I think he'll be there for a few hours, so he'll come and say hi in the morning. Brexit hit us quite hard, so we're trying to foster new business in America and the UAE at the moment. We have a wonderful new business development director, but Steven is finding it hard to delegate responsibility of that area." Rory thought it might not be just Steven who had kept his position as chief operating officer since his early thirties, who was reluctant to let go. Sylvia and Steven ran a successful international crane hire business and, now both in their 70's should really be looking to retire and hand the business over. Having been in Sylvias family for 180 years, she was reluctant to let the business go outside the family, but since Ruth had shown no interest in taking over, it was beginning to look like they had no choice.

Sufficiently fed and watered and caught up on life in general, they all headed to bed. "Do help yourself to breakfast when you're up in the morning" called Sylvia. "it's in the usual place. Sleep well"

Chapter 3

"I'll probably be gone only about an hour. I'm booked in for a slot for 10 minutes and the rest of the time will be travel." Rory was running through with Amelia when he was seeing Ruth the next day.

"Sounds good. Does she need us to get her anything?" Amelia knew Ruth could never resist a travel magazine or a galaxy chocolate bar.

"No, I asked Sylvia and she thinks she'll be out in a day or so."

"That's great news! Remember to send her my love." She said, before opening the door to the twin's room and diving headfirst into a room that was not filled with calm bedtime vibes.

"Mummy, please can we ride the horses tomorrow? Pleeeeeaase!!"

"It's not up to me Rowan, but we can ask Aunty Sylvia in the morning"

"Yaaay! Thanks Mum"

"Night night you two, I love you" Chimed Rory and Amelia.

Despite Sylvia offering Rowan and Emma their own rooms, they always insisted on sleeping in the same room, so she kindly moved two beds into one room and let them use the other room as a playroom. They hadn't been apart since birth and generally got on like a house on fire and Amelia knew this may not last forever, so she clung onto this closeness. It did occasionally cross her mind how they would cope in the real world when they were adults, but she was sure their independence would come.

Amelia was slathering moisturiser onto her hands tucked up in bed, thinking about the adventure they were starting. Over the last decade, Amelia and her husband had crafted successful careers in corporate law and IT. They had enjoyed their corporate careers as much as was reasonably possible with the pressure involved, and it had enabled them to have amazing holidays, give their children opportunities that money helps with such as private school and violin and flute lessons, but they were missing out on living life. They realised that there was more to life than living in their offices and having other people look after their children.

Both Amelia and Rory were coincidently from Coventry. They didn't meet in Coventry, they met in London through mutual friends and only later found out they were both from the same place. Warwickshire and the Midlands felt like home for both Rory and Amelia, so it seemed the natural place for them to gravitate back to. So, they concocted a plan to move back, to start up a small restaurant and make time to enjoy their young family. The plan had been 2 years since its inception and it was now actually happening. They had sold their family home of 9 years, Amelia had given up her job, Rory had taken on a consultative role at his company, rather than being directly client facing, meaning he could work remotely a lot more and they had got the kids a place at a new school. They had found a location for their restaurant and were signing the contract for the lease in January. A chef was ready to start working on a new menu, local suppliers were contracted ready to start supplying food when they opened, contractors ready to go, to install a new commercial kitchen and a marketing campaign all prepped to entice local business and influencers to their launch party.

Work had been so busy the last few months whilst Amelia handed over to her successor and tied up as many loose ends as she could. Her career in the IT industry may have been coming to an end, but she still wanted to leave a strong legacy and with her good reputation intact, taking a premature step back was not an option.

The whole move had been kept a secret from their friends and family because there were so many moving parts, it could fall down at any moment and they didn't want to put that disappointment onto other people. They also didn't want to have to keep on giving updates when there were so many unknown factors. Now, it was definitely happening, they could start to tell people. Amelia hoped no-one minded that they hadn't consulted them. Sylvia was one of the first people they had told of their impending move, but only this morning when Rory asked if they could stay at Beaudesert over Christmas before they moved house. Amelia was planning on seeing her Mum and stepdad tomorrow with the twins whilst Rory visited Ruth if she was well enough for visitors and she was hoping to broach the subject then. Her stepdad was always supportive of anything she wanted to do, but her Mum less so. Slightly more old fashioned in her views, she always wondered why Amelia worked so hard for her career, when Rory earned enough to support the entire family. In her Mum's eyes, women did not work but had children and kept a household running. A career was something her Mum would never understand. Amelia's Mum, Julie loved her daughter and her Grandkids, there was no doubt about that, but she had some morals that Amelia did not want imposed on the twins. Amelia was proof that hard work and dedication can get you to where you want to be and this work ethic was not inherited, but learnt through a want, a necessity to create and understand her own value and self-worth.

Chapter 4

Nathan got the WhatsApp from Gwen at 1.00 in the morning. He was still up because he was working on coding for a new project. He had many people to do this coding for him now, but this project was so ground breaking, with the potential to affect so many people for the better, he didn't want to delegate for fear of errors being made early on and the high risk of the idea and initial coding being stolen.

He sold his baby, "Groop" a dating app that brings people together through their hobbies, five years ago. You enter what your hobbies are in your profile and are then matched with people of similar interests. He'd made enough money to never have to work again, but he enjoyed his work and even more so now that he was doing it for fun. His latest venture was in conjunction with a private healthcare and research company; they were creating an app, that, along with some external monitors, would allow certain health conditions to be monitored and tracked at home, resulting in less physical time at the hospital, reducing strain on hospitals all round the world and reducing potential spread of viruses and diseases... something on all of our minds after the last four years of covid's presence. He'd secured funding from one of silicon valley's top software companies and had access to research and medical professionals to ensure he was using the right medical data and the future was looking sunny.

Ruth was one of his oldest friends from school and he wished it was in his power to make her happy. She'd always struggled with her mental health, battling depression and crippling anxiety as well as being diagnosed with borderline personality disorder. Despite this though, she had become so successful professionally and personally on her own, with no use of her parent's money or name. He was proud of her and would do anything to help her enjoy life. His invites for her to cross the pond and stay with him for some R&R were always turned down as she had too much work, or an ultra-marathon to train for, or was singing at a local bar. He'd always thought her work life and being permanently on the go was her attempt at concealing her sadness from the outside world. Nathan could always see through her and knew if she was lying about being OK. He wondered if he could create something within the tech industry that could help facilitate a way of being happy? He made it sound so simple and straightforward. He banked that thought for another time.

A quick call to Dominic downstairs and his flight was secured for 6am. Well aware of the extravagance and environmental impact of a private jet, Nathan had promised himself he wouldn't use it forever, just whilst he was flying between countries for meetings for this latest app, which he was adamant could reduce pressure on hospitals in all countries across the world. He made a feeble attempt at offsetting his carbon footprint by not having a private car and driver and getting public taxis everywhere if he needed road travel. His Jet was at an airfield only 10 miles away from his duplex condo, so shouldn't take too long to get there, but he didn't want to risk getting stuck in traffic and missing his slot, so got everything ready he needed straight away. He wasn't expecting to be away for more than 2 weeks, so wouldn't need that many clothes. No-one needed to know that he was away and nothing needed to be rearranged because all of his work calls could be done remotely. Tech guys weren't expected to be in the office, especially when they were working on coding. Plus, his investors would be breaking up for the Christmas break soon and heading off to their respective families. Sure, they'd still be working, but they'd also be at home, so it didn't matter what country he was in.

Four and a half hours later, Nathan was sat comfortably on his flight. Of course, he didn't miss it, he never missed anything, was never late, never omitted details, was fastidious in his planning, or at least Dominic was fastidious in his planning. That was part of his personality that had helped make him so successful, from being able to understand the intricacies of coding an app, to managing a multi-million-pound business (albeit that was only for a short amount of time before he sold it), to his attention to detail.

Looking across at Dominic, his ever loyal, hardworking, trustworthy personal assistant, he wondered what he should do with him. Dominic had been with him since he had launched his app, pandering to Nathan's every whim. His job title was PA, but he was so much more than that; he was fairly tech savvy himself and was a great person to bounce ideas off as he understood the industry, he was a confidante that Nathan needed, a constant in his life when he was always travelling around, moving from hotel to hotel, apartment to apartment and most importantly, a friend. It was because of this, that Nathan was considering letting him go. Dominic was single, seemingly had no friends or hobbies, spent the rare time that he took as vacation, by himself and never seemed to experience his own version of a fun of life, only living Nathan's version. Nathan worried that he was holding him back and stopping him from building a life he could call his own.

Nathan hadn't really had relationships himself before, and quite frankly didn't know what he wanted out of life long-term. He knew he was happy right now, he enjoyed working and when he stopped enjoying work, he would do something else. He had plenty of 'outside circle' friends, as he called them, that he saw on a regular basis in the US, whom he went out partying with, shopping, short holidays, and that sort of thing, but they weren't close, 'inside circle' friends like his English friends from school. The great thing about his inside circle friends was that, as much as he missed them, in a way, he didn't miss them, because he knew they were there for him always. It also went the other way; at a drop of a hat, he would be there for them, no matter what. Hence why he was now spending Christmas back in England instead of partying in Las Vegas.

Sylvia, Ruth's Mum had kindly been in touch, knowing that he was travelling from the States and had offered to put him up for as long as he needed. She said it was no trouble and that she'd enjoy having him there. He believed her, but he needed his own space and he was bringing Dominic with him, so it seemed fairer to rent somewhere for 2 weeks.

Chapter 5

This morning felt better. The events of the past fortnight were becoming a little clearer in her mind and the daily therapy was helping. It had been almost 2 weeks since her friend, well more like colleague and drinking pal, had found her in her flat, having overdosed after a night out. They were celebrating Sarah's successful onboarding of a new client and were partying to the limit, like they normally did, in their usual haunts across Knightsbridge. But this night was different for Ruth. She'd recently miscarried; her 4th miscarriage in a row and she felt her life was beginning to crumble around her.

To an outsider, she had it all, a high-profile job as a senior partner in a digital marketing agency, a great group of friends, parents who always loved and supported her in her desire to not join the family business, she didn't even need to work as her inheritance would be more than sufficient for the rest of her life. She threw herself into anything she tried, resulting in her becoming accomplished in so many areas, horse riding, skiing and fencing to name a few of her childhood hobbies, while her life in London resulted in her becoming an experienced ultramarathon runner, amateur singer songwriter and guitar player and a regular yoga practitioner. But what she didn't have was children and to Ruth, there was a huge space in her heart for them. She hadn't met the right person yet, so decided to do it alone, but multiple cycles of ivf and 4 miscarriages was having its toll on her mental health.

Sarah could see Ruth struggling; her friend had been back at work the day after her miscarriage, giving herself no time to process the trauma and loss she was experiencing and tonight she wasn't her usual self. Sure, she was normally a big drinker, but she was a happy, bubbly drinker and the life and soul of the party. That night, she had been drinking particularly heavily and just didn't want to talk, despite Sarah's attempts at getting her to open up, Ruth seemed to just want to drown herself in drink. They shared a taxi home, along with another colleague who lived in the same area.

"Thanks for everything guys, I mean it." Ruth slurred as the taxi dropped her off. As Sarah was shimmying into her Liberties silk pyjamas, Ruth's last comment didn't sit well with her. She'd normally have some sort of sarcastic, jokey comment to throw out, she was never one for serious goodbyes after a night out. Ruth wasn't picking up her landline or mobile, which wasn't surprising given how drunk she'd been, so Sarah decided to pop back over there. She didn't need a key; a mate of Ruth's, a tech entrepreneur schoolfriend had set up a secondary security system that overrode the physical electronic key that Ruth normally used, allowing entry to her flat, using retina recognition. It was installed 3 years ago, following a period when Ruth was struggling with her borderline personality disorder. Luckily, Sarah found Ruth in time for her stomach to be pumped and there was no lasting organ damage as far as they could tell.

Ruth spent the rest of that night in A&E before being transferred to a ward where she was stabilised. When she came to, she was violent, lashed out at the medical staff caring for her and started headbutting the wall, so she was sedated, which was when her parents arrived.

They made arrangements to transfer Ruth to the priory in Birmingham for psychiatric care once she was physically stable, but she was still quite heavily sedated so the journey was all a bit of a blur. She remembered her parents being around a lot, and then the girls, Maryam and Gwen had visited and so had Vanessa along with a basket of bread, or was that a bouquet of flowers. Ana had been there, definitely Rory and Luke and then she was sure that Fergus, an ex-boyfriend had visited...Pah! That was definitely the drugs working some cuckoo magic!

After multiple daily therapy sessions, talking to groups, people who looked like they understood and cared, people who really didn't, people who sat there in silence waiting for you to speak and pour out your emotions whilst they make notes, giving a label to your "illness", she was starting to feel better. She'd been here before and wondered what diagnosis they'd come up with this time...Schizophrenia, bi-polar, clinical depression, severe anxiety, alcoholism, psychosis, personality disorder. Ruth knew that these labels were supposed to help her focus and work through her issues and understand when she needed to get help, but for her, this didn't work. Her therapy was being around friends and family, she'd always been a social butterfly. She hated these hospitals and just wanted to get home, so was complying with everything she had to and knew the right things to say to make her seem safe and in control again, despite the fact that she really felt the complete opposite.

Each therapy session, she would plaster on a happy smile and talk about how she was feeling much more positive, and looking forward to the future, but she was thinking about her lost babies, she must be doing something wrong surely to not be able to carry a baby full term. The agonising period like pain that she went through in the days after her last miscarriage almost felt like a punishment, she deserved for losing those babies. She almost enjoyed having to rush off halfway through her presentation to a new vegan make up brand to throw up in the toilets because of the pain and almost fainting on the way to the breakout area because of her heavy blood loss, because it felt like she was pushing her body to the limit as a way of saying sorry to those unborn babies.

But this morning really did feel better. Her closest friends from school had individually visited over the past few days and today they were all coming to visit her at the same time. She also had a meeting this afternoon to assess the possibility of her moving back home; back home meaning into her parents' house for a while, to recuperate.

The gang had been together throughout school, some of the group joining a little later than others. They had been such close friends for the majority of their youth, but grown apart a little in recent years. Not to the point of not speaking, they just couldn't meet up as much as they wanted to, with work and family commitments, but whenever they did meet up whether it was in person, or over video calls, it was like they had never been apart.

It wasn't the first time they had all visited her in a psychiatric hospital, but this was the first time she'd tried to kill herself. She really needed to pull herself together. Quite how she was going to do that, she didn't know, but something had to change. For now, she was going to savour her friend's company.

The gang all arrived around the same time, waiting for each other in the foyer before going in to Ruth's room. If anyone of them felt awkward to start with, all awkwardness had melted away after five minutes. They hugged, laughed, gossiped, drank lots of tea, reminisced of the "good old times", moaned about work and relationships, celebrated their work and relationships, avoided talk of babies and that thing from school and made plans to meet up on Friday evening in two days' time at Steven and Sylvia's, providing Ruth was back home by then.

Chapter 6

Vanessa rang the ridiculous doorbell at Beaudesert at 6pm on Friday evening. She'd been coming here since she was a little girl, but never failed to feel a little intimidated. She'd never had a huge amount of money, managing to go to the same school as the group on a music scholarship, not because her parents could really afford it. She still didn't have a huge amount of money as aspiring musicians in London are as common as actors in Los Angeles. The gigs that Ruth did for fun, playing her songs were the sort of gigs that Vanessa did as her main source of income. She did of course get other jobs to write jingles for adverts and radio shows, but they were few and far between.

Sylvia came to the door, beaming that everyone had turned out for her daughter and welcomed Vanessa in. Considering she came from old money and was used to this lifestyle, Vanessa always thought that the airs and pretension that came with people with this much wealth were welcomingly absent in Sylvia. She of course loved nice things, but didn't seem to take them for granted.

She walked into the kitchen and saw she was the last person to arrive You would have thought that the musician of the group would be an extrovert and love being the centre of attention, but Vanessa didn't epitomise this stereotype, she preferred working behind the scenes and composing, so having all eyes turned to her, even if it was her closest friends, made her feel uncomfortable. She felt an arm at her side. Maryam steered her towards the bar area away from the main group, giving her the chance to greet everyone in smaller groups.

"Thanks, hun. Good day?"

"Productive thanks. Approved final payroll for December, paying it early this month, before Christmas. Snowball?"

"Mmm please, small one I'm driving."

Maryam poured Vanessa a snowball, making small talk about her day before joining Luke and Ruth. Luke was chatting animatedly about his current case at work. Trying to be as anonymous as possible, he was describing an organised crime case and explained that he was representing some teenagers that had got unintentionally caught up in it. Ruth looked great, maybe not her usual glowing, bubbly self, but she was cheery – surely a façade.

"Well, I certainly don't have exciting stories like that from my work" Chuckled Maryam.

"But you're not getting death threats because you're representing members of an organised crime gang either" said Luke dramatically. "Comes with the territory of being a criminal lawyer."

"Furball!" Gwen closed in on Ruth and linked arms with her affectionately, Ruth allowing herself to be herded gently by Gwen, inwardly rolling her eyes at Gwen's nickname that she hadn't been able to shake for thirty years.

"Remind me again why Gwen calls Ruth Furball" muttered Amelia to Rory.

"Because her hair was so curly and frizzy when she was younger that we all thought she looked like an adorable furball."

"You sure she doesn't mind still being called Furball?"

"Naaah, of course not, its endearing"

"Oh Mum, these mince pies…" said Ruth in disgust as she bit into a mince pie

"Yes Ruth, I made them this morning with the twins. Along with those flat looking muffins and that quiche. Don't worry, Valerie is still with us, she's just with her family this weekend."

"Ooooh, I was about to say they are soooo yummy!" Smiled Ruth cheekily as she put the rock-solid mince pie back down on her plate.

Validated, Rowan and Emma gave each other a "well-done" nudge.

"Right, bedtime you two", Said Amelia, shuffling the twins upstairs after they managed to make a quick goodnight to everybody last 20 minutes. Kids were so manipulative sometimes!

Ameila came back downstairs to find Sylvia and Steven had made their excuses and also headed to bed. Gwen was insensitively retelling her story of Sylvia calling her to give the news of Ruth's hospitalisation.

"…and when I heard you were being pulled out of your coma, I just HAD to come and see you furball"

Ruth inwardly rolled her eyes again. "I wasn't in a coma then; I was just sedated for a short amount of time."

"OK darling, you know what I mean. Well anyway, you have no lasting physical damage and we will all cheer you up like we always do" Gwen always meant well, but her words didn't always help, or show any element of understanding her situation at all.

"Excuse me one moment guys" Apologised Nathan, hurrying out of the room grasping his phone, looking uncharacteristically flustered.

"More drinks anyone? Steven entrusted us with the bar and I'm sure he'd be disappointed if we didn't make use of this lovely looking Cranberry liquor. Cocktails?" Asked Ana.

A murmur of consents and declines ran through the group and Ana set out making overly alcoholic cocktails.

"Actually, we have some exciting news," ventured Rory. "Amelia, myself and the kids are moving back up here permanently and we're giving up our jobs and opening a restaurant in Knowle"

"That's amazing news guys!"

"Ahhhh Congratulations!!"

"Oh wow, that's so exciting!"

"Fantastic!" Nathan had just reappeared, managing to put some enthusiasm into his voice, but looked a little shaken up.

Everyone was so happy for them. Rory and Amelia beamed and enjoyed the kind words and excitement from their friends.

"What are you going to call it?"

"Not 100% certain yet Ruth, but we were thinking possibly Renshaw's. Too narcissistic do you think? We have until Monday to decide, that's our deadline for getting our signage, menus and merchandise printed in time."

"I think its great guys. It's your own creation, so I think you can afford to inject a little narcissism. When are you planning on opening?"

"Second week of January, the Friday. You're all invited of course; I'd love to have you there."

"Wow, so soon! And I think I can speak for everyone and say of course we'll all be there. Is that enough time to prepare for opening night?"

"It'll be close, but I think we'll get it done. We've hired a catering recruitment agency to get some experienced front of house staff. The chef is one of Amelia's friends from school and is bringing her own sous chef, and we've already decided on the menu, which Leia is currently perfecting. We've hired an interior design company and they are designing and doing up the place, with a little artistic direction from us. Everything is ready to go, we'll just need to work over the Christmas period, which as a one off is fine, the kids can get involved. We just can't start on the physical preparations until the lease is finalised. Hopefully well be signing on the dotted line this Wednesday and the lease will start on the 27th December! We've come across a minor stumbling block in that the seller of the house we were meant to move into pulled out yesterday. We were meant to exchange today, so quite frustrating, but we're going to rent for a few months instead and Sylvia and Steven have kindly let us stay here whilst we find a rental property which should be fairly quick."

Rory looked at Ruth, trying to gauge her reaction and hoping she didn't mind them staying, but her expression was genuine joy. Rory relaxed. He was so excited for this new chapter in their lives.

Chapter 7

Vanessa was deep in thought on the drive back to her budget hotel. She'd declined Maryam's offer to stay at her apartment, just wanting some space away from the seemingly superior success of her friends. Listing them off in her head, she knew not everyone in the group was a millionaire, or even extremely wealthy, but they were all good at something, had succeeded at something. Rory was at the top of his game, doing whatever lawyers in the corporate world do and now opening a restaurant, Ruth was really senior at her company doing marketing stuff, yes her personal life wasn't all that peachy at the moment, but that would soon change, Luke didn't earn much money as a criminal defence lawyer, but he loved his job and always got the really high profile cases, so he must be doing well at his job, Nathan, well Nathan just flew in by private jet from LA so that speaks for itself, Ana owned a successful art gallery, which, OK, was started with family money, but she ran it so well and was so good at finding new talent and new buyers, that she felt she had earned the right to call herself a successful business woman, Maryam was a finance director at a large corporate property management firm, her next role would surely be CFO and you don't get much more senior than that in the finance world. And then there was Gwen, she didn't work, she didn't have to coming from old family money and marrying into more old money, but she had built a strong, happy marriage, had two happy young children, and always seemed to be winning, even when she was running around after the kids. Vanessa felt like the only one out of all of her friends who had nothing to be proud of in her life.

Well, next year, that was going to change. She'd had enough of just scraping by, doing gigs and bar work in crummy bars in London just to earn her rent, writing cheap jingles for the radio with no artistic licence, she felt like she was cheapening herself as an artist, all the while lying to her friends that she really was enjoying what she was doing. She really wasn't.

Children were definitely going to be a part of Vanessa's life, but she wasn't sure whether she was a strong as Ruth to do it by herself. She really did want to be in a relationship, but never seemed to be able to stay in a relationship for more than a year. She bounced from partner to partner, gradually refining her tick list of requirements in a man, till she was sure there was no-one out there for her. Perhaps she needed to try something new.

No, this coming year was her year. She pulled into the dark hotel car park with a renewed optimism and sense of purpose. Closing her door to the world, she rolled out her yoga mat and tried to focus. She'd always practiced yoga, but had just completed a yoga teachers class so she could run her own classes for a bit of extra cash on the side. But hopefully she wouldn't need to run those classes. She was going to finish this musical, she was going to get recognised, she was going to get her musical produced in a theatre, she was going to be known as one of this century's best composers.

Chapter 8

"Mum, Mum, Daaad"

"Daaaaad, DaaaaaadddddyyyyyY"

"Morning you two" Amelia's head was swimming a little after Ana's cocktails last night.

"Please can we go horse riding, please please please"

"Let's go and get some breakfast first and then we'll ask Aunty Sylv..."

"We've already had breakfast"

"Uncle Steven made us porridge"

"He let us put jam in it"

"I put loads in!"

"Uncle Steven said that Poppy and Joyce are at the stables this morning and he'll ask them to take us out on the horses."

"Well OK, if that's ok with ..."

"Thanks Mum"

"Thanks Mum"

"Rory, is this, ok? Our children have been fed by Steven and are now going out horse riding again with the stable girls. Are we using Sylvia and Steven's hospitality a little too much?"

"Hmmmmm? I'm sure they don't mind. Ill chat with them later. In the meantime," He grinned and lifted his eyebrows at his wife. She threw her head back and laughed.

The Renshaw's spent a lovely weekend together. The kids went out horse riding on Saturday morning and in the afternoon, Ruth came with them to see Santa at Evesdale farm and then Rory made everyone lasagne for dinner, while Sylvia made a bread-and-butter pudding. Sylvia and Steven were enjoying having so many people round the house and Ruth seemed to be looking a little more carefree.

Ruth was indeed starting to feel more like herself. She was slowly weaning herself off the antidepressants the hospital had put her on (not at the advice of her doctor). She knew she was depressed, but felt that antidepressants were not the right path for her this time. Being around her friends and family truly was helping, but she knew this couldn't be permanent. She acknowledged that you don't always need something to be fixed to stop depression, sometimes you may have a perfect life, but you're depressed. You don't have to have something that is broken in your life to explain depression. But this time, there was something broken and not right in her life. She wanted children; she had tried to have children and failed. This was why she was not happy; she knew the reason this time. To help her through previous depressions, she tended to focus on a project and this is what she needed this time. Currently signed off work, she decided to make use of that headspace and not start her new business plan that she wanted to present to the board on her return. Plenty of time for that. She'd start small and decided to sign up to another ultramarathon and focus on training for that. Much better than a thinking project given her current state of mind. Once she was feeling a little more well, perhaps she'd start thinking about planning that ultramarathon race through local countryside that she'd always wanted to run.

She put her planned project on hold for now and composed herself before meeting her parent's pretentious neighbours. They'd popped round under the pretence of wishing Ruth well, but really it was for a gossip. Sylvia hadn't kept the reason for Ruth's return a secret, telling anyone who wanted to know, but she hadn't gone out of her way to tell people. The Hartley's next door went out of their way to find out and spread gossip, which neither Ruth, nor her parents liked. They endured their neighbours through necessity, not through desire.

Ruth inwardly groaned as she came downstairs as slowly as she could without appearing like a moody teenager. She heard her neighbours congregating in the hallway, her parents refusing to invite them further into the house. Although the hallway at Beaudesert was more comfortable than most hallways and had sofas and a table, so still could be used for brief visits, or for visits where you didn't want guests to get too comfortable. She could also hear the voice of Louise, the Hartley's daughter, who must have come across with them. Of course, she did, she still lived there and loved a bit of gossip, just like her parents. Louise was one of Ruth's childhood friends, partly through convenience because they lived next door and there weren't many other houses or children nearby and partly because they really did enjoy playing with each other. They started growing apart from about age 10 and despite going to the same school, became distinctly not friends by year 9. Ruth thought Louise too prim, proper and perfect. Louise considered Ruth a diamond in the rough, who, if only she could get her hands on her, could be polished to high perfection.

"Ruthy darling!" called her shrill voice. She made a mental note to have words with Rory later; as soon as he heard the Hartley's were coming over, he quickly made plans to take the family to Warwick castle. Louise had a crush on Rory throughout school and wouldn't leave him alone, so whenever there was a slight chance that Louise might be around, Rory avoided the occasion at all costs – he could have at least left Amelia with me as back up thought Ruth. She politely greeted the three unwelcome well-wishers and answered their thoughtless and somewhat spiteful questions.

 "Why did you do it Ruth?"

"Did you not think of your poor parents?"

"Well, it's all over now isn't it."

"When are you going to settle down?"

"What about children, you're getting on a bit now aren't you, I mean…. Oh, gosh, the miscarriages, I completely forgot about that! Oh, you poor doll! Gosh, I won't mention children again"

"Actually, I'm going to focus on a new project for a few months, an ultramarathon race that I'm going to plan and also run myself, going through the Warwickshire countryside." She picked up her phone and showed everyone the route that she had in mind. She'd drawn this route on google maps years ago, so it would probably need changing, but it was a start. 'Thank you Mr and Mrs Hartley', she thought, you have just made me decide that this is happening.

"Good for you!" shrilled Louise in such a patronising tone, Ruth had to pause a moment to stop herself from slapping her.

"Thanks, I'm looking forward to it. You can be the first entrant If you'd like Louise?" Ruth knew full well that Louise didn't run outside – she might get sun damage on her alabaster skin.

"What a lovely offer Ruth, thank you. I'm sure I'd have a blast completing it, but I couldn't tear myself away for that long from the family with all the training needed. But why don't I give you the number of my yoga teacher instead? He's wonderful and I'm sure you could do with some stretching after all those long runs."

"Actually Louise, that would be great thanks. I was starting to miss my hot yoga class in London, so that would be perfect."

Steven quickly wrapped up the gathering using some excuse that he needed to run through a new marketing campaign with Ruth. Sylvia couldn't help noticing that Louise looked a little more shifty than usual, but then again, she'd never liked that girl, so she was probably biased.

Chapter 9

"How was Warwick castle folks? I love, that place, I've not been in years!!" Rory and the family were back at Beaudesert and were having dinner in the kitchen with Ruth, Sylvia and Steven.

"It was sooooo good, we climbed up all the towers" Said Emma

"And there were really smelly dungeons and a trebshay" Said Rowan

"Treb-u-chet" Corrected Amelia

"Trebleshay"

"Treb-u-chet" Amelia tried to correct again. She was enjoying this final informal dinner before Valerie came back after her few days off – they'd surely start having more formal dinners then.

"Yeah, that thing, and it was sooo cool"

"And we saw real horses with knights on them and everything!"

"Ooh there was a show was there? Amaaazing! I hope you took lots of photos?" Ruth enthused.

"Well, Mum won't let us touch her camera and Dad won't let us have his phone to take photos because he says we always start watching you tube videos on it, so not really."

"And DO you watch you tube videos on your dad's phone?" Asked Ruth, amused, even more amused by Rory and Amelia's weary faces.

"Yes, we do, and then he chases us to get his phone back, but can't catch us for a while"

"Because we're so fast"

"And it's funny!"

"Think you should change you pin number mate! Anyway, you and I need words! I can't believe you bailed on me earlier. You had a lucky escape because Louise did indeed come over and boy was she on top form! Dad saved me, saying he had to run through a new marketing campaign with him...a flat out lie and Dad hates lying, so that shows how little he likes them coming round."

"Anything for my number 1 child darling" Said Steven between mouthfuls.

"Your only child!" smiled Ruth. For a moment, Steven thought she looked at him with such innocent happiness, like she did when she was younger. Oh, if he could only bring an ounce of that back.

A car pulled up and the doorbell rang. Sylvia jumped up, about to answer the door, but Ruth stopped her.

"It's ok Mum, it's just Louise. She said she'd pop round this evening with her yoga instructor's number"

"Goodness me, why can't she text that to you!" Exclaimed Sylvia.

"I can probably guess why!" Said Ruth, her eyes twinkling at Rory who looked like he was trying to melt into his chair.

"Darling!" Louise shrieked as soon as Ruth opened the door. "Here's the number, he's a wonderful instructor and he is mobile as well as having a studio, so can come to you if you don't feel like leaving the house."

"Thanks Louise, I apprecia…"

"I saw another car outside; do you have visitors?" Louise edged herself past Ruth and somehow ended up standing in the hallway. Ruth grudgingly closed the door behind her to keep what heat they still had in this large, drafty house, inside the house.

"Yes, Rory and his family are staying with us for a short while, I'm sure he'd love to see you." Ruth rose her voice at the end of the sentence hoping to prompt Rory to pop his head round the corner. It worked and Rory dutifully bounded into the hallway. Ruth couldn't help but smile.

Not being one to flout normal social etiquette, he pleasantly greeted Louise, tolerating her fawning and non consentual touches and incoherent babble that was something to do with what she had been doing with her life since they last met. Louise was dancing around Rory so ridiculously that she bumped into the side table and knocked off the house phone and mobile. "Well, that knocked her out of that reverie" Thought Ruth.

"Whoops, sorry about that!" Gushed Louise, putting back the phones, checking for damage. "Here's your phone Ruth, I knocked it off the table. Well, I really must be going. Lovely to catch up, see you, I'll see you soon."

"Likewise, Louise."

"Thanks for dropping the number round Louise."

"All good?" Amelia enquired, looking slightly amused as Ruth and Rory came back into the kitchen. "Looking a bit red and blotchy there hun…"

"She was particularly touchy feely tonight. Poor Rory, you're always so polite, I don't know how you do it. She didn't quite seem herself though. What did you think?"

"Well I got my face stroked, she touched my arms and I'm pretty sure she managed to run her hand down my chest when she tripped over so, she seemed pretty normal to me…"

"Yeah, yeah I know that's pretty normal from her, but I just mean she seemed just a little more coy than usual and she wouldn't normally trip over, that's so unlike her and she couldn't even tell you anything meaningful that's been going on with her, like she had another baby two years ago, that's significant news right? She told you about new curtains her parents had just bought. She just normally has her shit together and this evening she most definitely didn't."

"Shit!" the twins repeated. "Shit shit shit!"

"That's a naughty word Aunty Ruth"

"You're not supposed to say that word!"

"Erm… yup correct guys, erm…right thanks for dinner, I'm off to bed. Night night" Ruth made a quick exit, Rory glowering at her

Chapter 10

Luke took the opportunity to pop out for coffee by himself in the morning. Mondays quite often ended up being working from home days for him, and it was nice to have a change of scenery. He'd put the offer out to the gang to see if anyone fancied meeting him, seeing as they were all back in the area and Ruth was planning on popping along in an hour.

He smelt the delicious cakes that were baked on site before he'd even turned round the corner. Corner three coffee shop in Kenilworth had new management and a new name, but he was glad to see it had kept the same rustic and cosy style of the interior that it had twenty years ago when him and the gang used to order hot chocolates and lattes there after school.

He settled down at a table overlooking the high street with his cappuccino and cheese scone and opened up his laptop. His case was going so well and he knew if he did well here, he could really start handling even bigger cases and doing a lot of good both in his career and in the community. He was representing five young lads that had unintentionally become part of an organised crime gang. They were used by the senior echelons of the gang to carry out their dirty work, including intimidation of local business to pay what they called safety money, trying to copy the mafia gangs of old. Along with possession of fire arms and grievous bodily harm of someone who borrowed money from the gang and didn't pay it back in time, these lads were definitely going to prison, but Luke wanted the jury to see that these young men were pulled into this world through certain circumstances that could have been prevented. One of the group he was representing was dyslexic, but this was not picked up early, so he had no additional help at school, struggled to knuckle down, was considered stupid and naughty, so left school at 16 with no qualifications, was kicked out of home because of behavioural issues and turned to a life of crime in order to survive. None of the group had strong family units, some of the group went through the care system, none of the group had any form of stability, even down to their social worker changing every few months and none of the group had access to any free community clubs or groups that might have provided role models, advice or counselling. This was just one case of many, but he ultimately wanted to change the whole prosecution system and his focus was on youths and he knew he was going to get there.

Luke was watching the quiet high street, giving his eyes a break after going through the fine details of another harassment case, to see a blast from the past walking up to the door. She looked around rather vaguely, before setting her eyes on Luke.

"Beverley Kingsley!" Smiled Luke

"Well, what a lovely surprise Luke! What are you doing here? In fact, tell me in a moments, I'm just going to grab coffee, do you want another one? Mind if I join you for ten minutes?"

"I'd love another cappuccino please and yes, that would be lovely!"

Beverley came back with the drinks, rushing to get to the table so quickly that she tripped forward over the chair that Luke had added to the table for her, spilling thankfully only his glass of water over the table. Luke just managed to whip his laptop out of the way and only got water on his trousers.

"I'm so sorry," Gushed Beverley. "Still as clumsy as always" she added sheepishly.

"No harm done, we're all good" reassured Luke. "So how are things with you? What brings you to Kenilworth, did you move from Bromsgrove?"

"Still in Bromsgrove, I'm just here scouting out the market for a new estate agent in the area. We opened our second one in Barnt Green this year and it's doing really well, so we're thinking a third one in Kenilworth or Leamington is a good shout." She added "and I love this place, so I thought I'd pop in for a quick caffeine fix."

"That's great news! Congratulations! I moved back here London a few years ago actually, with Laura. I still work in London; I just commute a few days a week."

"Oh wonderful, I didn't realise! So, is anyone else back in the area for Christmas? You meeting anyone? Got any plans over the break? Any parties? You and the gang usually get together over Christmas don't you?" Interrupted Beverley. An open question suggesting she was prying for more information.

Luke was trying not to give out too much information about Ruth as it was no-one else's business, but he also didn't want to lie, so gave out as little information as he could without coming across rude.

"Yeah, we're all back here now for Christmas. I'm meeting Ruth here a bit later actually."

"Oh, she's back here early. She normally comes home around Christmas eve doesn't she?"

"I, er, I don't know, but, well, Ruth's been in hospital for a short while so that's why she's back in the area before Christmas."

"Oh no poor doll! Is there anything I can do to help? Shall I go and visit? I'm guessing the whole gang is back then? When did you arrive? Is she still in hospital? Which one?" Beverley still had verbal diarrhoea and could never filter what was going on in her head. She had always been on the peripheries of their friendship group, being in the same year at school as them, she had always been invited to their birthday parties and big events and always hung around them, sometimes a little too desperately. They were generally kind to Beverley as she always seemed in need of a friend, but her personality never clicked with the group, so she was never part of the inner circle, but Luke was sure she was content with this, making an effort to stay in touch with all the group over the years since school finished.

"Yes, everyone's back in the Midlands to support Ruth, she's recovering at home with Sylvia and Steven. She might appreciate a message from you, just give her a bit of time before popping over." Luke managed to avoid too many details, but hopefully made Beverley still seem needed; he knew how insecure she was and feeling needed and wanted was important to her.

They caught up with their lives since they had last seen each other a few years ago before Beverley made her excuses about having to rush off. She asked for directions for the loos and then queued up for another coffee to go, whilst Luke video called Laura, his wife of three years, acknowledging Beverley's frantic wave through the window as she rushed off back down the high street.

Hanging up the phone after wishing his wife a good flight, Luke sighed, knowing he was going to miss his wife over the next few days. They were spending the lead up to Christmas separately for the first time since they had met. Laura was flying Edinburgh to celebrate an early Christmas with her mum who was in a home suffering from dementia. They normally alternated Christmases between their parents, but Laura was worried this might be her mum's last one, so she wanted to spend some time just the two of them. She was planning on flying home on Christmas eve, so Luke wouldn't see her for almost a week.

With Laura being a senior partner in a corporate law firm, and Luke being called to the police station at all hours of the day, their time together was far from frequent and made each moment together even more precious. Since their works had become more demanding, they had made a pact with each other that they would always have at least one night a year together on New Years eve. This year, they had booked a food delivery box from a two Michelin star restaurant they visited on one of their first weekends away together in York. They'd used these boxes before, but not from a restaurant, so this would hopefully be a bit more special. The box would contain a partially prepared five course meal, that only needed to be put into the oven and plated and Laura was sorting out some special wines. Cooking together was one of their favourite pastimes and if it involved Michelin starred food, even better.

Putting his phone away, he turned back to focus on his work. He had a lot of work to get through, and with Ruth meeting him for a coffee shortly, and then meeting up with Rory later, he had to get his head down.

Chapter 11

Driving down the Birmingham Road to Knowle, Luke was going over his chance meeting with Beverley. He couldn't help thinking it was strange that she was in the area. That particular spot was never one that they met Beverley at – there wasn't a bus route between Kenilworth and Bromsgrove, so she wouldn't have been able to get home; Beverley only met them in Coventry, after school, or in Birmingham, where she could reliably get a bus or train home to her neglectful parents, so it seemed strange that she would be in there today as she had no ties to that coffee shop like he did. But, then again, she did say she was looking to open up a third branch of estate agents, so that explains her whereabouts.

He shook his head and told himself he needed to be less judgemental and stop jumping to conclusions. Shrugging off his judgemental thoughts; he'd always found her a little clingy and she'd done a few things that made her come across as desperate and a little stalker-like. That time when she turned up uninvited to Maryam's sisters engagement party in Balsall Common; she said she'd just happened to walk past the restaurant on a Wednesday evening, dressed to the nines and simply had to come in to congratulate the happy couple that she had only met a few times. That time when she bought a Dalmatian the same time Gwen bought a Dalmatian and the time that Luke just couldn't get right in his head, when she turned up like a knight in shining armour, to help Ruth out of her car that had crashed into a ditch when the brakes had failed, ten minutes into her drive back home from visiting her parents – that one caused Ruth to suffer her first miscarriage. He'd raised his concerns with his friends before, but they didn't share his thoughts. They just thought she was an innocent lady, slightly desperate for their friendship, whose somewhat awkward personality made some of her actions come across more sinister than they actually were. He had quietened his suspicions, and remained kind and friendly but never really let his guard down fully with Beverley.

He pulled up outside the empty property on Knowle high street to see Rory pacing up and down.

"How's it going mate?!"

"Hey Luke. Not too bad thanks."

"So, this is it! Your new baby! How are you feeling about it?"

"Yeah! Sorry I can't show you round inside; I get the keys tomorrow. I mean, argh!! Am I doing the right thing here? It's such a huge upheaval and lifestyle change and what if it doesn't work out?"

"Heyyyyy, relax. Let's grab a drink and have a chat mate."

Luke reassured Rory that he was indeed doing the right thing. It would be hard work at first, but the time back he would get with his family would be so worth it. Rory had asked Luke to be a second pair of eyes and look through the lease. They went through the lease contract together, Rory pointing out the amendments that had been made at his request. Luke couldn't think of anyone better than Rory to run through a commercial lease contract. His attention to detail was top notch and his perfectionist personality meant there was little if any opportunity of him making a mistake to his detriment and getting screwed over. They agreed, the contract was solid, so Rory could sleep soundly and get excited to sign on the dotted line tomorrow.

"Well, if there's anything you can think of that you want to run through with me this evening, I'm just going to be chilling at Mums, so I'll just be on the other end of a phone ok?"

"Cheers man, I appreciate it"

"Right, I'm off. Promised Mum I'd come home with an Indian takeaway. See you tomorrow?"

"Thanks for your help, mate, I appreciate it. Yeah, see you tomorrow."

"I'll bring the champagne!"

Rory jumped into his car and headed back to Beaudesert, but not without noticing the white Toyota Auris parked on the other side of the road opposite his new restaurant to be. It pulled up about half an hour after Luke had arrived, no one had got out the whole hour and a half they had been there. He couldn't make out whether it was a male or female in the car or any distinguishing features really, but his curiosity was piqued.

He pulled into a driveway on the country lane and turned off his headlights. Feeling a little silly, like he was in a z-list spy film, he thought he'd sit in wait to see if he was being followed. Probably being completely silly, but still he waited. Five minutes was enough. Nope, nothing. OK, he was getting paranoid in his old age.

The white Toyota Auris carefully kept its distance behind Luke as he drove through the city centre towards his Mum's house in Coventry. Popping out for a takeaway just round the corner from his Mums, the car lay in wait, watching. Just watching.

Chapter 12

Rory walked into the bedroom looking sick. Amelia sat up in bed worried by her husband's unusual seriousness.

"Hey sweetie, what's wrong?" Rory had just been out for an early morning jog with Ruth and she thought he had perhaps pushed himself too hard trying to keep up with her and pulled something.

"Smith and Barts just called and said they are not willing to lease to us. They cited some ridiculous excuse of having had break-ins recently and the premises were being used as a place away from CCTV to sell drugs and they don't think we have the experience to be able to prevent and handle this." He was pacing up and down the room. "It's ludicrous! There was no evidence of any break-ins in the property, Greg would have picked up on that, and what experience do you need to know that drugs use in any capacity is a reason for breach of contract, so obviously, we would prevent it, using whatever security measures are necessary. Its Knowle for goodness' sake, it's one of the nicest places to live in the country! Well maybe I'm slightly biased, but that's not the point, there isn't a drugs problem here and, we gave up our jobs and moved the family and..."

"OK hun, you're babbling now. I get the picture. Take a deep breath. Let's figure this out" Amelia wasn't one to panic and although he knew she was only paying it lip service and was probably panicking inside, he was grateful for her serenity and calmness. "It's only eight in the morning, and everything was fine when you spoke to them at five yesterday, so this decision must have happened overnight, they can't have just got to the office this morning and suddenly decided to lose business like this. Can you think of anything that has happened that might have changed their mind between now and then?"

"No, not at all. Luke and I were there yesterday as you know, we hung around outside for a bit, whilst I showed off the front to him and then we went to the Bell for a drink, ran through the contract one last time with Luke and then we both headed off. I voiced my concerns to Luke about the family upheaval and whether it was the right decision for the family, but I don't think anyone overheard me and even if they did, it shouldn't be grounds for not giving us the lease!"

"OK" Amelia said slowly. She was thinking. How to make it better, how to fix this, how to calm Rory down. "Let's go out for breakfast" She decided.

Breakfast at Spirita in Coventry never failed to disappoint. A café spot near the cathedral that served a mixture between a greasy fry up and smashed avo on toast to suit all generations and tastebuds. Rory didn't want to discuss too much business at the table in front of the kids as he didn't want them to worry. As far as they were concerned, they were starting a new adventure with a new school, new house, new friends, and they would get to see more of their Grandparents and Mum and Dad. They were too young to worry about this.

"At least they gave us our deposit back." He muttered, tucking into his full English. "I just can't stop thinking about all that money we've already spent on contractors, planning the opening, I just don't know where to start."

"Let's enjoy our breakfast, enjoy our walk around the cathedrals and when Mum and Dad have the kids, we'll have time to think. Please don't worry. You still have your job and I can get another job here. It will all work out in the end."

"Nana!!!! Grandad!!!!" Shouted the twins through mouthfuls of chocolate crepes, as Amelia's parents walked in. Amelia and Rory looked up and smiled. The twins were so fond of her parents and it was definitely a mutual feeling. They lived in a small flat in Earlsdon, which was ideal for transport links and easy to walk into town to meet people, which happened a lot these days now they were both retired. It did, however mean that sleepovers at their house were few and far between; there was barely enough space for the twins to lay out their sleeping bags in the lounge, but that didn't stop them. They were having a sleepover there on Christmas night and the kids could not wait! Despite their obvious lack of wealth, they were one of the happiest married couples that both Amelia and Rory knew. They had been happily married for 45 years and had never had wealth, but had never wanted for anything. They had never had material possessions to excess and therefore never wanted for them. They always lived within their means on Amelia's dad's small salary and had managed to pay off the mortgage on their flat by the time they retired. Now they could enjoy their retirement, content in the knowledge that they had two dear grandchildren and a happy daughter as their legacy.

Amelia had briefly told her dad what had happened on the phone this morning, before asking them to come and meet them and take the kids off their hands for a few hours whilst they figured this out.

They ordered more coffees and had a quick catch up, before saying goodbye to the kids and Amelia's parents.

"Right," Amelia got her laptop out and went into business mode. "We need to figure out what contracts we can get out of, what can be postponed whilst we find another location, what can be cancelled or returned, see what deposits we can get back, what equipment can be sold, which is a tough one as it hasn't even been delivered yet and a list of contacts that we need to notify about the non-start. That is a good enough start for today. Are you happy to run through the contract with Smithshields farm? We have a bi-weekly vegetable order with them, starting third week in January that we need to find a break clause to – I'm hoping they will be fine with us cancelling for now, as long as they know this is just a small delay and we will be using them in future. Right, the crockery purchases are due to be delivered on the 29th December, now, are we able to store this somewhere for a couple of months, or is it best we cancel?"

"You're great babe! This is why I married you. Nothing phases you, and you are so positive always!"

"Oh, I love you!"

"OK, so before we start making phone calls to wind down our business that never even began, I have an idea. It might sound crazy, but hear me out, OK?"

Amelia listened.

Rory talked.

Amelia listed some more and started to feel a little excitement in her tummy.

"So, let's do it!" She agreed

"Baby steps OK, baby steps, I need to speak to Nathan first and there are so many other stumbling blocks we could come across, so let's treat it as an idea for now right!"

"Agreed Mr Prudent! Let's drive there now, it's probably best you see him alone, you haven't had a catch up just the two of you yet anyway. Why don't you drop me off at the Swan in Henley on the way and I'll work from there, whilst you meet him?"

Chapter 13

Nathan had just received a call from Rory, he sounded slightly flustered and said he really needed his help, the biggest favour he would ever ask for. Did he want a website created for his new restaurant perhaps? Maybe he was desperate for a PA and was going to ask to borrow Dominic whilst he set up the restaurant? Money? Who knew – he hoped he'd be able to help him though whatever it was.

He would be glad to see him, or any friend really. He hadn't seen anyone except Dominic since Friday, at the soiree at Beaudesert. He loved his work, he really did and the more he worked on this latest medical tech project, the more he got excited about the extent to which he could change entire healthcare systems, but he had to admit, being back in the Midlands made him realise how lonely his life was. He always convinced himself that he didn't need anyone around him permanently, as long as he had his long-term childhood friends around, or at least a phone call away, but he was beginning to see this was not the case. A partner to sit and have dinner with, discuss your day with, or sit in comfortable silence with, make a cup of tea for, just to generally be with, would be nice. He just didn't know what his type was yet; what interests would his partner have, what qualities did he desire in a soulmate, was intelligence more important to him than a sense of humour, what trade-offs would he be willing to make, if any. Gender, hair colour, build, he just didn't know what he was physically and emotionally attracted to. He probably needed to start dating a mixture of people to find out.

He turned his thoughts to the break in at his condo last Friday. He'd received a notification on his phone of the break-in and looked at the cameras which were also linked to his phone, in time to see someone rifling through his study. He couldn't tell who it was as they were dressed head to toe in black, just like it was a burglar in a film. Except it wasn't a film. It was his home. His alarms notified the concierge and police immediately, who arrived within seven minutes. One of the benefits of living where he did in Silicon Valley was that he was in between two police stations, so response time would always be fairly quick, especially for America given the huge distances they cover.

Nothing was taken, just a lot of mess made, but it wasn't obvious to Nathan what this person was looking for – there were plenty of easily stealable items in the hallway and study of considerable value, but they weren't touched, which made Nathan slightly nervous. What unnerved Nathan even more was that this break in was done in broad daylight. Given the amount of time that Nathan had spent working from home in that study over the last few months, it was very unlikely that this was an opportunist action in the hope that no-one was home. No, someone had to have known that he wasn't in, which meant someone in his close team spread this news, or even worse, he was being watched.

He had to put it out of his mind, otherwise he wouldn't be able to enjoy Christmas, It was probably someone trying to steal his work and luckily for him he never left that lying around. His laptop always stayed with him and his work was saved on the laptop, or in the cloud with a serious level of security to get past before you could access it. People had tried stealing from him before and had not succeeded. His housekeeper would tidy everything up and by the time he returned, everything would look exactly how he left it.

The intercom rang. It was Rory.

"Come on up mate, Ill buzz you in. Don't park the car by the gates remember, the farm house is still a four-minute drive from the gates, so stay in the car till you see the house" He'd rented the farm house he had used before on air bnb in the countryside near Henley in Arden. Sylvia had offered him a room at Beaudesert, but he liked his own space and having Dominic around all the time meant it was a little more awkward staying at a friend's house – it would be rude to ask for another room for your assistant. The farmhouse was perfect; it had two large log burners in the lounge come hallway, which he had on at the moment to keep it nice and cosy, a double aga in the spacious kitchen, which he didn't know how to use, a dining room and three bedrooms upstairs. One of which was taken by Dominic, who Nathan had still not decided what to do with. He'd chosen this place, or rather Dominic had chosen this place because it was so private, set back far off the main road, which you could hardly call a main road, and allowed enough indoor and outdoor space for both Nathan and Dominic to live together and not be on top of each other,

"Cup of tea?" Nathan swung open the big farmhouse doors and ushered Rory inside out of the cold.

"I'd love one"

"I've just put another log on the fire. Living the good life here!"

"This is a tad different from your pad in California, right?"

"You know, I'm really enjoying having minimal tech here and just getting back to basic living."

"Blimey mate, you make it sound like you're living in the Outer Hebrides...you've got central heating here and running water, and a motion sensor operated intercom with a video function no less at the gate." Rory baited cheekily. "Great home for the next week though"

Nathan chuckled realising how frivolous he was being, renting out an entire house like this, but didn't mind his old buddy teasing him.

"Listen mate," Started Rory, "I've run into a problem, but I've got a business proposition for you and thought perhaps we could, well, I haven't thought it through properly yet, but, let me start at the beginning"

Rory told Nathan how the lease of the restaurant had fallen through. Nathan empathised, being a businessman himself, albeit a completely different type of business. Rory went through all the contractors and suppliers that he still poised, ready to go to set up a new restaurant from mid-December. He'd seen a small house up for sale on one of the smaller roads just off the high street in Knowle and it looked to him like an older person lived there and may have died, leaving the family hopefully wanting a quick sale.

"So, what makes you think someone died there? And why are you interested in a 2-bed house in Knowle, surely you need something a little bigger?"

"Well, the garden of this house is pristine, even for winter, and I always assume an old person lives there if the garden is perfect – not always correct, but quite often true. Then I looked the house up online – it's been so well looked after, but not been updated for at least 30 years, which again makes me think an old person has lived there, their whole life and maintained, rather than updated. Soooooooooo. OK, well the reason I was interested in this is because, well, you know this lease fell through, and we are going to be dependent on this restaurant for our income in 4 months when I stop my job and Amelia has already left her job and this place would be the perfect size for a restaurant, with a bit of work and well, we do have the money from the sale of the house in Surrey, but..."

"But you don't want to spend that money on the business, you want to ringfence that cash for a family house for you, Amelia and the kids. You're asking me to buy the house for you am I right?"

Nathan felt a little disappointed that he was being asked for money, but tried to shake it off. Whenever he was out with his "friends" in the US, he was always expected to pay. Huge bar and restaurant bills were racked up by his "friends" on his behalf. He always paid up, knowing full well he was being taken advantage of, but it went both ways, he was, in effect, buying their friendship and company, and he would continue this relationship with them until he had had enough. On the contrary, no-one in his close group of friends had ever asked him for money; they may have teased him about it, but never taken advantage, so it came as a surprise Rory asking for money. Him and Amelia had made plenty of their own money, but he knew they had invested heavily in their house, overpaying their mortgage as much as they could each year.

"Yes. The money from the sale of the house in Surrey is going straight into our house that we're moving into up here. We can probably scrape up to 50% of the asking price for this other house if we sell shares and other investments we have. The only trouble is, I was hoping to make a cash offer for the entire amount, so we could bypass a lot of the paperwork and painful waiting around, which I think would be amenable to both sides. I was going to propose to you that you fork up the other 50% of the house and then you could have a stake in the restaurant, get involved in decision making and eventually share in profits, when it becomes a money-making business and of course, I'll pay you back then too."

"Mate, you're such a hard worker and between you and your lovely wife, you will absolutely make a success of it. I'll send you the money today, just pay me back when you are able. And thanks, but I don't want to be involved in your business – the only interest I have in restaurants is eating in them and I won't have any useful input into your business decisions unless you count my sarcasm as useful, so with all due respect, thanks but no thanks."

"Nathan, you're a lifesaver, thankyou thankyou thankyou!!! I have to go and tell Amelia. Sorry, so rude of me. How's everything going with you? You looked a little worried the other night at Beaudesert, anything wrong?"

"No problem at all. Yeah, I'm quite busy with my latest project thanks, really enjoying it though. The flat got broken into the other night."

Rory had visited this so called flat before and knew it was very much more than a flat, but Nathan tried to tone down his wealth a lot of the time.

"I've got cameras everywhere, so I was able to see them rifling through my things, which wasn't nice to see. I think perhaps they were after the work I've done on my current project, but I had it all on me, so they got nothing. I just don't know how they knew I was away. I didn't tell anyone, Dominic arranged everything and I know he wouldn't tell anyone – loyalty is his middle name."

"Ah man that sucks. Such a violation of privacy. Could it be that someone saw you leave and took the opportunity to break in?"

"It could be that, yes. I mean, they didn't take anything of value, they saw my watch collection and didn't even touch it, so I feel like it was definitely targeted at me and my work, rather than an opportunistic thing, but never mind, I'll probably never know, so I have to get it off my mind. Anyway, don't you hang around here, go and chat to Amelia and get things moving. Text me your bank details and I'll send the money over now, to bring up your fund to the asking price. If that's not enough, just let me know."

"OK let's just write up a quick contract and we can both sign it. I mean it's a lot of money to invest so, I'd feel better if we had something in writing and then you know that I am 100% going to pay you back."

"No need mate, really. We've been friends for decades, I completely trust you, but thanks for the offer. You go and find Amelia and get that call in to the estate agents.

Nathan ushered Rory out of the farmhouse, trying his best to listen and respond appropriately to his friend's grateful, excited chatter and waved him off. He needed to focus. It was happening soon and he had to stop it.

Chapter 14

Rory caught up with Amelia back in Henley in Arden.

"That was quick!" She said "You were barely twenty minutes after dropping me off."

"Nathan practically kicked me out to come and speak to you."

"And?"

"He's lending us the money!! Al the money!! He's completely saved our bacon. He doesn't want to be involved in the business at all, and just said to pay him back when we are able to."

"That's great news! Wow, what a friend! And well done for thinking outside the box! It would never have crossed my mind to look at a domestic house to turn into a commercial premises, let alone a restaurant."

"Thanks, you truly are my muse, you drive me forward to achieve more and more. We wouldn't have got here without you."

"Did you get a contract written up and signed? Something informal at least?"

"No, he wouldn't let me. He said he trusts me and knows well pay him back. In fact, "Rory was replaying his encounter with his friend, "he didn't even let me counter argue, he wanted me out of his house so badly, he just talked over me, took my tea cup off me and told me to go and find you. I hope he's ok. He's working on his new project, I'm sure that's what it is." He shook his head to focus. "Right, let's call the estate agent to put an offer in before they close for Christmas!!"

Chapter 15

Ruth and Rory had only made it to a village down the road before Rory got a phone call and had to turn home. She hoped everything was ok. He always landed on his feet, so fingers crossed it would be. She decided to carry on and ran to Evesdale and had a browse round the shopping village there. She grabbed a drink and wished she'd brought a book as it was a nice place to sit and relax for a while. She got out her phone and began texting Gwen to see what she was up to when a familiar face walked past. It looked like one of the teachers at her school, but she couldn't be certain. She managed to sneak a quick picture of her and send it to Gwen, who was much better at facial recognition that she was.

*Ooh That's Mrs Teedale, History teacher. She didn't teach me, and I'm guessing not you either if you don't remember her, but I think everyone else had her. Gwen text straight back.

*Ooooh, good memory. Fancy meeting me at the café at Evesdale for a natter?

*Sure, what time?

*Well, I'm here now, so now if you're free?

*Yep. Can I bring Alfie? Winona's at school."

*Of course, you never need to ask!

Gwen swanned through the doors twenty minutes later, with one year old Alfie on her hip.

And planted a kiss on Ruth's cheek.

"How are you darling?"

"Not too bad thanks. I ran here so I'm feeling quite invigorated."

"Crikey love. I get the same feeling by blasting the aircon in the car on cold for five seconds. Much less taxing."

Ruth smiled. She did love her friend; she was not to everyone's taste, but she made Ruth smile, and she was loyal.

"Can you just take Alfie for a second, whilst I get a drink, please. Do you want anything?"

"Oh sure, erm I mean, I'm kinda smelly, I ran in these clothes you know."

"He won't mind, and I'm normally covered in baby sick, baby drool and snot behind closed doors, so he's not exactly used me being sweet smelling either. Drink?"

Ruth shook her head. Looking Gwen up and down, judging her external appearance, she could hardly believe that she would ever let her Versace shirt and Miu Miu skirt get covered in any form of bodily fluids, but she knew that not everyone showed their true self on the exterior, even to their best friends. Behind closed doors was when the true you came out. Ruth had seen the true Gwen once, when she had visited her a few days after giving birth to Winona, seven years ago. She got to see the raw emotional challenges of parenthood. Gwen was finding the nights hard; she was finding the days hard. Ruth saw her struggles, but through this, she saw the love, the selfless unending love that Gwen felt for her child. Gwen had no make up on, no designer clothes, no overly cheery façade, she was herself and she cared about this little human more than she cared for herself, so she knew that the breezy, ostentatious, materialistic exterior that Gwen showed the world was only a wall to protect herself.

Alfie had managed to fall asleep on Ruth in the two minutes that Gwen had gone off to get drinks.

"Oh, I'm sorry, it is his nap time and he's extra tired because Adie took him out to soft play this morning."

"Ah, bless him. Where is Adie by the way?" Ruth wondered where Gwen's ever present nanny was.

"Nannies need time off apparently." Joked Gwen. "Do you want me to take him?"

"I don't mind him sleeping here if you don't? It's quite therapeutic, hearing his breathing and knowing that he felt safe with me. Children are just so...pure - It must feel so special when your children laugh with you and show their love to you because children don't lie, it's such a true emotion for a child to laugh with you, they don't do it to be polite or to not hurt your feelings, they don't fake their feelings."

"I feel truly blessed Ruth, I really do. I'm so sorry about your miscarriages and pregnancy struggles. We've not talked about it recently. Tell me, how are you?"

"Gwen, I feel loads better now, you know me, I struggle with my medication for my bi-polar and sometimes I feel super low and other days super high, I struggle to regulate. But one thing I do know, is that I cannot be happy without children in my life, I know this. I don't need a man in my life, although if I meet one, that would be nice. I just know that I need children."

"OK, well does that feel good to realise you now know this is one of your core needs to be happy? Perhaps now you know this is a non-negotiable for you, you can look at other methods of getting a child."

"Getting a child!! Oh, Gwen you have a way with words!"

"You know what I mean, not like buying one! Shush you! Stop teasing me!"

"Yes, in a way," Ruth continued seriously "But I've known for a while that this is a non-negotiable and it makes me sad that biologically I can't make it happen. So, I've actually started looking at adoption. I'm looking at the routes to adoptions at the moment. Don't broadcast it though, I'm not sure I'm ready for a conversation about it yet with my folks and everyone."

"Oh, Ruth that's great! Well, I'm so happy for you and I'm here for you if you need a sounding board or just a few cocktails to numb the pain."

"You're telling your friend who just overdosed on pills and alcohol to numb her pain with alcohol?" Laughed Ruth

"Sorry darling, just know that I love you ok, even if my words come out insensitive." Purred Gwen. "Anyway, "Gwen lowered her voice conspiratorially "I think Mrs Teedale who you spotted earlier is sat at the table just behind you. Let's say hi!" Gwen walked over to her and tapped her on the shoulder. Ruth was glad she was tied down to her seat by Alfie as she wasn't in the mood to make small talk with strangers.

Mrs Teedale recognised Gwen straight away. She was of course head girl at school and every teacher's pet, she knew how to keep people on side and that meant manipulating all of her teachers. She was always a hard worker though and intelligent, giving her a good reputation in the teacher's staff room.

"She retired a year ago you know. Quite early for retirement mind you, I think she's late 50s, not much younger than my parents, so I wonder what happened there. Ooh I think I'll have to have a little dig." She whispered, chuckling to herself at the detective work she had in front of her.

Chapter 16

Sylvia knocked on Ruth's door. She was sat at her desk, focused on her laptop screen. She had started planning this ultramarathon through Warwickshire in earnest. She was really enjoying planning her runs through fields and smaller lesser-known public rights of way to recce this run. She was then finding out who owned the land, to figure out who she would need to speak to, to get permission to put up feed stations, medical tents, portaloos and everything else needed to run a smooth ultramarathon.

"Darling, we need to have a chat." Sylvia sat on the chaise longue at the foot of the bed and patted a space next to her, inviting Ruth to sit."

Ruth obediently sat next to her Mum.

"Now, we had Alastair bring the post to Breakfast this morning. He brought yours too, but seeing as you had already been up and had breakfast, I said I'd bring it to you. Now." She paused dramatically. "All these leaflets about adoption have come through for you, and whilst I think that this is great that you are moving on with your life and trying to start the next chapter, I feel you should wait a little before considering adoption. I'm not sure you are strong enough mentally to cope with this yet."

Ruth stared, confused at all the adoption leaflets in her Mum's hand.

"Mum, I admit, I have been considering adoption, but I haven't sent off for any booklets, I've just been looking online at what the process is. I'm not planning on progressing anything yet and I certainly didn't send off for anything – If I did, I would get it sent to London, not here."

"Ruth dear, you don't need to hide this from us, its ok, I'm not saying don't do it, I'm just saying wait a while. You obviously did send off for those information packs, I certainly didn't, perhaps your medication isn't working properly. Do you think you're having you know, another one of your, erm," Sylvia paused, trying to be diplomatic and instead being the exact opposite. "episodes?"

"Mum, how can you even jump to that conclusion because some adoption leaflets have come through the door! I'm fine, my medication is fine, but understand me when I tell you I did not send off for those leaflets and I'm not having a psychotic episode thank you very much. Thanks for your concern. I'm busy right now, working on a project, so see you at dinner."

Ruth was cross that her Mum didn't believe her, but she also started to question herself. Perhaps she did send off for these booklets, rather than keeping it online, or perhaps somehow the cookies on the website were able to pick up her address details somehow and illegally send her mail. She'd have to check with Nathan if that was possible. The more plausible explanation however, was that Gwen thought she was trying to help and sent off for all these leaflets on her behalf. She was the only other person she had told about her potential adoption plans.

She decided to call her and confront her before she saw her at the Christmas Eve party.

Gwen answered straight away.

"Ruth darling. Lovely to hear from you again!"

Ruth was sure she sounded guilty already

"Gwen, why did you send me loads of adoption leaflets? I told you in confidence and now my Mum thinks I'm losing it."

"What on earth do you mean Ruth?"

"Gwen, stop playing games, I know it was you, I haven't told anyone else about my adoption plans and then a few days after telling you, a load of leaflets come through the door telling me about local adoption agencies."

"Ruth, I have no idea about this. I would never."

"You would Gwen, I know you would and you would do it under the pretence of being a good friend. Quite frankly, I wouldn't be surprised if you called my Mum straight after our conversation and told her. It's not like you to keep secrets is it?"

"Really Ruth, I haven't done anything."

"Fine, Gwen, if you're not going to admit, can you at least promise not to mention it to the rest of the gang? I don't want them overly concerned about me too. I wish you'd just said the other day that you were going to send off for these leaflets for me."

Ruth paused and realised she was being a little venomous for the crime committed. All Gwen had done was send off for some leaflets about adoption for her and probably thought she was helping. Ruth had convinced herself that it was Gwen and decided to drop it.

"OK Gwen, I forgive you. See you at the Christmas Eve party." Ruth hung up, not thinking anymore about the severe chastisement she had just given her friend without allowing her to speak.

She settled back at her desk, continuing her portaloo research when a new email popped up.

POOR LITTLE RUTH. LIFE NOT DEALING YOU AN EASY HAND? THAT'S IT, RUN HOME TO MUMMY AND DADDY. DON'T COUNT ON IT GETTING EASIER.

She shivered. What cold hearted moron would send her such an email, taunting her of her failures. More importantly, who would actually care enough to send this sort of message. Picking up her phone, she called Nathan.

"Nathan! I've received an email!"

"Hey Ruth. Yeah, Im good thanks. How are you?"

"I'm being serious."

"OK, you received an email. I think I need a bit more than that hun."

"It was horrible. Let me just find it." Ruth scrolled up and down her emails on her laptop, but the email wasn't there.

"Ruth? You there?"

"Yes, I can't find it, one sec." Ruth went to her emails on her phone. It wasn't there.

"Nate, it's gone!"

"You're telling me you received an email and now you can't find it? That's what you phoned me for?"

"I guess. Sorry."

"Any time Ruth." Nathan said sarcastically, but not unkindly. "I gotta go. Work stuff. You going to be ok?"

"Yes yes, of course. Sorry, I'm fine. Bye."

Ruth was so confused. The email was there. She read it. It was there. At least, she thought it was there. She thought she read it. She can't have seen that email. Her mind must have been playing tricks on her.

Chapter 17

Ruth had spent the day decorating and preparing for the Christmas Eve party. Sylvia and Steven had always had a Christmas Eve party for their nearest and dearest, and extended nearest and dearest which included neighbours, friends colleagues and family, for years, but the last few years, Ruth had taken over more of the hosting and planning duties, meaning she got to choose the music, food, decorations and staff that were working. Shame she still didn't have control over the guest list.

Everything this year was all last minute as Ruth had not done any planning in the lead up and it was the last thing on Sylvia and Steven's minds, not even knowing if they should have one, for their daughter's sake. But Ruth thrived on other people's energy and they thought this would be good for her to reconnect, plus having it at home, meant she could retire to her room whenever she wanted.

The party was a success as it always was. The staff at Beaudesert were all considered guests on Christmas Eve, so there was no-one swanning about serving drinks and assisting the guests. Drinks and glasses were laid out in the hallway for everyone to help themselves, buffet food was laid out on a table next to it, music played from an ipod through speakers and most of the guests knew each other at least from previous parties, so the atmosphere was laid back and joyful.

Ruth excused herself and headed to her room to take her medication. She was still trying to wean herself off the daytime drugs but hadn't changed her evening dosage, to help keep her sleep routine stable. Buzzing from the night's excitement, she felt her ears ringing from all the laughter, chat and music going on downstairs. She took a moment to assess herself and realised she felt happy. Yes, this was definitely happiness, even if it wasn't going to last, she allowed herself to fully feel that happiness. Prancing into her bedroom, she kicked her shoes off for a moment and posed barefoot in front of her mirror for a few moments, savouring this feeling. She reached round the corner into the bathroom cabinet to get her drugs and couldn't find them where she thought she had left them, so she turned the light on to have a look. She couldn't see them because they had been knocked out of the cabinet onto the floor. In the cabinet was a snake. She froze in horror. She didn't care if it was poisonous or not, she hated snakes, it wasn't just a fear, it had been a debilitating terror since her childhood, for no reason that she or anyone else could remember. She backed away slowly, not daring to breathe and then when she got to the landing, let out a blood curdling scream that continued whilst she ran downstairs to the party.

The room went silent to see Ruth screaming, arms flailing, running barefoot down the huge staircase as Wham's Last Christmas began to play. Nathan was first to her side.

"Breathe, breathe. What is it?"

"A snake, there's a fucking snake in my room!"

"Oh Christ, what sort?"

"I don't bloody know Nathan! Somebody go up there and get rid of it! It was in my bathroom cabinet and had knocked everything off, I don't know how it got in there!"

Luke and Steven bounded up the stairs to her bedroom. Seeing that her daughter was being looked after by her friends, Sylvia mingled with the guests to put everyone at ease, making light of the situation. "We probably left a window open and it crawled into the warm from the fields", "Yes yes she's always been terrified of them poor girl".

Luke and Steven came downstairs ten minutes later. Steven went straight to Sylvia and Luke to Ruth. "Hun, are you sure there was a snake in your bathroom?"

"Yes Luke, why?" Ruth was irritated.

"Well, we didn't see one, we checked everywhere and your bathroom is perfectly tidy, your medication is still neatly on the shelves and erm the door was closed when we went in so it can't have got out. Do you think it could have been the light playing tricks on you?"

"No, it wasn't the bloody light playing tricks on me! I know what I saw! It was in my bathroom cabinet above the sink and had knocked my medication onto the floor. Someone must have put it there...I never leave that cupboard open; Id bang my head on it when I left the room if I didn't close it. I'm not making this up!"

Sylvia came over and put her arm round Ruth's waist. "You've got a lot on your plate at the moment darling do you think you could be being a little paranoid?"

Ruth knew what she saw, but didn't have the strength to argue about it. She grudgingly agreed that she was probably being paranoid and decided it was time for her to go to bed before she caused more of a scene. The guests would all be going home in a couple of hours anyway, so she wouldn't be missing too much.

Ruth heard a knock at the door twenty minutes later. "Mum I'm fine, I'm going to sleep. Night night, love you"

"It's us hun, Gwen and Maryam."

"Oh, come in guys"

"We came to say goodnight and just check you're ok."

"Thanks girls. I'm fine, really, I am, just tired." She looked up at their concerned faces hovering by the door. "Want to snuggle in bed with me and watch a trashy Christmas film on Netflix?"

Both girls grinned and kicked off their heels and jumped into bed. Just like old times when they used to have sleepovers and snuggle up in bed watching films till the early hours. At that moment, those three girls didn't realise how much they needed each other. Ruth was glad for the comforting friendship, free of effort and judging, Maryam was happy to not be going back to an empty room and empty bed and Gwen was happy to be needed as something other than just as a mother.

Chapter 18

Christmas came and went rather uneventfully for Maryam. She managed to completely switch off for a few days and not think about work which was partly thanks to having Vanessa over for Christmas day and boxing day as she often had done before. Maryam's Dad, Keith, came over for

Christmas lunch, bringing with him far too many side dishes and treats for a dinner for 3, but he always had done. The three of them stayed over in Maryam's modern apartment in Birmingham on Christmas night, drinking, playing games and enjoying each other's company.

The smell of bacon and fresh coffee wafted around the house on boxing day, waking up Maryam and Keith shortly after 9am. They had slightly delicate heads and appreciated the bacon and sausage sandwiches that Vanessa had knocked up for them.

"So, remind me, what's your plan for today, Vanessa?" Asked Keith good naturedly. He'd known Vanessa since she and Maryam were friends at school and thought of her as a second daughter.

"Heading back to the hotel to work on my new manuscript. I know we said no work over Christmas, but this really is fun for me and if I don't get my ideas down soon, Ill forget them."

"Well, as long as it stays fun, remember, we all agreed – no work over Christmas. As soon as it starts feeling like work, you put down your pencil Ness and get yourself outside into the fresh air. Go and feed the ducks at Ryton pool, that's just round the corner from your hotel, isn't it?"

"Yeah of course Keith!" Vanessa jokingly rolled her eyes in Keith and Maryam's direction. They all knew the hypocrisy of Keith's comment, him being the hardest worker of them all, running his own car garage, working all hours of the day since they were little. "Some fresh air and a walk is also on the cards for sure. I think I need a walk after that ridiculous amount of food I ate yesterday." She grinned.

Maryam and Vanessas' phones pinged at the same time.

"Probably one of Nathan's meme's, this time about Boxing Day hangovers perhaps?" Maryam assumed it was their group what's app that they'd had going for years.

"Oh gosh...Maryam, look...."

Maryam quickly read her message before looking at Vanessa's. "Mines the same message. Do you think we should go over? Do you think she's joking?"

"It's not funny, no-one would joke about that"

"What's up kiddos?" Said Keith who had begun clearing up the dishes. Looking at the girls' worried faces, he was genuinely concerned.

"It's Ruth, Dad. She's sent us both the same message saying she is quote "Going to do it properly this time." So, I know she's with Sylvia and Steven today, she's definitely not alone and I'm sure they'll be keeping a close eye on her ,but why would she say this? It seems like a cry for help."

"Give her a call girls, it does seem like a cry for help and given what she's just gone through, she might not be joking."

Before Vanessa could unlock her phone to make the call, their phones pinged again. This time, it was Nathan on another group chat without Ruth, usually reserved for talking about her birthday plans.

Nathan	**Just got this message from Ruth guys "Going to do it properly this time." I'm worried, I think I'm closest to Beaudesert, shall I drive over?**
Maryam	**So have myself and Ness**
Gwen	**Me too**
Rory	**Guys, I'm still staying at Beaudesert, I'll go and knock on her door, 1 min.**

An agonising five minute wait, Maryam went through the worst scenarios in her head. Had she reached out to her friends in the hope that they would be there for her to talk to? She'd possibly not been able to access a therapist the last few days because of Christmas, could that have tipped her over the edge? Were there subtle signs that Maryam didn't pick up on, she seemed fine when they left her on Christmas eve after the snake incident.

The phones went again, but this time it was Rory starting a group voice call.

Gwen	**Hello?**
Rory	**Hi.**

Maryam	Hi. It's me and Vanessa here.
Rory	Hi guys
Nathan	Rory. What's going on?
Rory	So Amelia, the kids and myself were in the lounge playing twister. I ran upstairs to her room, she let me in and said she was fine. Showed me notes she's working on to do with some sort of ultramarathon race she's going to organise. Here's what's strange, I showed her the message and she said she didn't send it. She was adamant that it wasn't her. She showed me her phone, and there was nothing in her sent items, which doesn't mean she didn't delete it straight afterwards, but I kinda believe her.
Gwen	Okaaaaaay. Soooooo, what now, we just pretend we believe her and carry on as if she's not about to kill herself?
Rory	I mean, I guess so. What can we do?
Nathan	Perhaps she it was a message she wrote a while ago and accidently sent it now instead of deleting it...
Gwen	Sure sure, Ruth accidently messaged all of her friends individually and then realised it was an accident and then deleted her sent messages and lied about it, something which she has never done in her life. Yes of course, believable." Gwen's sarcasm was not lost on the group, but no-one had anything articulate to add.
Vanessa	You've got to tell Sylvia and Steven so they can keep an extra close eye on her. I know you have your family there and its Christmas time, but can you just pop your head into her a little bit more?
Rory	Yeah, you're right hun, but guys, I really do believe her and she really does seem fine. We're probably overthinking it.

Gwen	I do have to tell you though, everyone, she accused me of something the other day, I wont tell you what as I don't want to betray her confidence, but I didn't do what she accused me of. We ended the conversation with her thinking she was being the bigger person and dropping it, but I know she didn't believe me. I think we need to keep an eye on her.
Vanessa	What did she accuse you of?
Gwen	I'm really not going to tell you but I didn't do what she thinks I did. She did it, but she seems to have forgotten.
Rory	We'll keep an eye on her. I think she's good though, I really do.
Nathan	I'll leave a message on our group chat so Luke and Ana know we've checked on her when they see her message, assuming she's sent it to all of us.

Everyone hung up cheerily wishing each other a speedy hangover recovery, but silently wondering if they should be doing something more.

Chapter 19

40 minutes later, Vanessa was back in her hotel room, feeling a little drained. They were definitely not overthinking it, like Rory had suggested. After their phone call with Rory, they had discovered that Luke and Ana, so the whole group had received this message from Ruth and although Nathan was going to look into where the message had come from, he wasn't confident about being able to find any further details due to the high level of encryption used on the messaging platform. It came from Ruth's phone number too, so they had no reason to question this, other than the fact that she said it wasn't her. They had agreed to share any further weird messages they received like this over the Christmas period with each other on their shared group and they were all catching up on the 30th December with a stroll round Shelly Park anyway, so they could voice any concerns then quietly when Ruth was out of earshot.

She wasn't in the mood to do any work on her manuscript, so she went out for a brisk walk around Ryton Pool, grabbing her phone and headset to listen to a new comedy podcast. Something nagged at her inside to call her Mum, but this close to Christmas, she'd probably still be coming down off a massive festive excess high, so decided to leave it at least another day. Her Mum's drug problems were something she had battled with for decades and Vanessa had had enough of seeing her Mum's decline, never mind being taken advantage of, used and abused physically and verbally by her Mum, so three years ago she had decided that her Mum needed to hit rock bottom if she was going to stop using. She had to make this decision herself, no-one could decide for her that enough was enough and Vanessa cut ties with her Mum. At first, her Mum didn't care and she had no contact for the two years, but this last year, Vanessa had received messages on her birthday and the anniversary of her dad's death, and the few phone calls they had had, made Vanessa feel like her Mum was beginning to want to start turning her life around.

Emptying her mind of all her worries and problems, Vanessa put her headphones in and started walking, mindfully appreciating the sun glistening through the trees onto Ryton Pool where the swans were milling about by some children who were feeding them.

"Let's manifest this musical" She thought.

The driver of the white Toyota parked up and pulled out some binoculars. Ryton pool was a circular walk with minimal trees and this parking spot was the perfect location to sit and watch the ducks.

Chapter 20

Ruth closed the door behind Rory, slightly confused. He'd just asked her why she sent him and the gang a message suggesting she was going to kill herself. Firstly, she wasn't currently feeling like she wanted to kill herself and secondly, she hadn't sent anything, so she was understandably surprised.

Feeling good first thing, she had already been for a run and had a few more ideas for the ultramarathon race she was organising, so after showering and getting dressed, she got comfy at her desk and started planning. She had left her phone in her bedroom this whole time, so she couldn't have sent anything.

Rory knocked on her door just after 9.30 and asked if he could come in. He was treading on eggshells so much more than he normally did, he practically tiptoed into the room. Rory and his family had been staying at Beaudesert a couple of times a year for years, he knew Sylvia and Steven almost better than Ruth herself knew her parents, he knew the staff and he knew his way around, but it still wasn't home and Rory always liked his own space. Ruth thought the poor guy was probably so uncomfortable staying in her parents' house with his wife and kids and with one of his best friends who really wants children, but can't seem to make it happen and who also just tried to commit suicide. Maybe he felt like he was flaunting his happiness in front of her. That wasn't the case though; Ruth was indeed openly jealous of the fact that Rory had some lovely children, but that didn't mean she didn't want him around and she still loved him, he was one of her oldest friends. She just wasn't great at telling her friends how much they meant to her.

Rory insisted that he had received a text from her and so had the rest of the gang and that they were all concerned for her. Ruth thought this was ridiculous and grabbed her phone to show him her sent messages – nothing. Whilst they were on the subject of stray messages, she tried telling Rory about the email she'd received before Christmas that subsequently disappeared, but he obviously didn't believe her, just agreeing that it was weird.

"All right mate," conceded Rory. "As long as you're sure you're fine? Its ok if you're not ok though, you know that right? You've been through a lot. You can talk to me about anything, I'm here for you."

Ruth was fed up of hearing people say that they were there for her. What did that even mean anyway...her Mum and Dad were here because they lived here, Rory and his family were here as they had space for them all to stay. Why couldn't they just give her space and let her talk when she wanted to.

"We're going to make some brunch in twenty minutes if you want to join us? Pancakes, sweetcorn and courgette fritters, poached eggs and smoked salmon and hash browns, deep fried of course"

"What a mixture, sounds almost healthy if we pretend it's not deep fried!" Snorted Ruth, forcing a smile. "Sounds good, I've not had breakfast yet."

"Wish I could say the same thing. The twins were up wanting breakfast at 6."

"They're welcome to make their own way down to the kitchen you know. They can't cause too much damage in the kitchen you guys use and they can reach the fridge and all the cupboards they need right?"

"Oh yes, thank you, we and they are verrrrry much aware of this thank you. No, no they insisted on our company at breakfast because they didn't want us to be alone upstairs." Rory rolled his eyes jokingly.

"See you downstairs in twenty minutes then!" Said Ruth.

Rory backed out of the room. Ruth didn't want to go downstairs for brunch, she was on a roll with her race planning, but she felt like she had to prove that she was ok, so forced herself to make the effort. She tried to brush off her annoyance of her overly inquisitive friends and forced herself to think about which would be the best way to run over cuckoo field; via haystacks and deal with the muddy exit through a stile at the bottom of the hill or down the priests way and deal with the overgrown meadow in the middle. After fifteen minutes of thinking, she was no closer to a solution, so she threw on some lounge wear, leaving her towel dried hair hanging loose. She glanced at the screen of her laptop before she put it on standby and saw she had a new email. Her heart skipped a beat before she opened it. It was another one.

HA HA. YOU THINK CHANGING YOUR PASSWORD WILL STOP ME?!

She'd only changed her password to her email account last night. She'd not even sent any emails since the password had been changed. She knew that it wouldn't stop anyone sending her emails, but how the bloody hell did this person know she had changed her email? She had been in her bedroom last night when she changed her password, so the only way someone could have known that was if they had been looking through her window. Her desk backed onto the side window in her room, which had views out over the driveway; someone with a long-distance lens could be looking into her room. She always slept with the window and curtains open. There must be someone out there permanently watching her in her room. Or. She froze. What if there was a small camera actually in her room.

She rushed downstairs to tell Rory..

Ruth burst into the kitchen where Rory was helping the twins whisk up some pancakes and Amelia was sitting at the counter, enjoying, watching them. She grabbed Rory's arm, knocking the bowl with the pancake mixture onto the floor, splattering the twins, and the kitchen cabinets with mixture.

"I changed my password and someone knows so they must have been watching me with a long-distance lens from the driveway or there's a camera in my room and someone is spying on me Rory!"

"Why is someone spying on you Aunty Ruth?"

"That's really exciting though" the twins jabbered.

"Is it your friend?"

"Can you talk to them if there's a camera in your room?"

"Is there a camera in our room?"

"I don't want a camera in our room."

"Nor do I, Mummy, please can you take the camera our of our room?"

"Kids, kids. There's no camera in your room, I promise you. Rory, do you think you could…" Amelia nodded her head at the door asking Rory and Ruth to take this outside. Rory took the cue and gently took Ruth by her elbow and led her out of the kitchen.

"OK Ruth, tell me what's happened?"

"I got another email. They said they knew I'd changed my password, which I did. I changed it last night! How do they know that? Someone is spying on me, I'm telling you Rory."

"OK, ok, lets walk through this, what password did you change?"

"My email password!"

"OK and who is "they"?"

"The bloody people or person who has been emailing me!" Ruth was getting more and more frustrated with Rory's questioning.

"Right, so show me this email you received."

Ruth sighed, exasperated, but ran back upstairs to get her phone. Clattering down the stairs twenty seconds later, she fumbled to get into her phone.

"Calm down mate. It's going to be fine."

"It's not though Rory! The emails disappeared before." She opened her emails and scrolled up and down frantically. "See it's gone!! The last email I had was from farmer Ted saying he was happy for the race to cross his field on the South side near the brook, nothing from, I mean it's not even a name, the email address is just a load of numbers and letters."

"I don't know what to say Ruth. There's nothing there. Let's go back into the kitchen and have something to eat. Can we try not to talk about horrible emails and being spied on in front of the kids please? They've just got very active imaginations; they can turn the bubbling sound from a radiator into a unicorn running on the roof. I mean in their heads. You know what I mean. Shall we go for a walk this evening and have a chat? I've got restaurant challenges I need to offload too."

"Sure Rory." Ruth mumbled, "Sorry about the pancake mixture." More of her confidence drained away. No-one believed her.

Walking back into the kitchen, Amelia looked up and gave Rory an attempt at a subtle "Is everything ok, and did you have the conversation and ask her to be mindful about how she speaks in front of the kids?"

look. Ruth pretended not to see and put on her "fun Ruth" act to break the awkwardness.

"So, guys, who wants to make a fresh batch of pancake mixture and flip some pancakes? Ill let you put loads of sugar on them? Quick, Mum and Dad are looking the other way, I won't tell!"

Chapter 21

Ruth and Rory met in the hallway at 9 that evening for their walk. Ruth was dressed head to toe in reflective clothing, she had added reflectors onto her wellies, her running leggings had reflective strips down the side, her jacket was one big reflective piece of material, she had a dark hat on, but was wearing a head torch and was holding a hand held torch.

"Woah there Dazzler!"

"Huh? Dazzler?"

"Oh, she's a comic book superhero who converts sound to light, you know what, it doesn't matter who she is, why are you dressed like that?!"

"Walking at night time in December in the countryside is pretty dark mate."

"I thought we were going to have a wander round the gardens which I believe are lit."

"Change of plan." Ruth hand a head torch over to Rory. "we're going to explore a track behind the stables. I'm thinking of plotting it as part of my race, but it will be run in the dark for most competitors as I think it's going to be the last section, so I need to see what it feels like at night."

"I'm not dressed for this Ruth." Rory said, reluctantly adjusting his headtorch.

Ruth looked him up and down, assessing his smart black coat, neatly tied up scarf, dark jeans and very white trainers. "No, you're not!" She chuckled. "Never mind, it's not like we're going to be crawling through hedges or climbing trees, its literally a walk down a slightly muddy track in the dark, so you'll just get muddy and we can clean you up again!"

"Fine. You know I'm a city boy in all senses of the word, right? Muddy walks at night time are not the sort of thing I do for fun. I have a token pair of hunter wellies that have never even seen mud."

"Yes darling, I know. Come on, thirty minutes is all we need and then you can be safe back home, snuggled up with Amelia, moaning about how awful your friend is for making you get exercise in the evening."

"It's not the exercise." He started, but realised Ruth was baiting him. She gave him a cheeky smile and pushed him gently out the front door.

They started walking towards the stables, one side still lit up beautifully with Christmas lights and Ruth steered them behind a hedgerow, joining a path that Rory never even knew existed. It was overgrown with brambles and nettles and extremely muddy, but was quite clearly meant to be a path.

"Just try to keep the noise down for now, "whispered Ruth, "Just until we're past the stables. Don't want to spook the horses."

"Trying Ruthie, but it's kinda difficult walking, no, sliding through mud in trainers with absolutely no grip."

They climbed over a stile and the path took them through a cluster of trees too small to call itself a wood, but definitely big enough to block out any miniscule amount of moonlight they were enjoying.

"OK, we can chat from here, we're far enough away from the horses. Don't step on that log, you'll fall through, its rotting." Ruth started making mental notes about the work needed if she chose this path to be part of the course; she wanted a natural countryside experience, but if she could minimise the potential risk of injury to the runners, she would.

"Remind me how wearing head to toe reflective gear is going to help you to see better in the dark. I thought reflective clothing was to help you be seen. There's not going to be any cars at all on our walk!"

"Oh, you know, the light from your head torch will light me up and help us both see better I'm sure and we don't want to scare any animals in case they attack us in fright, its best they see us coming."

"Oh yeah, killer foxes." Grumbled Rory.

"So, tell me about the restaurant."

"Ugh. Well, I can't stop think about the last-minute lease refusal. It's just such a strange thing to do. They must have had a meeting in the evening to make the decision to not lease to us. I mean saying that we were too inexperienced to be able to protect the property from drug users is ridiculous."

"Sounds like they just wanted an excuse to not lease to you. I mean, I agree, they really are clutching at straws. Eyes up Rory, there's a tree branch a metre in front of you at your eye level"

"Argh. Thanks. Yeah, possibly, but I have no idea why. Anyway, we and by "we," I mean Amelia, contacted the suppliers to retain but postpone start dates, equipment that we purchased is going to be delivered at a later point in time and we're not actually incurring that many additional costs because of this, thankfully. The biggest cost is going to be the chef that we were supposed to be employing from the beginning of January. We can't not pay her, that's not fair, so we'll just suck that up and task her with creating an even better locally sourced menu. You know, I don't know where we'd be without Amelia."

"Give yourself some credit mate, the initial set up was so well co-ordinated, you wouldn't have been able to contact everyone and make these last-minute changes so quickly and easily if you hadn't been so organised."

"Ah cheers. Well anyway, you know the offer got accepted on the house and they're keen to progress this quickly like us, so the biggest piece of work we have is all paperwork in getting the property changed from a domestic property to a commercial one. I'm not too worried about it being approved, I just know it will take time as the council has to be involved and I'm pretty sure they won't start work again until mid-Jan. But at least it will give me a chance to get the paperwork in order."

"Public sector eh, they get so many holidays! Proud of you mate."

"In other news, we're hoping to be exchanging contracts on the house for us to live in soon. Hopefully first week of January. We've sent off all the paperwork now, so just waiting on the solicitors to do their bit. So we'll be out of your hair soon."

"Ooh exciting times! Although we'll all miss you here. Careful, I wouldn't follow my path through this section, go left, it's really muddy where I am."

"Can we walk back along the road Ruth?"

"What road? This is the countryside mate! Wait Shhh Stop. Did you hear that?"

"Nope, all I can hear is my inner dandy lamenting the destruction of these new trainers."

"No seriously, I heard a phone. It was the sat nav lady giving a direction on a phone."

"You're hearing things Ruth. There's no-one out here. I can't see any other lights; I can't hear any sounds apart from us and the trees blowing. I can't even hear any animals."

"Rory, I heard it."

"There must be animals out here, foxes make weird noises don't they, could you have heard a fox?"

"Foxes can't use sat naves. I heard it, I heard it!" Ruth was breathing faster.

"Why didn't I hear it then?"

"Because you are not in your comfort zone out here, you were concentrating on where to walk like I'd just told you to and you were listening to your inner bloody dandy!"

"Ruth there's no-one out here, can we please go back, I'm really not enjoying this and from the looks of it, neither are you, you are so on edge." Rory spoke softly to try and calm Ruth down and stop her from spiralling into an episode of hypermania.

"Rory, what if there's someone out there waiting for me? I'm sure I can see someone moving out there now!"

"What would they be waiting out there for? What would they want with you?" Rory tried to get her to rationalise her own thoughts, something Ruth had told him she had been taught as a coping mechanism when her intrusive thoughts began to spiral out of hand.

"I don't know, but someone's moving over there!"

"The only things moving out there are animals. I'm pretty sure next doors dairy farm has a field that borders this side of your property right? There's probably some cows out there. And if not cows, we're in trees, so there's going to be sleeping birds that we might have disturbed, owls, badgers, mice, squirrels. OK? If there's a human out there, they would probably be just as surprised as us."

"The sat nav voice was unmistakeable. And the border of the Nelson's farm is like a mile that way, not here. We're now in public land."

"OK well I can't explain the sat nav voice."

"You don't need to explain it away, you could just believe me! I'm not lying about these emails you know; Ill prove it to you somehow. Someone is out to get me." Ruth was shaking out her hands like she'd just washed them and was trying to dry them. She always did this when she was getting agitated.

"No-one is out to get you Ruth. Do you think you could be getting spam emails and you're not reading them properly?"

"For fucks sake Rory. No! They are emails of a photo. The photo always has some sort of threat typed out on it. I read it and then it deletes from my emails. After I've read the email, they don't show in my inbox, deleted items, junk, nowhere. They just disappear."

Ruth stepped backwards and someone grabbed her head, pulling off her headtorch. She realised someone was trying to break her neck. Why is someone doing this? Did she know something she shouldn't? Had she unwittingly witnessed a murder? She gave a panicked scream and then realised they had let go of her head so she might be able to break free, so she carried on screaming. Rory was tackling someone on the floor in front of her. Why was she frozen? She should help him. She was frozen in fear.

Rory was stood in front of her now. His headtorch shining directly in her eyes. Someone was screaming. She couldn't hear what Rory was saying to her. He looked like he was shouting at her.

He grabbed her face, "Ruth, stop screaming!" She understood eventually. She didn't realise she was still screaming.

"Rory thank God you're ok. I thought they had you!"

"Who had me? What do you mean?"

They grabbed my head and tried breaking my neck but then they let me go for some reason, I think because you came at them and then I saw them tackling you on the ground. Thank you for not running off Rory"

"Ruth!" Rory didn't know where to start. Facts. "Your hat got caught on the branch and you twisted away. The hat is still attached to the tree, see? Look!"

Ruth did indeed see her hat stuck to the tree.

"You started screaming, I turned round to see what was wrong and lost my balance and slipped over which is why I was rolling around at your feet. You just carried on screaming Ruth. What on earth did you think was happening?"

"I thought someone had grabbed my head, trying to break my neck and then had started on you"

"Your hat is the only thing that you are wearing that is material, which is why it snagged on a branch, everything else is either gortex or lycra, so wouldn't catch and the hat is tight, right, which is why it felt like some was tugging at your head or neck when it was coming off. I swear, there was no-one here. There's even footprints to prove it, see, just yours and mine."

Ruth nodded. Still incredulous that her mind had let her think that someone had grabbed her from behind, when it was just her hat snagging on a branch.

"Hey, it's all good, let grab your torch and put your headtorch back on."

Ruth just watched Rory struggle to walk over to the tree with her hat and headtorch still hanging on it and then reach into some brambles to get the hand held torch.

"Ruth, are you still taking your anti-depressants?" Rory decided a different tack would work better as right now, talking about the tricks her mind was playing was not helpful.

"What?! That's none of your business" said Ruth, still frozen to the spot.

"Hey don't get defensive, and I think it is my business. I'm your friend and I want to help you get to the bottom of this." He put the hat and headtorch back onto her head.

"OK, fine. No, I haven't. Anti-depressants have never worked for me before, they make my moods spike and I don't see how this time is any different. I want no drugs in my system and going cold turkey for me is the best way."

"Ruth, you know that's so dangerous! You should be doing this alongside a consultant who can make sure the dosage is correct, but at a reducing volume over the course of a few weeks, months, however long it takes."

"No, this time is different because I want it to be. I have started to feel more in control of my life. I feel good, I have a plan for the future, I have a project to focus on, I have projects in the pipeline that aren't work related. I'm even considering the family business. Life is definitely looking up."

"That all sounds good in principle and I really am happy if that's how you feel. It's just that." He paused tentatively, trying to pick the right words. "It doesn't come across to myself or anyone that cares about you. You just seem preoccupied."

"Well, it's not been that long since I came out of hospital, so give me at least another week before you see true party Ruth emerge again."

"I just want to see happy Ruth."

"She's there inside, she wants to show her face, I promise!"

"You know you can talk to me, right?"

"I know, thanks. I know you're only concerned for me, sorry for getting cross."

"No worries, I can deal with you getting cross. What I can't deal with is my feet getting any colder and wetter than they already are! Can we please leave this awful place, No more adventures and meaningful conversations in the woods, right?"

"Right. We can go round the garden next time. If you stick to the path, you can even keep your slippers on!" Ruth grabbed Rory's hand and helped steady him as he walked back through the mud, trying to be the front man.

Had she heard something? Sometimes the quietness in the countryside is deafening, especially at night-time and the mind makes up sounds, conjures images of things that aren't there. Maybe Rory was right and he would have heard it too. She couldn't help feeling she was being watched as they made their way back through the woods. The feeling stopped as soon as they reached the end of the woods and made it back onto the muddy path. They probably were being watched, just by the animals of the wood as Rory pointed out. They were making slow progress because Rory, bless him, was trying to take charge but wasn't sure of his footing and kept stopping to hold back every branch, nettle and bramble for Ruth, wrapping her in bubble wrap. Lovely gesture, completely unnecessary, but it made Rory feel like he was helping so she let him, but now she just wanted to get back.

"OK, I'm back." She announced with a clap of her hands.

Rory looked at her. "You good?"

"Yes, thank you." She snapped. "Ok swap places." Ruth took control "Right, walk on this grass verge over here, I didn't see it on the way, it'll be less slippery. Ah there we are, see the lights, we're almost back at the stables."

Rory was too busy concentrating on the ground to see the lights but grunted acknowledgement.

Back at the house, they shook off their muddy shoes in the hallway, both ready for bed.

"Hey Ruth," started Rory "you know I really am here for you."

"I know. I'm so lucky to have such great friends. Thanks for the walk"

"No worries, anytime!

"Ha ha, you definitely don't mean that!" chortled Ruth, halfway up the stairs.

"You're right, I don't mean that. Chats and garden walks, absolutely anytime."

"Sorry about your trainers. And your coat. And I hope those jeans weren't anything special."

"Just a bit of mud, easy to wash off like you said."

"Night!" Called Ruth over her shoulder, already at the top of the stairs.

Rory stood for a moment staring at his once white trainers, shaking his head before heading upstairs.

Chapter 22

"OK everybody in!"

Ruth was driving herself and the Renshaw's to the park to meet up with everyone.

"OK, checklist guys," announced Amelia. "Wellies and spare socks?"

"Check" Chimed the twins.

"Kites?"

"Check!"

"Thank you cards for Aunty Maryam."

"Check!"

"Both been to the loo?"

"Yes!"

"Great, and most importantly, backpacks with drinks and snack in? This village we're going to is mostly independent business and I don't know if anywhere will be open to get a drink, ok?"

"Yes, we've got them Mum!" Rowan obediently replied.

"Right, let's get you clipped in!"

Ruth sat patiently in the driving seat, in admiration of Amelia, she was definitely a catch. She always seemed to have everything together, nothing seemed to faze her. As far as she was aware, she'd never been intimidated by the fact that one of her husband's best friends was a girl and she showed the kind of capability and self-assurance that meant most people trusted her with most things.

"You are amazing Amelia."

"Oh goodness, thanks! Why do you say that?" responded Amelia as she got in the car.

"You're just so on it. You know what I mean?"

"Oh, all I did was get some snacks ready and spare clothes. It's basically the same checklist whenever we leave the house, whether it's a long journey or short journey."

"I hope I can be a mother like you one day."

Amelia clipped herself into the middle seat in the back and leaned forward to squeeze Ruth's hand. Rory came running out the house carrying some muddy wellies.

"You sure your dad won't mind me borrowing these, Ruth?"

"No worries, of course he won't mind. They're filthy, but I did have a hand in getting your trainers muddy, so I guess this is me fixing it! Anyway, jump in, we've been waiting aaaaages, let's go!"

"You definitely still owe me a pair of trainers Ruth!" Laughed Rory.

They arrived at Shelly village just after 10 and managed to nab the last available electric vehicle charging point on the high street. Ruth plugged the car in and saw the café across the street was open.

"Guys, I'm going to pop across the road and grab drinks for us all. What do the kids want?"

"Oh, great idea thanks! The kids are good thanks, they've got smoothies in their backpacks."

"Perfect. You guys unload and lock up and I'll see you outside the café in 5 minutes." She threw the keys to Rory and headed over to the café. She thought she saw Luke and Laura crawling down the high street looking for a parking space, perfect timing for those drinks she thought.

5 minutes later, Ruth emerged from the café clutching 2 bags of assorted cake slices and 8 drinks. She couldn't be bothered to message the group for individual drinks orders, so everyone was getting a large cappuccino with chocolate sprinkles, apart from Gwen who got an oat one as she was dairy free. Gwen had already arrived with Winona and Alfie, Vanessa and Maryam were also just crossing the road and waved at the group.

"Hi guys!" Beamed Ruth, handing out the drinks. "So, let's save the cakes for when were in the park. I got a selection so we can all share. I'm pretty sure I saw Luke and Laura driving down the high street looking for a space five minutes ago so they'll be here soon. Shall we head over to the park and message the group chat so they know where we are?"

"Sound good. Ana is still not coming today, family thing going on." Confirmed Gwen.

They entered the park and the twins took it on themselves to look after Winona and ran off to play. Gwen strolled in front with her Louis Vuitton pushchair in one hand, coffee in the other, one eye on Winona and one ear open to the conversation behind her. Amelia skipped forward a few paces to walk next to her.

"So how was your Christmas Gwen?"

"Oh, wonderful thankyou darling! Pretty low key actually, we cooked ourselves as Penelope, our chef has Christmas off, so no delicious culinary delights unfortunately. We did a small turkey crown, did some roast potatoes, parsnips, brussel sprouts, stuffing and gravy and a microwave Christmas pudding. Not a huge amount of food as it was just the four of us. If I'm being honest, even cooking roast potatoes is a stretch for me. I'd be happy with a pizza if it's just the four of us!"

"How lovely! It really is family that makes Christmas special though, right? I'd love to have something simple for Christmas dinner one year, rather than killing ourselves on Christmas eve trying to prepare everything. Did you catch the new Christmas film on CBeebies on Christmas day?"

"God, unfortunately yes, I thought we'd be able to avoid it, but Winona's friends at school told her about it and she wouldn't let it go. By that point of the day, I'd already made here jam sandwiches twice, first time because she decided she didn't like dinner, including the potatoes and I had to remake her jam sandwiches because I cut them into squares instead of triangle, how dare I?! How was your day?"

"Really good thanks. We all got stuck in making Christmas dinner and ate with the Dillons and then we went into the gardens in the afternoon and flew the kids' new kites that they got from Santa. The day went so quickly."

"Oh, you still have Santa? That's wonderful. I want to keep that going for as long as I can. Winona! Winona! We'll go into the play park later sweetie. Let's have a little walk first. Why don't you go and climb in those little trees over there. Yes, over there! Stay with Emma and Rowan. There's a table we can sit at and its much nicer than the play park." Gwen pointed to a table facing the trees and some muddy open space in the park.

Amelia looked Gwen up and down, taking in the beige suede shoes, the long camel coat, cream trousers and dusty pink gloves, wondering if Gwen really meant to encourage her daughter to play near the muddy trees.

"What?!" Laughed Gwen, knowing exactly what Amelia was looking at. "Darling, this is outdoorsy for me, my heels are barely there, I've got a polo neck on and I've got a cross over bag, I draw the line at backpacks.

Plus, Winona's got a puddle suit and wellies on, she's the one getting muddy, not me!"

Ruth plonked herself down on the bench in front of the small copse of trees the kids were playing in and she started opening the bags with the cakes in, carefully balancing each cake slice on top of the paper bag on the bench. The kids had a sixth sense for sweet stuff coming out and suddenly ran over for their portions. Ruth let everyone help themselves, but kept looking around for Luke and Laura. They should have been here by now, there were plenty of spaces at the bottom of the high street, it should have taken them an extra five minutes perhaps, not twenty-five minutes. She was beginning to think she should say something when they appeared at the edge of the park, waving. The couple got their power walk on and made it over to the group in time for a nibble of cake and cold cappuccinos.

"Sorry we're late guys, the taxi arrived twenty minutes late."

"Taxi?!" Said Maryam. "But Ruth said she saw you driving down the high-street when they pulled up."

"Nope, couldn't have been us. Our car's been in the garage since the 28th. It's at your dad's actually Maryam, we never stopped using him, even though he's the other side of town. Thankfully he was open during the Christmas period. We had our catalytic converter stolen and can't use the car. It was when we were at Beaudesert on Christmas eve actually; we started the car to drive to my Mum's on Christmas day and it made an awful sound and we knew what had happened. Keith said they need to order the new cat in, so it's going to take a few days, so we've just been getting taxis everywhere."

"Oh such a pain." Empathised Maryam. "How did you get to your Mum's in the end?"

"We walked. It was quite nice actually." Smiled Luke.

"Guys, was the taxi the same car as your Lexus?"

"It was the same colour, a white Prius, but..."

"I saw your car on the high street about half an hour ago! It must have been you!"

"What can we say! It really wasn't, we got a taxi here. I can show you my uber receipt if you want?"

Ruth wouldn't let it drop. "Guys, it was your car! I saw it! It had your sticker on the back from Vietnam, the green one, I recognised it"

"Ruth, you surely can't have seen the car that closely. When it drove by, didn't you have your back to it whilst you were crossing the road?" Reminded Rory.

"Yes, but I turned round to, to erm. I turned round, OK? I can't exactly remember which way I was facing but I saw Luke's goddamn car!" Ruth had jumped up and was pacing in front of the bench.

"Hey, hey. Let's chill." Soothed Maryam. "So, Ruth saw Luke's car. Let's accept this for now guys, ok?"

"What do you mean accept this for now?" flared Ruth. "I'm saying it happened, so just accept it, period!"

"Yes, yes, we accept it, period." Answered Maryam.

Ruth stopped pacing, temporarily placated by her friends saying they believed here, even though she knew they didn't.

"So, ahem, Ruth, the message you sent on Boxing Day, erm." Vanessa had spent the last five minutes thinking how best to start this conversation and got cut off straight away without being able to get her full spiel out.

"I know, weird right?" Said Ruth, starting to pace again. "I didn't even have my phone on me in the morning, I went out for a run. So, I don't know how that got sent." Shutting the conversation down.

"Darling don't shut us out." Said Gwen, wanting closure on this. "We all received an individual message from you, not on the group chat and you essentially said you are going to kill yourself. Now given recent events, can you blame us for being concerned."

"Just give me some space guys. I know you all mean well, but it's too much. Too much ok! Too much!" She picked up what should have been Ana's coffee and walked off to where the kids were playing and joined in climbing on the trees, lifting up Winona, so she could get as high as the twins. She snuck a quick message to Nathan.

Wish you were here. Hope works ok. Can I swing by later?

Nathan hadn't been able to make the park as something work related had come up. He never questioned her sanity or wrapped her in cotton wool whenever she had been ill, he was the only one of her friends who carried on treating her normally, something which she was craving. Right now, though, if she wasn't going to get any normality from her friends, tree would have to resign herself to tree climbing and kite flying with two 10-year-olds and a 7 year old, which secretly she preferred anyway.

The gang didn't stop Ruth from walking off or playing with the kids. They realised they had probably all been a little intense and she just needed space. Space in the fresh air, running around with kids is so wholesome. They didn't manage to fly the kites in the still air at all, but it didn't stop them from trying, running madly across the park dragging the kite, futilely hoping a tiny gust of wind would sprite it up into the sky.

Three nature wees later, and all snacks and drinks consumed, it was time to go.

"So, I'm heading back on the 3rd Jan. Got work on the 4th. So maybe see you before then?" Vanessa was saying as Ruth joined the group, reuniting three tired children with their parents.

"Brunch on the 2nd?" Suggested Gwen. "Nathan will probably need to head back around then too, he mentioned something about an investor meeting, so it will be good to have a final catch up of the season. Come to mine and Ill cook"

"Or we could go that cute farm shop down the road from you?" Suggested Luke, not wanting to experience Gwen's cooking.

"Don't worry darling, when I say Ill, cook, I mean Penelope will cook. She's back on the 2nd." Reassured Gwen.

Everyone agreed and started to head back to their cars.

Rory and Amelia hoisted the twins onto their shoulders. The rested their chins on their Mum and Dad's heads.

"Have fun guys?" Asked Rory

"Mmhmm."

"Aunty Ruth tired us out."

"Oh, she did, eh?"

"You're welcome!" Said Ruth, winking at Rory and Amelia

They arrived back at the car and Ruth stopped, tilting her head sideways. "The cars unplugged."

"What?!" Sais Rory and Amelia together.

"The cars unplugged; I don't know how. Its ok, there should still be a bit of charge left." She started the car, but it only had 6 miles left. They wouldn't make it back to Beaudesert.

"I. I. Don't understand!"

"You forgot to plug it in!" Said Amelia, frustrated. The kids were starting to get really tired and she needed to get them dinner soon. Being stuck in a Warwickshire village, most the shops closed, 10 miles away from home with hungry tired children was not ideal.

"I'm sure I plugged it in. I mean that's why I parked there."

"Well you didn't, obviously because its unplugged and only you can unplug it right as you have the release button on an app on your phone?"

"Yes. But. Let's call Anthony, he'll come and get us."

"He's not working, he's still on his Christmas break remember?"

"Uber?" Said Ruth sheepishly. She was so frustrated with herself. Not only had she let her friends down, but now they were going to think she was not able to look after herself. It was a simple mistake though surely.

Chapter 23

After waiting 45 minutes for an uber home, the Renshaw's and Ruth made it back to Beaudesert.

Ruth headed upstairs to her room, turning her laptop on to get stuck into ultramarathon planning. She had received another email.

I'M GOING TO MAKE YOU SUFFER. JUST WAIT AND SEE WHAT I HAVE IN STORE FOR YOU!

Ruth picked up her phone and messaged her group of friends.

Ruth	**Someone is emailing me threats guys. I just received another one, they said they've got something in store for me and that I'm going to suffer. What should I do?**
Maryam	**That's awful. Is it definitely meant to be sent to you and it's not spam sent to like a million email addresses?**
Ruth	**It's only sent to me!**
Nathan	**Forward the email onto me. N.Render@Render.com**
Ruth	**Its gone!**
Ana	**What's gone?**
Ruth	**The email. It's been deleted**
Nathan	**Check deleted items.**
Ruth	**I'm not stupid Nate. Already checked.**
Nathan	**How can the email have gone then?**
Ruth	**I don't know!**
Ana	**When did you receive the email?**

Ruth	About two minutes ago!
Ana	Probs spam hun. Ignore it.

Ruth gave up. Her friends thought these emails were spam mail and wanted her to ignore them. They felt pretty personal to her though.

Needing a change of tact, she picked up the card of the yoga instructor that Louise had dropped off before Christmas. Joshua Hartlepool, trained under the British School of Yoga, specialises in Hatha and Vinyasa yoga. "Perfect, just what she needed." she thought and called him up to book a class.

Chapter 24

It was moving day for the Renshaw's. Their house in London had been packed up for weeks, since they came to the Midlands at the end of December, so not much work was needed there. Rory had gone down there early this morning to make sure that the removal company picked everything up and the house was left in a decent condition.

Amelia had already picked up the keys to their new house this morning and was over there now, along with carpet layers and a plumber. She'd managed to source carpets and a carpet fitter to come and fit carpets before all their furniture was delivered in the afternoon and a plumber to fit a new bathroom and sink in the downstairs toilet. So Ruth had the important job of collecting the twins from school at 4pm.

She was so worried she was going to miss the school pick-up, she'd set two alarms on her phone, an alarm on Alexa and had asked Alastair to come and check that she was getting ready to leave at 3.30.

She'd originally planned for them to go horse riding after school as she knew the twins enjoyed that, but then realised it would be dark by the time they got home, so decided on baking a cake and then a film with popcorn and pizza.

Ruth was over 6 hours early, but she wanted everything to be perfect, so she was measuring out ingredients in the kitchen for later, so the baking would be quick and easy. She didn't know how tired the kids would b when they came back from school, so wanted it to make the activity use as little brain power as possible. But then she thought, what if they needed to burn off some energy from sitting still all day, maybe she should have some fun physical activities organised. What if they'd had a hard day and wanted to talk, they'd only been at their new school for just over a week, they might be struggling with something, what would she say?

The doorbell rang, forcing Ruth to drop her uncertainties. She didn't know what she was she worrying about anyway, they were great kids, she loved being around them. She just lived with them for almost three weeks and knew them really well. They'd be fine.

Joshua was at the door for Ruth's 10am yoga class. He'd been coming over almost 5 times a week since the beginning of January and they normally did a vinyasa flow together. He had started hanging around after their class for a drink and sometimes they would go for a walk around the grounds and the fields together. Ruth found him an easy person to talk to. He was charming, never judgemental, funny and interesting, with an anecdote to tell about everything, but not in an annoying way.

Ruth found herself telling Joshua about the emails she had ben receiving from this anonymous sender. She had stopped telling her friends about them because they didn't believe her. Joshua had no reason to not believe her, he just sat and listened, empathised, agreed with her how unpleasant it was to be on the receiving end of them. The latest one was this morning.

I CAN SEE YOU EVERYWHERE. EVEN SLEEPING AT THE HOSPITAL. YES, I WAS THERE!

Someone was wanting her to feel unsafe, to feel paranoid, question herself. Well it was working. The yoga classes she had with Joshua were her only escape at the moment. When she wasn't with him, all she could think of was when she was going to receive the next email, was she being watched, why was she being watched, why was she being targeted, what was going to happen to her, her family, her friends. Why?

"Morning Joshua."

"Hey Ruth, how's it going?"

"Fine thanks. Joshua, do you mind if we just do a half hour flow this morning? I'm quite tired and my mind is all over the place, I can't focus."

"Another email?"

"Yes! How did you know?! Its like you're in my head, I swear Joshua!"

"Well you don't look yourself Ruth. You look quite pale. So, yes, lets do a half hour flow and then perhaps a walk around your beautiful garden?"

"Sounds like a plan!"

Joshua ended up spending most of the day with Ruth. They talked about Ruth's ultramarathon, that Joshua promised to enter. Ruth gave Joshua a beginner's horse riding lesson, had lunch together and went for swim. Before she knew it, the day had gone and Alastair was coming to find her to remind her to pick up the Renshaw kids.

"Thank you Alastair, I'll be leaving in five minutes."

"The Tesla's out the front Ma'am"

"Thankyou." Said Ruth gratefully. She hadn't even asked Alastair to bring the car round for her.

"Ma'am?!" Repeated Joshua, mocking Alastair.

"I know. He's known me since I was a baby and still calls me Ma'am. I've told him so many times that he can call me Ruth, but he prefers to keep formal boundaries when it comes to work. Anyway, I've got to go and get Emma and Rowan. Are you happy to show yourself out?"

"Sure. We've not got another class booked in for now. Shall I come over tomorrow?"

"I'm not sure for now. My friends Rory and Amelia are moving house today and then they're opening a new restaurant in a few weeks, so I want to be around for them if they need me. Can I call you?"

"Sure. See you soon."

Ruth had a blast with the kids after she had picked them up from school. The cakes came out flat, but they licked the spoons to an inch of their lives. The pizzas made such a mess, but were delicious and they fell asleep snuggled up on the sofa watching the lion king. Amelia and Rory crept through the door at 8 and carried their two happy children upstairs for their last night at Beaudesert.

"Thanks for watching them Ruth. Was everything ok?" Asked Amelia

"Yeah, we had a great time thanks, I don't know who had more fun! We made a cake, pizza and watched a film. I can watch them again if you want? How did the move go? Congratulations new home owners!" Said Ruth, beaming for her friends.

"Thanks Ruth! I'm so glad it went ok. Yeah, the move went well. I can't believe Amelia managed to get new carpets laid before the removal trucks got there. We've not opened any boxes yet, so I don't know if there's been any breakages, but erm, yeah, the house looks, well, a mess, but we're excited right?" He looked tiredly over at Amelia who also looked exhausted.

"Look, you guys get yourselves off to bed. If you want me to watch Emma and Rowan this weekend whilst you unpack, I can, or if you need someone to help you unpack, I'm here. Or if you want some time just you two, then just ask. Day or night, you know, I'm here. I mean, I know you've got the restaurant opening in a few weeks, so you have a lot on."

"Thanks Ruth. I think we want the kids to get settled as soon as possible, so we'll have them at the house this weekend thanks. They can sleep in sleeping bags if we don't get their beds up in time. It'll be exciting. Ugh, don't talk to me about the restaurant. We have so much to do, but we're having to park that for a few days and focus on moving. Right, we need some sleep. Night night."

Rory and Amelia headed upstairs to bed, leaving Ruth feeling self-conscious as she knew how needy she'd just come across. She had just wanted to offer her help seeing as she wasn't working at the moment and she knew how busy Rory and Amelia were, with the house move and restaurant opening, but it all came out wrong.

She went to her room and opened her laptop. She had some planning to do. Thinking about the latest email she had received, she was horrified to think someone she didn't know had visited her at the hospital in December. Tomorrow, she was going to visit the hospital and find out exactly who had visited her and when, if Rory and Amelia didn't need her of course.

Chapter 25

Ruth's services were not needed the next morning, so after the Renshaw's had said their goodbyes, she jumped in the Tesla and drove to the Priory in Birmingham.

She hoped that no-one there would recognise her. The chances were fairly slim, especially as she looked different, wearing clothes, having brushed her hair and generally not looking like a homeless drug addict.

She put on a podcast listening to a couple of long-distance runners talking about a race in Wales that was on her to do list. They talked about training, nutrition, the gear they used and the ups and downs of the course. She thought how amazing it would be if her race was featured on a podcast like this one day.

She pulled up in the car park at the hospital and confidently strode through the front doors and up to the desk.

"I'm here to see Ruth Dillon."

"Sign in please." Said the receptionist robotically. Ruth was hoping to get this sort of greeting. She grabbed the visitors books and started reading back through all the visitors in December, she saw her friends, her parents a number of times. The receptionist looked up.

"Who did you say you're here to see, Ruth who?"

She obviously couldn't find her on the system Ruth thought. She only needed another thirty seconds to finish running through these names.

"Dillon." She said "Ruth Dillon." Knowing the receptionist would at least find a patient under that name, even if she had been discharged a month ago.

She carried on reading through the book. Then she saw it. There was his name. Fergus Goodheart. He had visited her, it wasn't a dream. She quickly took her phone out and took a photo of his name and the date he visited.

"Sorry, it looks like Ruth checked out last year, I'm afraid."

"No worries. Thanks for your help" Ruth put the visitors book back, opening it on the newest page and left.

She pulled her phone out as soon as she got back to her car. She was surprised Fergus had come to see her; he was an ex from many years ago. They had vaguely stayed in touch after they split up, which was all very much a friendly and mutual affair, but he was a doctor in the army and was always to track down. The last she knew; he was based in Northern Ireland. She decided to email him to catch up and thank him for his support.

She didn't even realise her friends had told him she was in hospital, she wished they had told her so she could have been prepared.

It didn't seem worth a confrontation, so she left it and drove home, deciding to do a short five mile run when she returned.

She came back from her run and saw she already had an email back from Fergus. It was lovely to hear from him. He'd been working in Cyprus since they last spoke and hadn't left the country in over a year, so it wasn't him that had visited her. Well, someone with his name had definitely visited her. She saw his distinctive face with his red hair and imperial moustache, she had never met anyone who looked like him, so someone who at least looked like him had visited her too. Unless someone was impersonating him.

Wringing her hands, she tried to stop thinking about it. Paranoia was a symptom she showed related to her borderline personality disorder and that's probably what she was being; paranoid. Standing in-front of the mirror, she looked gaunt, thin and pale, despite all the running outside she had been doing recently. She had to get a grip, all this worrying was making her age prematurely. She had vowed not to get Botox till she was at least forty.

Chapter 26

Ruth got a call from Nathan at lunchtime that Monday, which she welcomed as she hadn't seen him or spoken to him for ages and she had received another email that morning and she needed to take her mind off it.

"Hello stranger!" She said.

"Hey Ruth, how's things?"

"Fine I guess. How was your Christmas and New Year? I haven't spoken to you for so long, have you been avoiding me?"

"Well, sort of." Nathan said shiftily. "What do you mean 'fine, I guess'?"

"Ahh, just more emails. I've had a few more emails over the Christmas period and then they disappear so I can't show anyone. They're really making me question everything, you know, am I ok? Should I be telling my psychiatrist that I keep seeing these emails or am I actually receiving these emails. Got me thinking about a dream I had when I was in hospital. I really thought I saw Fergus. You know, the army doctor?"

"Yeah, I remember him, red hair?"

"Right, red hair, and the moustache."

"The moustache, yes! Unforgettable!"

"Anyway, I was sure I saw him in hospital, I must have been heavily sedated as he was quite blurry, but it was unmistakeably him. I had a look at the visitors book at the hospital today and he did visit me."

"Wait, you looked at the visitors book at the hospital?"

"Yes, Nathan, I went to the hospital today and read through the visitors book. According to the book, Fergus visited me. He signed in using his full name and I even took a photo of it."

"Well, that's nice of him to have visited. Ruth, hun, why did you need to see the visitors book? Couldn't you have just asked him? I mean, you're still in touch aren't you?"

"I had to see the visitors book because I had another email, telling me that they had watched me sleeping whilst I was knocked out in hospital. I had to see if I recognised any names in that book. Do you think Fergus is messing with me?"

"Ruth, I, really don't know what to say. I mean, you and Fergus are friends right? Why would he do that?"

"Oh yeah, sorry, I'm feeling confused. I know, so I emailed him, and he's been in Cyprus for over a year, so it couldn't have been him that visited me!"

"So, Ruth, what's your point?" Asked Nathan exasperated.

"So, someone impersonated Fergus!" Ruth shouted down the phone. "I even have evidence that someone signed in to see me as him, I took a photo of the entry in the visitors book. I'll send it to you. Wait! It's gone. The photo, it was on my phone!"

"Ruth, are you sure you took a photo of this visitors book? I mean did you even leave the house today? Are you sure you didn't imagine this?"

"What?!" Ruth was angry. "How dare you question me! How can you not believe me!"

"Look, Ruth, I'm sorry, OK? I've been in hospital myself since the 30th December."

"Oh Nathan! Why, have you been ill?"

"No, not ill. The morning we were all due to be meeting in the park on the 30th December Dom and I popped out to get some food from Tesco first thing. We really just needed to get out and get a break from our screens as we'd both been working all night. We got a couple of miles down the road and I thought I'd left my hair straighteners on. Well, you know me, I wouldn't be able to focus on anything if I didn't check, so we had to drive back. I ran in the house, ran straight upstairs, and checked the hair straighteners, incidentally they were off. I ran back downstairs again, about to run out the house when someone took a swing at me as I was running down the last step. I completely blacked out for a second and hit the deck. I then got beaten up to an inch of my life. I was on the floor so I couldn't fight back." Nathan fought back tears. "I was completely helpless. I thought I was gone. I was just losing consciousness again when Dom came in and scared them off."

"Nate." Ruth was stunned.

"So, Dom called an ambulance for me and they kept me in until the 4th January. I asked Dom to not tell you what had happened, I just didn't want to talk about it. I had a collapsed lung, broken ribs, my face was black and blue, I was a mess. I'm still bruised, just, more mentally bruised now. I was completely taken off guard. I'm a fit guy, I could have fought them off, but I stayed on the floor and took the beating. I don't know what came over me."

"Survival Nate. Your body did what it thought was best to survive." Ruth whispered.

"Yeah. So anyway, I've got a black eye still and my nose is swollen and that is why. Fancy meeting for a coffee/"

"Yes, want to come over here?"

"Yes please." Said Nathan. "See you in thirty minutes."

Nathan was at Beaudesert 25 minutes later. Ruth pulled him into a big bear hug, realising she'd been so self absorbed lately, she had hardly checked in on any of her friends.

"Ouch, still a bit tender on the ribs there Ruthie!"

"Sorry Nate. I, I didn't think. Look, I really am sorry for not being there for you, or at least I'm sorry that you didn't feel like you could come to me.

I've been completely wrapped up in myself, these emails, feeling like I'm being watched, I just don't know what to do with myself."

"Hey, it's fine, I had Dom with me; he's been looking after me. I honestly don't know what I'd do without him." Nathan followed Ruth down th hallway to the kitchen and perched on a stool, whilst Ruth made coffee.

"He is pretty great. Good old Dom." Agreed Ruth. She couldn't remember first meeting him, it was just like he had always quietly been part of Nathan's life.

"So show me these emails Ruth, what's going on?"

"Well, that's the problem, I told you, I can't show you, they keep disappearing."

"That's ridiculous, how can they just disappear. Check your deleted items again. Emails don't just disappear unless you delete them and if you've accidently deleted it, it will be in your deleted items folder."

"Well you know I've checked all my folders and they aren't there. I can't explain it." She paused. "Nate, I had another email this morning. It just said "I know what you did". I think its referring to what we did at Linkertons."

"Jesus, stop jumping to the worst conclusion. You're such a catastrophist! Do explain to me why you think this is to do with Linkertons." Said Nathan, cocking his head to one side, ready for Ruth's elaborate but implausible story.

"Fine. I know you don't believe me, but I will explain to you. So, everyone knows that my biggest fear is being sectioned when there is nothing wrong with me. I'm fairly eccentric and sometimes do things out of the ordinary and have also struggled with mental health illnesses in the past, so this could happen. I was fairly vocal about this at school wasn't I? I even did a speech about it for debate club. It's no secret. So, I think someone is sending me these emails, to scare me, make me feel threatened and insecure and then they are putting a timer on them to delete after a certain amount of time, so that no-one believes me when I try to talk about them, leaving me completely alone. This person is making me think they are watching me in my room and have access to even places like the hospital. This person obviously dressed up like Fergus and came to visit me."

"And why would they dress up like Fergus?" Asked Nathan, humouring Ruth.

"It's obviously part of their ploy to make me question my sanity. Fergus is an easy person to dress up as, you know, red hair, *that* moustache."

"And how would this person know what Fergus looks like?"

"Facebook! I see him probably once every two years and we'll generally go to a pub for a few drinks. He always talks photos and posts them on Facebook. It would be clear to anyone that we are friends and his name is on his profile. He doesn't say where he works though, so this person probably wasn't banking on him being in Cyprus right now."

"OK, so Linkertons? What's the link? Hee hee." Nathan giggled at himself and the pun.

Completely ignoring Nathans chuckles, she carried on explaining. "Its one of the few things I've done wrong in my life. One of the few things I've done that could have repercussions. You know this right? You are aware of possible repercussions yes?"

"Of course I'm aware. I still think about it, but its pretty old news. It was years ago."

"Some people don't forget. Remember Ivor? He might still be annoyed with us."

"Naah, not Ivor, so he found out he was adopted. Big deal, I mean his parents should have told him sooner and anyway it's not like he had a bad life, in fact his parents gave him a great life."

"But he shouldn't have found out that way. I just mean, there could be a lot of people out there still not happy with us."

"I think you have an answer for everything Ruth, so can we just drop it please? I think you're wrong, lets just agree to disagree. You're safe here ok, your parents have got your back. So what happened on the 30th anyway? I hear you forgot to plug the Tesla in?"

"That's the point, Nate! I did plug it in, I know I did! Someone is following me and trying to discredit me!"

"No-one is doing that. I think you have so much on your mind that you're forgetting to do things."

"Who told you that anyway?" Flared Ruth, getting annoyed that her friends had been talking about her behind her back.

"Rory. I only spoke to him over the phone as I lent him the money for the new Renshaw's location. I didn't tell him about being beaten up, it really was just a quick chat. He just said he was worried about you."

"OK." Said Ruth Sullenly.

"So anyway," Nathan tried to brighten up the conversation, knowing he was going to find no common ground with Ruth talking about the emails. "How's it going having your house back. Must be quiet without the Renshaw's?"

"Yeah, its actually too quiet, I miss them, but they've been really stressed recently, focusing on the restaurant so I think it was good for them to have their own space. Everything seems to have happened really quickly, thanks to you and a friend of Mum's on the council who helped push their application to use the premises as a restaurant through. They had all the contractors ready to go so they had already done most of the ground work. Gosh they're so resilient to be able to bounce back from having their lease cancelled at the last minute. Credit to them, they're going to be great business partners."

"Totally agree, I'm so proud of them."

"Are you going to be in the country for their opening night?" Ruth asked anxiously

"I've got a lot on over the next few months getting the app finalised and launched, but hopefully.."

Chapter 27

"Welcome to Renshaw's!" Corrinne beamed as Vanessa, Maryam and Keith walked through the doors of the newly opened restaurant into an already buzzing room. Vanessa was already starting to feel overwhelmed and she had barely entered the room. The smart casual dress code was definitely adhered to and less so on the casual side. She had never seen so many designer shoes and handbags at a 'smart casual' event. Most people in here were probably wearing designer clothes too. She tugged self-consciously at her h and m blazer and 10-year-old bag from somewhere in Camden Market that was definitely not designer. Maryam sensed her fidgeting at put a gentle arm round her, protectively pulling her between herself and her dad. Vanessa took a deep breath.

"You can do this. You are good enough" she told herself.

"The bar is open," Corinne recited "you'll find canapes being served throughout the evening, using produce from local farms as much as we could. Each canape is a smaller version of a meal that will be on the menu this coming season, so you are having a cheeky taster of the menu to whet your appetite."

"Thanks Corrinne, Exciting! How are you finding your first day?" Maryam asked.

"Yes, so exciting! Well, I've been here a week now, just helping Rory and Amelia get ready for opening night, so I know my way around now, and I love speaking to customers, explaining the spirit and ethos of Renshaw's, so I'm in my element."

"Well, it looks like you're doing a great job. I'm sure we'll catch you later."

Amelia came over as soon as she had spotted them and gave them a big hug.

"Thanks for coming guys! It means so much. Look, there's so much going on tonight and I really want to chat to some of the local chicken farmers and see if we can establish some sort of supply chain arrangement, and the gazettes here, along with some food bloggers and..."

"Go go go!" Laughed Vanessa. "You can chat to us anytime. Go do some business boss lady! Shout if you need us to do anything. We're here for you both."

"Thankyou. I think the evenings all organised, so you guys just enjoy yourselves. The rest of the gang are here somewhere, canapes are going round, they're…."

"Yes, mini versions of dishes on your menu this season as a pre-taster. Brilliant idea! Your front of house employee is obviously fully trained up and is telling everyone about the local produce."

"Ah great, I was a little worried as sometimes she seems a little off and we took her on through a recommendation, rather than via the agency and haven't seen any references and er…anyway that is not your problem. I'm just glad she's doing her job. Right, I am going to go upstairs to the kitchen and have a minute to chill and calm down, everything seems in hand down here. You guys, have fun."

"This place looks great." Maryam called as Amelia darted off to the kitchen to calm down. "Wow, I've not seen her that wired, I think, ever"

"Me neither" Vanessa agreed. "This is a huge deal though. It's got to be a success for the sake of their family and with all the roadblocks they've come across so far, the delay on opening has probably caused a lot of stress. Look, there's Gwen, lets head over"

"You know Ness," Maryam grabbed her arm before she walked off, letting Keith walk on a few paces "No-one here is judging you by what you look like, or comparing achievements. This is a group of people who have come to support the opening of a restaurant. Nothing more. Be kind to yourself, relax and enjoy the evening."

Vanessa just looked at her friend and nodded. It was like Maryam knew her innermost thoughts before she had even understood what she was thinking herself.

Gwen was mulling about near the bar with some guests and Beverley and had just got a round of drinks in for everyone. "Keith! Nessie, Mimi! Just in time, what can I get you? Wine? Whisky? Gin? They have a fair few craft gin here. Or shall I get 3 more glasses and you can have some of this champagne?"

"Some champagne would be great thanks."

"Not for me," piped up Keith. "Glass of Malbec if they have it, please. Never been a champagne lover myself, I'll leave that to you ladies."

"No problem," said Beverley handing champagne glasses to Vanessa and Maryam.

"You must try the tuna and asparagus tartlets with quail's eggs by the way. Simply divine." Announced Gwen as she floated over to greet the three of them with kisses all round."

"Keith, can I introduce you to Lois and Edmund Teedale. They both worked at our old school, Lois taught History and Edmund was a lab technician." The Teedale's raised their glasses in Keith's direction at Gwen's introduction.

"This is my good friend Maryam's Father, Keith Suncliffe."

"Nice to meet you both," beamed Keith. "Now you must tell me how you managed to work with children every day, it must have been so difficult having to teach, discipline, mentor and counsel on a daily basis, especially with such low pay and long hours." Maryam smiled, happy that her dad didn't need babysitting; he could talk to anyone and more than that, he had the charm and charisma that meant most people not only wanted to talk to him, but liked him. Very rare to come across a likeable car salesman in her experience. He obviously chose the right career. She looked round for Vanessa, but she looked comfortable, deep in conversation with Beverley, so she wandered off to find the others.

Maryam found Luke in a corner with Sylvia and Steven, having a conversation with furrowed eyebrows that she wasn't sure she wanted to interrupt.

"Hi guys. How's everyone doing?"

"Hi Maryam! Lovely to see you! We were actually just talking about you." Sang Sylvia

Luke gave her a hug.

"Oh dear!" Chuckled Maryam. "Good or bad?"

"Oh, good things of course, always good things." Said Steven." We're going to float the company on the stock exchange."

"Oh wow, that's so exciting! What's your reason? I mean, I don't want to sound negative, but there's a lot more regulatory requirements when you do this, so a fair bit more work."

"Yes, well that's exactly why we were talking about you. We've obviously never done this before. We know how to run a company, but the reporting requirements behind a listed company are completely new to us. We've only ever used an accountant to make sure we are paying people correctly and paying the right amount of tax, so we're not sure where to start."

"Well, we do know where to start dear," interjected Sylvia, "we need a finance director, or at least a finance director level consultant to help us through the preparation of and floatation of the company, with around 6 to 9 months of hand holding afterwards."

"Our lawyers are ready to go," continued Steven, "as soon as we have a finance director appointed to assist us with any financial compliance we need. We were hoping to offer the role to yourself. It's a fully paid role of course, we wouldn't be asking you to be giving us pro bono advice, it's much more than just advice we are after, so it would be a full-time commitment."

"Oh gosh, thanks! I'm flattered that you'd trust me with this task, I know how important this company is for you. Well, I would definitely be interested. Perhaps you could send me over some more details regarding your requirements, expectation etc. Let me give you my card, it's got my work email address on."

"Exciting stuff, eh?!" Smiled Luke. "Ah here's Laura and Ruth with the drinks."

Laura was snaking her way through the crowd holding a bottle of champagne, closely followed by Ruth who was cradling an orange juice.

Laura handed over the champagne to Luke who obediently started pouring. "Top up Maryam?"

"No thanks, I've barely touched this one. How's things Laura? Long time no see! Great thanks, I've just got a new jobs, still corporate law, but only in London once a week, which is brilliant. I have a bit more time on my hands, now I'm not travelling as much, so I've also started a podcast, something I've had in the pipeline for a while, just never had the time to actually get it going."

"That's amazing Laura. Congratulations on the new job. And what's the podcast going to be about?"

"It's going to be talking about mainly lifestyle choices that I have made, follow, trends that I might try out, things I enjoy, like. Basically, me talking about a whole load of stuff that Luke doesn't want to listen to me jabber on about."

"Well, it's a great way to do it and you can potentially make money out of it too, so bonus! Ruth, hey! I was sure I saw you just behind Laura and then you disappeared."

"Hey love. I was right behind her, then Beverley caught me, so I stopped to say hi briefly. I didn't know she was coming here tonight. In the space of me stopping to chat for like 2 minutes, she managed to bump into me twice and spill half of my orange juice and her champagne over both me and Vanessa!" She rolled her eyes, pointing at her half full glass and now sticky top.

"Oh, bless her! How are you doing anyway?".

"Fine Maryam, really, thanks for asking. Fine" Ruth was fed up of everyone asking how she was. She thought was doing well. She felt good, stable, happy, had plans for the future and didn't believe there was much that could swerve her off this path she was on. Everything felt right at the moment, apart from those emails. "OK, so I'm going to down the rest of this orange juice as there's like only a sip left and get another from the bar so I have a drink for the speeches in a bit. Catch you later."

Maryam knew Ruth was trying to get out of talking about her feelings; Rory and Amelia hadn't planned speeches to be for another hour. She let her go though and turned to catch up with Luke and Laura.

Rory looked around the room, proud of what he and his wife had achieved. He was certain they were going to make this a success, creating a legacy for the twins. The setbacks had not been easy, but they had overcome them and managed, in two months, to create from scratch a restaurant with character and an indulgent, modern menu and all within their ethos of buying as local as possible. It was a luxurious restaurant but being a small space, it still felt intimate. All of the downstairs area was completely full with guests, friends, family, suppliers, contractors who had been involved in the speedy makeover, press, local councillors, even an ex-teacher and her husband. Most people invited had actually come, which was unexpected. He'd anticipated only around a 40% acceptance rate from guests, but evidently lots more people were excited and happy to support this new restaurant than he had expected.

Amelia pulled him out of his daze, putting her arms round his waist.

"So far so good right?"

"So far so good" murmured Rory. "I don't know how we did it, but we did."

"Grit and determination. And of course, we couldn't have done it without the input from the twins in the menus." They'd let the twins help design one meal on the menu for the season and chef Leia was kind enough to facilitate this. She was a good egg; someone she'd known since her university days and she trusted her to do a good job. She had worked all around the world in high end restaurants and was ready to head up her own kitchen. She'd initially approached her about the chef role at their restaurant over a year ago, just floating the idea of her as head chef to see what she thought of it and she practically accepted the hypothetical job offer straight away. Fast forwards a year and she was indeed head chef. She had spent weeks perfecting a menu, and testing out all the kitchen equipment, making sure she was comfortable with everything. Being such a small restaurant, they were not going to have any other kitchen staff to start with, so it was essential Leia was competent in the kitchen. Leia had made every course on the menu last week, which the three of the sat down and critiqued. A few minor tweaks and the menu was finalised, so she certainly seemed competent in the kitchen.

"Of course, our 10-year-old food aficionados." Said Rory affectionately. "By the way, have you had a chance to take a peek at the piece of art that Ana gifted us from the gallery? I must admit, I haven't had a chance to look"

"No, me neither. That's fine though I think. We can see it at the same time as everyone else at the unveiling, in about 30 minutes." Amelia checked her watch. "Which reminds me, I must catch up with Greg Tanner, he's the chicken farmer that we were talking about getting regular deliveries from. Oh, look there's Nathan coming through the door, go and say hi from me. Oh, and don't forget to get a few words in with the guy from the gazette, I can't remember his name, but he's milling about somewhere, he's the one with an SLR round his neck."

"Got it sweetie." He kissed her gently on the cheek and went to greet Nathan.

Ruth had also seen Nathan and was bounding over to the door, drink in hand, but wobbled on her heel and down in spectacular style. Rory saw it happening in slow motion, she wiggled her hips deftly to the right to avoid bumping into someone, but her momentum was still propelling her top half forwards, which she realised only too late, tried to slow herself down by jerking herself the opposite direction and backwards, but her ankle gave way, she wobbled on her heel and went down with a loud squeal., her shoe skidding across the floor. The buzz in the room died down to a quiet hum, for a moment everyone staring at Ruth. Rory and Nathan both ran over and picked her and her shoe up.

"God Ruth, are you ok? That was a dramatic greeting!" Nathan was a tad concerned she'd been drinking, but then he couldn't smell any alcohol on her.

Ruth starting laughing hysterically." This is why I don't wear heels guys! Oh, my goodness. Ah ha ha ha, my eyes are streaming!" she cried as she mopped at her eyes. "Thanks for picking me up, I'm fine, I'm just erm, I just going to sort myself out in the bathroom. Back shortly."

Nathan and Rory exchanged a quick knowing glance, but never spoke about it.

"Congratulations on everything you've done here mate, this looks incredible"

"Cheers man, obviously we couldn't have done it without you, I can't tell you how much we…"

"I know mate, I really do. Anyway, come and catch me later, go and mingle and do business. I'll find my way around"

"Amelia says hi by the way. She was running off to speak to a chicken farmer."

"Of course, she was" Smiled Nathan "Because that's a normal thing to do at a party! Give your beautiful wife a big kiss on the cheek from me and tell her I'll see her later too."

Nathan had got himself a lemonade from the bar and made his way over to the corner that Luke, Sylvia and Steven hadn't left all evening by the time Ruth had emerged from the bathroom. She wasn't in hysterics now and looked a little out of sorts. She was slouched and walked with more of a lop-sided swagger than her usual elegant saunter and although her make up looked perfect and not a hair was out of place in her stylish updo, her could tell before even speaking to her that she was under the influence of something.

"Ruth," he called, hoping to speak to her without the rest of the group overhearing, "Do you want to talk?"

"Nathan! Yesh, lests talk about this shirt. Ish sho unique." She said fingering Nathans silk pink and orange "I-refuse-to-be-seen-as-a-boring-tech-guy" shirt.

"Ruth, you've been in the bathroom for 20 minutes, have you taken something, you can tell me"

"Of courshe not! I've not drank or taken any pills since before Christmassshhs! I feel good"

"Really Ruth? Because you're slurring your words and wobbling and…"

"Shhh Rory'sh abour to shpeak."

Rory gently tapped the microphone, coughed nervously and then started talking into it.

"Thanks everyone for coming. Amelia and I are grateful to each and every one of you for making the effort to come out tonight and celebrate Renshaw's opening night! It's not been smooth sailing, but I'm pretty sure Christopher Columbus didn't complain of that when he crossed the Atlantic. He he, erm, so we'd like to...Oh Hi Ruth! Erm..."

Ruth grabbed the microphone from Rory.

"Ssso my name is Ruth and I want to thank my friendsss for life itself. For being at my ultramarathon races, for holding my tights together when they fall down and to Mum and Dad for not shelling the businessh and woops...!"

Ruth fell backwards and Rory could see it all in slow motion again. She was grabbing at the air to try and break the fall, but there was no-one there. She glanced behind her to see what she was falling into, realising it was a table with loads of full wine glasses, she twisted and ended up falling just to the right of the tables, where the yet to be unveiled painting from Ana stood, knocked it off the stand and put her foot through it. The room went completely silent.

Nathan ran to Ruth and picked her up, motioning to Rory to carry on with his speech. Completely thrown, Rory stood there in silence until Amelia appeared by his side with the retrieved microphone and started speaking about the local farmers who had supplied tonight's ingredients for the canapés.

Sylvia and Steven rushed over in a panic, but Nathan held them back at a distance. He knew and they knew that something was up with Ruth, whether it was drink or drugs, they couldn't be certain. What he did know was that Ruth's night was over, but Sylvia's and Stevens night didn't need to be.

"I'll drive her home, my cars just round the corner and I'll stay with her till tomorrow. You guys don't get much time off together, so stay here and enjoy your night, ok?"

"Oh Nathan, you're a good friend. I don't know what she's been drinking, I've only seen her drink orange juice tonight, so she must have snuck something in without us seeing. Did you see her drink anything Steven?"

"Nothing."

"Ok. We're going to go through the back door so we don't disturb Rory and Amelia's speech any more than we have already done. Please say my goodbyes to them."

"We will do of course Nathan. Here's my set of keys to the side entrance, you know, the one next to the staff kitchen, to the right of the front door. The security light isn't working there at the moment, which reminds me we really must get that fixed, so you may need to use the torch on your phone."

"I've not actually got a phone on me right now, I'm having a screen free evening so I left it at the farm, but I'll find it. I think I know the door you mean."

"OK, I'll leave it with you. Thankyou!" Called Sylvia, staring worriedly after her daughter.

Nathan half carried; half dragged Ruth out the back door. He had forgotten that he was actually in what used to be a house and the back door led into a somewhat overgrown garden, rather than onto the street, so he had to find the gate to the street. Once he found it, there were wheelie bins blocking their way, so he had to put Ruth down on the ground for a moment to move them out the way. Ruth was lying flat on the floor moaning when he came back to her, so he scooped her up and carried her to his car, where he gently laid her on the back seat. He clipped her in as best he could and drove to Beaudesert.

All the staff were sleeping when he arrived at Beaudesert, they didn't cross paths with anyone, which was a blessing for Ruth as it meant there would be less chatter and gossip about her. They made it to Ruth's bedroom and he carefully laid her on the bed, took her shoes off and tucked her in. He debated taking her make up off for her, but he figured she could cope going one night without taking it off and besides he was a tired from the flight from Germany this morning.

Ruth stirred and tried to sit up. "Naaaathan? I'm, I'm shorry I…"

"Ssssh it's ok, lets chat tomorrow."

"I didn't drink."

"You didn't drink? I believe you hun, I couldn't smell anything on you, but you took something else, didn't you? Its ok, go to sleep. We'll get you the help you need."

Ruth fell back asleep and Nathan tried to get comfy on Ruth's chaise longue. Sylvia had called him a number of times over the past few weeks to talk about Ruth's deterioration. She was becoming more and more delusional, seeing things that weren't there, suffering from crippling paranoia, thinking she was being threatened by somebody by these non-existent emails, forgetting things and just generally showing uncharacteristically strange behaviour. Then of course, there was the drugs; Sylvia and Steven have had their suspicions for a few weeks, but couldn't prove anything. Tonight, was all the evidence Nathan needed to agree with Sylvia that the best thing for Ruth right now was to get her admitted to hospital. She needed professional help now; friends and family were not going to cut it and this drugs usage needed to be stopped now before it got worse.

He was just dozing off, when he heard a light tap on the door. "Mmmyes come in." He called. Sylvia and Steven both walked in as he was getting up off the chaise longue trying to shake off the sleep. "Nathan, thank you for bring her home." Started Steven. "We're so worried about her."

"No problem, Steven. Look, I've been worried too and tonight I think, shows she needs more help. She's obviously taken something and I'm pretty sure it's not alcohol, I mean no-one saw her drinking and I couldn't smell anything on her. I feel like we may be facilitating her behaviour accepting everything she has been saying and doing, like its ok, rather than challenging it. I think we need professional help now."

"Nathan, I'm so glad you agree. I know we don't need your endorsement for this, but as one of her closest friends, I think it's important that you are involved in this decision, so it's not just her parents forcing this on her. I'll make the calls this first thing in the morning."

"Oh, my baby girl, I just want her to be well." Lamented Steven.

"She will be, she will." Reassured Nathan. "This time will be different. We'll make sure of it."

"Do you need a guest bedroom setting up for you?" Asked Sylvia.

"No thanks, Ill head back to my Airbnb. I've got the place on the farm down the road again. All my stuffs there, I dropped it off just before I headed to Renshaw's, I came straight from the airport. Plus, Dominic will be expecting me too. He'll send out the search parties if I don't come back soon!"

"Very well. We'll call you in the morning when we have a plan. Thanks again."

"You can see yourself out? We'll stay here with Ruthie for a little while." Nathan's heart ached when he heard Steven refer to Ruth as "Ruthie", something he hadn't heard him call he since she was a child. Steven really was hurting for Ruth.

Nathan quietly closed Ruth's door behind him and walked along the hallway, down the immense staircase and stood in the downstairs atrium for a moment. It really was quiet here, eerily so. Letting himself quietly out the side door, he suddenly saw movement near the stables. He froze, wondering who could be out with the horses this time of night. He stared at the same spot that he saw movement for a good 5 minutes, but saw nothing else and decided it must have been a fox or his tired eyes playing tricks. He jumped back into his car and drove to the farmhouse of a long-needed rest.

Chapter 28

Ruth stretched, looking outside. It was a beautiful day outside, the sun was shining, it looked a little chilly, not too windy, perfect day for a run. She jumped out of bed, but then remembered last night.

She had most definitely not been drinking, nor had she been taking pills. At least she didn't think she'd taken any pills. She couldn't remember if the pills she remembered taking were last night or the ones she took a few months ago that left her in hospital. What if she didn't take any pills? Then someone must have given them to her. But she had a history of taking pills, so she probably did. She must have hidden them somewhere in her room. Yes! That was it, she needed to see evidence of the hidden pills in her room so she knew what was real.

She started by stripping her bed and taking the mattress off. Nothing.

She emptied her wardrobe, checking all the pockets she could find. Nothing.

The desk, she must have hidden them in her desk. Nothing.

Bathroom cabinets emptied onto the floor. Nothing.

She stood in the middle of her room that she had managed to tear up in about 10 minutes, running her hands through her hair. She knew she must have been on drugs last night, so where did she hide them? She wouldn't dare hide them in any other part of her parent's house, they must be in her bedroom, but she'd looked in all her old hiding places and found nothing.

Think. Think. Think.

She bent down on her hands and knees in a half-hearted attempt to look under her bed, which was so heavy, she knew she couldn't move by herself, but worth a look.

Her parents burst into the room as she was running her hands through her hair, trying to make sense of what had happened last night.

"Oh, Ruth darling." Sylvia ran over to Ruth, sat down and cradled her in her arms. "It's ok. its ok. We're fixing this. We're getting you help now."

"Mum, what, what are you on about?"

"Ruth darling, what happened to your room?"

"I was …just…looking for something."

"Of course, darling. Its ok." Sylvia started rocking Ruth backwards and forwards. "It's all sorted. Anthony is going to drive you there in an hour when your escort arrives. It will be two weeks of intensive therapy and then we'll know more about your recovery plan after that."

"Oh God Mum, what's sorted, I have no idea what you're on about. I speak to my psychiatrist once a week and I know exactly what my recovery plan looks like, I'm not driving anywhere today as I'm running one of the last sections of the race that I'm planning, plus, it's his day off and Frank works weekends remember, not Anthony."

"Darling, you're not well. Your therapy sessions and your current recovery plan are clearly not working. After what happened last night and now this morning, I mean, your room…" Sylvia paused, trying to gather her words and continues very slowly. "Well, your Father and I, and, well Nathan too have decided that it is in your best interests to spend a little time away at a retreat to erm, allow you to recover more quickly."

"What the fuck, you're sectioning me? I have no idea what happened last night, but I swear I'm fine!"

"Ruth, it's not just last night, it's the build-up of the last few months. The threatening non-existent emails, struggling getting on with your life, I mean you've not been plugging your Tesla in, "

"That's was once Mum and I swear I plugged it in!"

"OK fine, but the substance abuse, I'm sure this has been going on for a while now, "

"No no no!"

"Basic tasks you seem to be struggling with. You are so paranoid that people are watching and following you, which is so not the case, we have security footage to prove this! And now your room…" Sylvia was lost for words. She really needed Ruth to agree to go to this facility on her own free will as she really didn't want to section her.

"Mum, I can explain all that behaviour and as for the emails I'm not lying, I just can find them after I've read them. Yes, I've been a little paranoid that someone is following me, but I'm sure someone is, I've seen the same car a number of times in different locations, our home security footage proves nothing, only that whoever is following me was clever enough to avoid the cameras. And my bedroom…well…I was looking for something and it's my bedroom, so I can do what I want in it!" Ruth was very aware that she was sounding more and more unstable with every word that came out of her mouth. Truth be told, she now wasn't 100% certain that she was being followed and was starting to think she was being slightly paranoid. She honestly didn't know what had happened last night, and realised how it looked, walking into your daughters room the morning after she was off her face on a concoction of pills and she has just completely trashed the room.

"Dad, any input?" Demanded Ruth, knowing full well he would agree with her Mum.

"Ruthie, I want you to be happy and right now, you don't seem happy, so yes, I think you need some time away in this retreat. It's in Wales, in the mountains, so should be very therapeutic."

"And Nathan?!" Ruth couldn't believe Nathan was in on this.

"Yes darling, he brought you home last night. We mentioned it then and he agreed, given the state you were in last night and have been the last few weeks."

"OK fine, so how long do you need me to agree to be away for?"

"Two weeks for the initial intensive treatment."

"Fine, and this is all voluntary and private right? So, I can leave whenever I want?"

"Yes, but…"

"Yeah, yeah I know, it's for my own benefit that I stay."

"We'd hoped you'd agree, without us needing to get power of attorney. We've given Anthony an extra day's work to drive you there as I know you know him better than Frank. A representative from the Rhyddid centre in Wales will be here in about an hour to escort you there. They will be there for you to talk to, as an ally, a counsellor, a friend, mentor, whatever you need, but we will be signing a form to allow them to physically restrain you, should you try to take any form of drugs or try to harm yourself in any way on this journey."

Ruth inhaled slowly. She was in a good place in her life, she didn't want to harm herself, she didn't think she had a drugs problem and she had a plan for the future, but if this was how she could prove to her family and friends that she was OK, then she would do it. She looked at her parents, taking in their concerned faces. They suddenly looked old, with a lot of pain in their hearts. Realising that this pain was mainly caused by her, she exhaled and stood up.

"You're right. Ill pack. I'll be downstairs in 20 minutes, then maybe we can have breakfast together before I go?"

"Ruthie I'm so proud of you for deciding this." Steven managed a small smile. Sylvia gave Ruth one last squeeze before they both left the room.

Ruth knew she had to see this as an opportunity to mend anything that was still broken and hurting inside of her, but she couldn't help feeling like it was a betrayal, she'd expected this from her parents, they'd done it before when her erratic behaviour had warranted cause for concern and professional help was needed, but she hadn't expected this from Nathan. This can't have been a spur of the moment decision by the three of them last night that's too rash even for her parents, and for Nathan to have known what she had been doing the last few weeks, they must have been speaking to him, updating him behind her back. She thought Nathan was an ally, but seemingly she couldn't trust him anymore.

She picked up her phone to message her yoga instructor, apparently the only person she could rely on being supportive at the moment, but saw a new email message pop up. She took a deep breath and clicked into her emails, hoping it was a junk email. It wasn't. Another email.

SLOWLY LOSING IT. IS IT ME OR IS IT YOU? EITHER WAY, YOU'RE GOING TO LOSE EVERYTHING SOON.

Ruth took a screen shot straight away and sent it her yoga instructor. If her friends didn't believe her, at least he would. She stared at the screen, willing him to respond. Throwing her phone across the room in frustration, she decided she should probably pack; rather she chose the underwear she wanted for the next 2 weeks than the burly, self-righteous escort who was coming to collect in, now less than half an hour.

She packed a bag, if throwing some knickers, leggings, t shirts and a toothbrush in a bag is considered packing and retrieved her phone. Her friends still didn't believe her about these emails she'd been getting so she didn't think they deserved to know where she was going, but Joshua had been a constant relief for the last few months since her first session with him. He listened, let her offload and didn't judge. She'd become reliant on him recently as he had a way of helping her to calm her thoughts and think more rationally, although thinking rationally was quite difficult when someone was threatening your family, friends and livelihood on a weekly basis. Joshua deserved to know where she was going and she should at least cancel her sessions with him for the next 2 weeks. She messaged him to say where and why she was going and rushed downstairs for a quick breakfast with Sylvia and Steven.

The escort arrived at 10.30, not someone that Ruth was expecting; Not burly, no overly kind, patronising eyes, no nurses uniform, no "I used to be an addict too and I completely understand what you're going through" stories and no threats of 'If you try to run away, I will do this' kind of thing. Ruth was no longer dreading the car journey as much as she had been earlier this morning.

The time came for her to hand over her phone to Amy, her companion as she called it. She did so grudgingly but knew it wouldn't be forever. Taking a quick peek before handing it over, she saw she had no messages from Joshua; she'd just have to talk to him in a few weeks and hope that the messages she had sent were enough to cancel her classes.

"Please don't tell anyone where I am, Mum." She begged. "I don't want anyone breathing down my neck when I come back, asking me how I am."

"Of course not Love." Said Sylvia. She and Steven gave Ruth a big hug and waved her off, hoping this would be the last time they would be stood here waving their daughter off to another course of rehab.

Chapter 29

Ruth didn't panic as the car was driving away. She didn't feel resentment towards her parents or Nathan for forcing her to do this. More sadness that her parents no longer trusted her and sadness in the loss of the friendship she had with Nathan. He surely didn't care about her the same way now if he thought she had lied so much.

Had she lied so much? Was she lying about what was going on to get attention, to make herself feel like she had a better hold on things than she actually did. She was sure she had plugged her car in to charge just after Christmas, but then, coming back and seeing the car unplugged, did she do that? Did she intentionally not plug her car in, or perhaps just forget?

She was certain she had been receiving emails from someone, threatening her, but when she had taken screen shots or tried to forward them on, no-one had seen her forwarded messages and she hadn't been able to find the emails to show her friends. Perhaps they were a figment of her imagination. Un-said fears manifesting themselves as emails from someone else, so she could distance herself from these terrors, which were in fact her own real nightmares.

Last night. She didn't remember drinking at all. And she didn't remember taking any pills. But then, she did remember taking pills at some point. Perhaps it was last night and her memory is blurring timelines.

She probably did need help, maybe, but she wasn't sure what exactly she needed help with, or how someone could help her. Was she really losing her grip on reality? The more she thought about events over the last few months, the more she realised she wasn't making sense. Her extreme paranoia of being followed was just ridiculous, she was starting to see that now; there was no reason for someone to follow her and she was living in the middle of no-where, it would be pretty obvious if someone started following her on those empty country lanes. She had no enemies, did she? Who would sending her those ridiculous emails? She'd never received anything like them before and it did seem fishy that they started as soon as she'd come out of hospital, when she was at her most vulnerable, she'd been in a long time; she was possibly still experiencing side effects from the drugs in her system and the anti-depressants they'd forced her to take. Yes, she must have been imagining these emails as a coping mechanism.

Her thoughts were starting to spiral, she wasn't able to make sense of anything. What was real, what wasn't. What had happened recently and what had happened month, years ago, it was all merging into one. She couldn't trust that she was going to make good decisions, how can you when you don't know what is real

She was slowly accepting that she needed this "retreat" or whatever it is she was being driven to. She leant back in her seat and closed her eyes, trying to calm her thoughts, settling in for the journey.

Chapter 30

Those pigeons were so loud. That wasn't even the problem, they just made a really really annoying noise and Rome was bloody full of them. Wait, he wasn't in Rome anymore. Where was he? He tried to trace his footsteps last night. He walked off the plane and Dominic herded him into a car and then they arrived home and he went to bed. Nope, too early, he decided, he couldn't remember, he needed a few more hours, so rolled over back to sleep. The pigeons carried on. Wait! That was his phone ringing, not pigeons cooing! What was with the ridiculous ringtone?! He glanced over to his bedside table, looking for his phone. Not where he was expecting it. Looking round the room, he saw a desk which also had his ringing phone on it. He half stumbled and half bounced over to the desk and grabbed his phone, which stopped ringing as soon as he reached it. Typical. At least he knew where he was now.

Squinting at the screen, he tried to see who had called, but gave up. Even when his eyes weren't blurred by sleep and he wasn't stood in a dark room, without his contacts in, he couldn't see a lot. He was trying not to have his life dictated by his phone and live life according to his own schedule a lot more and vowed to check who had been ringing when he was dressed. He was clumsily putting his contacts in, when Dominic burst into the room without knocking.

"Morning Dom! You ok?"

"Nathan, its Gwen," His eyes looked panicked.

"What's she doing calling you?!"

"You need to take this."

Nathan grabbed the phone from Dominic." Gwen?"

"Nate! They've taken them!" Gwen was screaming. He'd never heard her like this. "The kids, they've gone!"

"What?!" Nathan didn't know what to say or do.

"The kids have been taken Nate!" they're gone! They're not here!"

"Right," Nate collected himself. "What?! Have you called the police?"

"Yes, I've fucking called the police!" She screamed back to him.

"Gwen, I'm at the farm down the road. I can be at yours in 20 minutes. What else do you need from me?"

"Nate, Ruth was telling the truth about the emails, the messages. She's not losing it; I believe her now." Gwen sobbed.

"What makes you say that? Tell me Gwen, what else has happened?"

"I received an email last night, exactly how Ruth described hers. I saw the message but didn't bother opening it as I was going to bed. I need you to trace this email and help me find my children"

"I'll be there in 20 minutes Gwen. I'll be bringing Dom too, ok?"

"Nate?" Gwen whispered.

"Yes?"

"They left an old Linkerton's badge on the kid's beds"

Nathan paused, this information sinking in.

"See you in twenty, OK?" Nathan looked at Dominic and just stared.

"What do you need from me Nathan?"

Nathan just kept on staring. What did he need? He didn't know. Where to start? He couldn't think. Linkertons badge. Well, it couldn't be clearer what the motive was.

"OK Nathan, you get yourself dressed." Dominic took charge.

"Gwen's kids have been…"

"I know, I heard. So, let's start by tracing the email Gwen had and we'll go from there"

Nathan just nodded.

"I'll grab everything we need and see you downstairs in 5 minutes ok?"

Nathan nodded.

"Nathan, I need more than that from you. Stand up, snap out of it,"

Nathan looked at Dominic blankly, like he didn't understand what Dominic was saying.

"What's the problem? So its related to your misdemeanour during your school days? Is that what's spooked you? Fine, we'll figure it out. Right now, you need to move, your friend needs you."

Nathan sat up straighter. Happy that he had his boss's attention now, Dominic carried on. "The suitcase closest to the desk has clothes for today; jeans, t shirts, jumpers, boxers, socks, everything is clean, all you need to do is get dressed. Do you need me to pick you some clothes?"

Dominic's forceful tone snapped him out of his trance and Nathan stood up, shook his head and cleared his throat with a little more conviction. "Glasses." He mumbled as Dominic whirled out of the room.

"On the desk." He called over his shoulder.

How the bloody hell did he not see them earlier. OK, it was a glasses day today. Trying not to think about one of his closest friend's children being taken, he got himself dressed, instead, thinking how grateful he was to have Dominic in his life.

Chapter 31

20 minutes later Nathan and Dominic were driving through the gates of Gwen's estate, Heronfield, having been buzzed in by Mike, the estate manager. All the lights inside and outside the house were on and 2 police cars were on their paved semi-circle driveway.

The front door had been opened for them to let themselves in and Nathan led the way through to their main reception room, where Gwen was pacing the room with 2 police officers trying to ask questions. Gwen ran over when she saw them and Nathan hugged her tightly.

"We'll get them back, ok? We'll get them back." Nathan reassured her. Not entirely sure how, but he knew failing was not an option.

"OK, so let's start by tracing this email, Gwen." Nathan and Dominic fired up their laptops.

"Morning sir. I can assure you, that is not necessary. We already have a team looking into this thank you." One of the police officers had obviously been briefed on what Gwen had asked Nathan and Dominic to do and disapproved.

"What do you mean they're already looking into this? You're telling me your cybercrimes team is in the office from 7 in the morning?"

"Err no sir, but they will be starting work at 9 this morning and they will have a report on their desk to look into this email Gwen received straight away." Fumbled the officer, backtracking slightly

"Not good enough. That's already 2 hours away from now before they even enter the office, then another 10 minutes for them to say good morning to each other, then they make themselves a cup of tea and get back to their desks for possibly 9.30 when they may or may not choose to read the latest reports they have in their inbox. They may choose to respond to emails first, who knows. Feel free to have your team look into it, but we will be working on this on the side and will indeed share everything we find with you. Treat it as a free consulting service."

Dominic gave a wry smile. His boss was obviously over his initial shock and when he was this focussed, Dominic had seen him achieve so much. But when he was focussed and livid at the same time, there would be no stopping him.

5 minutes later and Dominic had the ip address that the email had been sent from and Nathan was busy trying to hack into the email account that had sent the email. He hadn't kept quiet about what he was doing, giving a running commentary throughout, partly for the police's benefit and partly for his own, to keep him focussed. The police either didn't care or didn't understand that what he was doing was actually breaking the law, and they continued milling about looking a little lost.

"Nate just tell me where the email was sent from. Please."

"Gwen, patience please," Nate replied, realising straight away that that was the wrong thing to tell someone whose children had just been taken. "Look, I just mean, it's not helpful to know where it got sent from until we know context. I mean, why, erm, who. You know, I just. Well, it was..."

"Stop trying to make up excuses. Where was it sent from?" Gwen demanded.

The police glanced over at Gwen's raised voice then continued their muted conversation with Penelope in the corner of the room.

"Gwen, we still need to investigate this, but ok we'll tell you" Nate looked at Dom for reassurance he was doing the right thing. Dom gave a slight nod.

"Beaudesert. The email was sent from Beaudesert."

"What?!"

"Yes, I recognised the ip address straight away because I hacked into Ruth's emails when she said she was getting those messages. Have a go at me about that another time ok, I realise its wrong and an invasion of her privacy, but just know I was doing it all for the right reasons. I didn't find any emails in Ruth's inbox that looked sinister FYI."

"But who? Ruth's obviously not there right now, but they have so many staff working there, it could be anyone!"

"I'm almost in Gwen. Let's have a look at this email account and see if they have left any clues. Don't get your hopes up yet though, they could have set this account up just to send this one email."

Gwen had started pacing again. One of the police officers noticed and came over. "Everything ok?" she asked.

"Yes yes, he's still digging." Gwen feigned ignorance allowing Nathan to keep this information to himself a little longer. She had more faith that her friend could get results than anyone. "Just frustrated that we've had no ransom note yet"

"Yes ma'am, I completely understand."

"Do you? Do you really understand?"

Nathan looked up hearing Gwen's voice crescendo. He saw her eyes flaring and her lips pursed and knew there was no use trying to save the police officer from the torrent of abuse she was about to receive so he looked down again and busied himself with his laptop.

"My children have been taken from their beds whilst I slept!" Gwen screamed. "How the hell can you possibly understand!"

The police officer remained calm and nodded her agreement at Gwen, who was breathing faster and faster, only just warming up.

"You're absolutely right, but I too have had a child taken from me."

"What?!"

"Yes, my ex took my son when he was 8. It was the middle of the night; he took his passport and they went to Spain for 5 weeks. I got him back un harmed. I really do understand."

"I'm sorry" breathed Ruth. "I'm so glad you said that, I was about to unleash, I'm not quite sure what, but a lot of anger in your direction."

"It's ok Ma'am. Completely understandable and not taken personally. Now can I please just run through this list of staff on the property just to check we have interviewed everyone."

"Of course, but interviewing my staff won't be necessary, they've all been background checked and I completely trust them all."

"Thank you ma'am, it's just protocol and they may have seen or heard something that seems insignificant to them, nut may be useful intel."

"OK sure. Soooo Mike our Butler and estate manager, Penelope our chef, Adie our nanny, who your colleagues are still speaking to next door I believe, Sunita our maintenance lady, Sarah the driver, errr, yes, they were all here last night. Adam is on annual leave until Friday I think, maybe Saturday, and then there's just Lydia, our cleaner. She comes twice a week and does a deep clean of the, you know what, it doesn't matter. She doesn't live here, but she'll be here by 10 today."

"Thankyou. Penelope also mentioned another member of staff." Flicking back through her notebook, the police officer added, "Mark?"

"Ah yes, Mark, he comes over on the weekends and mainly works in the gardens, but he helps out with maintenance of the estate too. He reports to Sunita, she could probably tell you more about his work and the hours he works. Erm, there's no-one else, just my husband who is working away at the moment."

The intercom buzzed. Penelope excused herself from the police officer to answer it, and came back shortly. "Gwen, your parents are here, they're just driving up. Mike is in the hallway and will let them in."

"Thank you, Penelope."

Adie walked into the room, her eyes red, her face blotchy, unable to stop crying. Gwen looked up, trying to feel sympathy for the woman. Her bedroom was in-between both children's bedrooms and Alfie even had a camera in his room and the monitor was on Adie's bedside table, so Adie was feeling a lot of guilt for not hearing anything. If Gwen hadn't been using every fibre of being trying to hold herself together, she would have given her a hug, but instead a nod towards her was all she could muster.

"Gwen, come and look at this." Nathan said quietly. He had hacked into the email account that sent the email to Gwen last night.

"OK, what am I looking at. Ah, yes that's the email the fucker sent me!"

Nathan and Dominic both looked up at Gwen's uncharacteristically colourful language, but let her continue.

"What's this a list of? Oh of course, sent items. OK, soooo?" She looked at Nathan, questioning the significance of what she was looking at, her patience wearing thin.

"Yes, and the last one sent before yours, was back in March, to Ruth. "Slowly losing it. Is it me or is it you? Either way, you're going to lose everything soon." Jeez that's nasty. That was just before she went away."

"You mean just before you and her parents sent her away?"

"Again, it was for the right reasons. Or I thought it was. Look here." He was scrolling through the sent items in this account. "These are all the emails that Ruth said she received. Well, some of them, I guess she stopped telling us about them because we didn't believe her."

"We need to fix this with Ruth, but first, we need to find out who took my children and get them back. How is this helping?"

"Agreed. Gwen, all information at this stage is helpful. Information gathering first then analysing and sifting. Let me just finish looking through these sent items. There's a few to some other email addresses. One to someone at Smith and Barts. Ever heard of them?"

"Nope. What's on the attachment?"

"Smith and Barts is a commercial property leasing company." Announced Dom, quickly looking up the recipient of the email. "Gregory who received this email is one of two managing directors of the company."

"OK and any message?" said Gwen, looking up to see her parents walk through the door. "Mum, Dad!"

"Just a photo of two people in a car kissing." Said Nathan, trying to keep their detective work quiet.

"The man in that photo is Gregory, judging by his linked in profile." Piped up Dominic.

"I'll bet that woman isn't his wife." Added Nathan before Gwen's parents came over.

"Gwendoline!" Spoke her mother. "I can't believe this has happened. We'll pay whatever they ask of course. Have you managed to get hold of Rupert?"

"Oh Mum, that's the thing, we've not had a ransom request at all. I don't know what to. Ruperts flying home from Abu Dhabi in the next hour. Should be here for this afternoon."

Mike came over with a tray of tea.

"Thank you, Mike." Said Gwen's dad.

"My pleasure Mr. Pinecastle."

Nathan and Dominic had been working their way through the sent items and had a plan. Not wanting to make a scene, they excused themselves, Nathan giving Gwen a knowing look to reassure her they were working on something and they left.

Chapter 32

"Turn right out of here. Sat nav says ETA 8am, about 20 minutes."

"Got it." Said Dominic, turning right out of Gwen's estate. "Do you think he'll be there? "

"Well, he's an MD so more likely will want to be there before the rest of his employees and especially today as he has his son's violin concert at the school at 6pm, so he'll probably be leaving work earlier than usual."

"Does no-one have any privacy from the all-seeing eye of Nathan Render?" Smiled Dominic.

"If they're good guys, sure they do!"

20 minutes later, dead on 8am, Nathan and Dominic pulled up in a visitors spot at the offices of Smith and Barts. "Over there, look." Nathan pointed to a black Land Rover in a reserved parking spot with a registration number of **B4rts.** "Think our guys in the office."

There was someone on reception, so they tried their luck and strode into the small office building.

"Good morning. Can you kindly tell Gregory Barts that Nathan Homes and his solicitor are here to see him."

"Good morning, Sir, certainly, although I can't see that he has a meeting with you in his diary."

"We're happy to wait a few minutes." Nathan boldly continued "But we really need to discuss the particulars of the last-minute changes made to our contract that is being signed this afternoon."

"Of course, Let me just call him." She picked up her phone.

"You know, "Nathan was looking around the office and thought he could see the MD's office towards the back. "If he has no meetings in his diary, why don't we just head over and knock on his door. Save you the trouble of calling him."

"Erm, right, let me show you."

"Thank you kindly. No need to get up."

Nathan walked confidently towards the office he was really hoping contained Gregory Barts. When he got there, thankfully, it did.

"Solicitor?" Dominic raised an eyebrow.

"Yes, you wear many hats. OK, let's do this. Although I'm not really sure quite what this is yet."

Nathan knocked on Gregory's door before letting himself and Dominic into his office.

"Gregory. I'm Nathan. I'm going to cut to the chase. You received an email last year containing this photo." He flashed his phone, showing the photo of Gregory in a car with the unknown woman.

"I don't know you, but how dare you blackmail me with this again, I thought we were done!"

"I have not yet blackmailed you; it was not me" interrupted Nathan. "Yes, I thought you had probably been blackmailed when I came across this and I need to find out what you did to keep this photo a secret, who did this and why."

"I don't bloody know who did this, Nathan!" Gregory looked a little despairing. It looked like the blackmailing had taken a large toll on this man. "I don't know why and I'm not going to tell you what I did, I don't bloody know you! If you aren't blackmailing me, then I wish you a good day and I will send you on your way."

"Now I didn't say that I wasn't going to blackmail you. I said I haven't blackmailed you yet. I didn't send you that email in December, I just know about it. I really don't want to threaten you at all, but lives are at stake here, so if I have to, I will. Tell me what you did."

"What's it to you? That photo is out there now, who knows who has copies, so I'm not sure I can stop the inevitable. I'm going to speak to my wife tonight and tell her about it. The affair is long finished, but that of course doesn't excuse it. I only hope she forgives me."

"Very noble of you." Said Nathan sarcastically. "So the people that took that photo, how do you know they're not watching you now, or your wife at home, or your son? Perhaps they'll be at his violin recital tonight?" Nathan paused for dramatic effect, watching Gregory's reaction, hoping that he wouldn't jump to the conclusion that a bit of perfectly legal Facebook stalking of his wife's account had found out all this information. Gregory started running his hands through his hair.

"You don't touch my son." His voice came out in a weak growl, a pathetic attempt at being threatening.

Nathan took pity on the man and decided he wasn't the gangster type and couldn't pull off this tactic, so took a chance and went for the truth.

"Gregory, this is the short story of what has happened. My friend had an email last night, threatening to take her children. This morning, she woke up and her children have gone. The police are involved. I hacked into the email account of whoever sent this email and found the same person sent you this photo. This person is involved in the er, kidnap." His voice faltered. It was the first time he had said the word kidnap out loud and it made it seem all too real. "The kidnap of my dear friend's children. You must be able to give me something."

"Christ, I'm sorry about your friends' children, that's terrible. I know very little. A few months ago, we were going backwards and forwards with a client, fine tuning a contract for a commercial premises. It was a couple that were going to set up a restaurant. I believe they were moving here from London to start up this restaurant. One morning, I had a note appear in my inbox, my physical mail tray, not my emails, saying I had to find a reason to not fulfil the contract with this couple, i.e., not let them rent the property. They said they had photo evidence that I was having an affair. Of course, I didn't believe them, but then the email came later that day with the evidence. We've had our share of marital strife, but my wife and I were in such a good place that I didn't want anything to ruin that, so I threw the contract. I cited drug usage on the premises since it was un-occupied for a few months and said we would not be letting to them as they did not have the expertise to deal with this. A complete bullshit excuse. Someone didn't want us to let to this couple and with the threat of this video getting to my family, I didn't ask questions Other than that, I have nothing. I haven't heard from them since and I hope not to."

"I don't suppose this couple's name was Renshaw by any chance?"

"You know, I think it might be. Let me check." Gregory tapped away at his laptop to find the old file. "Yes, the Renshaw's. Man called Rory who I mainly dealt with. Shame, he seemed like a nice guy. Property's still empty."

"Thanks Gregory. I'd definitely tell your wife about the photo and the affair as soon as you can so you can't get blackmailed again. And by the way, your son isn't in danger of being watched as far as I'm aware."

"How do you know about his violin recital then?"

"Just a bit of old-fashioned Facebook stalking. I found your wife's page and she's very proud of your boy, posting all of his upcoming concerts on there."

Signing with relief, Gregory nodded and looked for the first time at Dominic. "So, who are you then? You the muscle?"

"I'm his PA." Dominic replied.

Nathan nodded his thanks at Gregory and left the room, closely followed by Dominic.

Chapter 33

Settling back into the car, Nathan was trying to piece this together. The break in at his condo in LA and then again in the UK, the sabotage of Rory's restaurant, Ruth's emails, strange behaviour and her consequential sectioning, Gwen's kids. It had to be what he had originally thought. But who? Who would want revenge on Ruth, Gwen, Rory and himself specifically and who would be willing to take children to sate their thirst for revenge?

"I think we need to speak to the rest of the gang." Said Nathan eventually. "Are you ok to drive me back to Gwen's please? Then you should take the rest of the week off. You've been travelling as much as me and you need a break."

"Of course." Said Dominic, entering her address back into the satnav. "Don't worry about the time off. This is more important and I can help. With the tech stuff at least, maybe not actually running down and physically catching some criminals though."

"I don't know, you managed to run off that guy who was beating me up last year pretty well. I really appreciate you Dom."

They drove back to Gwen's estate, being buzzed through the gates by Mike shortly after 9. Ana's Yellow Porsche 911 was on the driveway and Rory's Lexus. Only one police car was left, but there was now a white Toyota, probably a detective who had been assigned to the case. Mike wasn't at the door to greet them when they walked to the house, and the door was now locked, so they had to ring the doorbell. Penelope let them in and ushered them into the lounge where Ana and Rory were now huddled around Gwen. They looked up and gave a quick wave.

"Any news?" Asked Nathan.

"They've left a team with us that will monitor our calls so hopefully when the people who tool the children get in contact, they can trace their whereabouts and we'll find them easily. Simple." Dominic knew that Gwen was living in a dreamworld if she thought ending a kidnapping was really that easy.

"Ok, well that's good I guess?" Nathan asked. "Guys, I'm glad you're here actually, we need to talk, away from parents and police."

"Kitchen" said Gwen.

"Do you even know where that is?" joked Ana.

"Mum, Dad, hold the fort please, I need wine."

"Darling, really, it's not even 10!"

"Mum" Gwen voice warned her Mum not to question it as her and her friends headed to the kitchen.

"Go on then." Said Gwen more abruptly than usual when they were all sat around the breakfast bar in the kitchen. Nathan briefed the group on his and Dominic's meeting this morning following hacking into the email account of the potential kidnapper. Rory was furious after finding out that Smith and Barts had dropped his contract because of a stupid photo of a man having an affair, but then didn't really know exactly who to be mad at, so dropped it for now.

"And then Gregory confirmed, when I asked, that it was your contract, Rory that he refused to sign. Apparently, the premises are still empty."

Nathan looked around at his friends, unsure whether to continue with his theory, but he was pretty certain he was right, so carried on. "Did Gwen mention what was left on the kid's beds?"

"Yes." Said Ana gravely.

"So, are you all thinking what I'm thinking?"

Ana looked over at Dominic uncertainly.

"It's OK." Nathan assured her. "He knows. He knew before he applied to work for me, he did his research on me and I filled him in on what was not public information, so we have no secrets from Dominic."

"OK then. Well yes, I am definitely thinking that someone associated with Linkerton's is out to get us somehow. I don't think its improbable that each one of us could be targeted individually. But guys, before we go into this, I think I need to talk to you all about something too." Ana leant forward, ready to tell her story.

Nathan was about to respond when a polite cough came from the doorway. Mike, alerting everyone to his presence. "Excuse me for interrupting, but DC Banks would like another word with you Gwen, if convenient."

"Oh goodness you've been in there with him for ages. Thank you for answering all of his questions. Of course, I'll go to him right now."

"Of course. He's in the dining room. Quieter in there. Shall I bring you tea?"

"That won't be necessary thankyou Mike." Gwen looked at the group anxiously, "Can we continue this in 10 please?" to which everyone nodded.

Before anyone could leave, Dominic piped up "How long have you been in with the detective Mike?"

"About 25 minutes sir."

"But you buzzed us in about 5 minutes ago." Persisted Dominic.

"That wasn't me sir. I only buzzed you in this morning."

"Well, who buzzed us in then?" Said Nathan. "It was a male voice, it sounded just like you."

"I can assure you; it wasn't myself; I have been indisposed in the dining room. We have no other male staff working today"

"What other visitors have you had today?" pressed Nathan.

"Just your good selves," Mike responded, referring to Nathan, Dominic, Ana and Rory, "Mr and Mrs Pinecastle and their driver Wayne, and the various police constables, sergeants and detectives."

"Could it have been Wayne speaking to us over the intercom?"

"Not if he sounded like me." Said Mike.

"Why not?" questioned Nathan?

"Well, his accent is very strong sir. He's French."

"He's French? Wayne is French? There is a man called Wayne and he is French?!" Nathan repeated.

"Yes." Mike allowed himself a slight smile. "Rather English name I know. I believe he was born in England and moved to France when he was a baby."

"OK fine. So, you didn't open the gates and neither did anyone else in the house that we know of..."

Gwen jumped off her stool, willing Nathan to do something. Nathan ran to the main reception room where the rest of the household were congregating. "Who buzzed Dominic and myself in 5 minutes ago?"

Everyone looked up in Nathan, like this was the strangest question he could have ever asked.

"Who.Buzzed.Us. In?" Nathan repeated slowly. "Mike was in the dining room with DC Banks and did not buzz us in. We were buzzed in by someone who sounded awfully like him. Who opened the gate?"

There were murmurs of "Not me" and "I don't know" from Gwen's parents and the household staff.

Nathan looked directly at the two police officers in the room. "There's someone else in the house. There is someone in the house. Find them!"

The two police officers sprang into action radioing in an update before running off to find the detective and search the house. Rory and Mike went with the Police officers as an extra pair of hands.

Gwen helped Adie who seemed to be falling apart again, to a chair. Gwen's parents sat stoically. The room fell quiet, so many thoughts entering their minds.

Nathan was pacing the room now. What had he missed? He had been to Gwen's so many times before, each time speaking to Mike; he knew his voice very well, he would go as far as describing Mike's voice as distinctive. How could he mistake it? Was someone impersonating him? What was he missing? What?

The police car. The two cars that were at the house first this morning were small Corsa's. The car that was there now was some sort of estate, so the four officers that were here this morning had gone and another team had arrived. That made sense as there was now a detective in the house and Gwen said they now had a team to monitor phones. Nathan had assumed the White Toyota on the driveway was the detective's. It probably was. He looked outside and it had gone. Why would the detective have left, just when they had realised there was someone else in the house. Surely, they would need more man power right now?

Gwen was muttering about being right about having cctv on the estate and screw personal freedom.

"Whose was the white car out on the driveway?" interrupted Nathan?

Everyone ignored him.

"Who owns the white car on the driveway?!" Nathan raised his voice.

"Nate, the cars on the driveway are Ana's yellow one, some police cars and Ryan's car. Wayne, did you park the car in the garage like you normally do?" Gwen looked at Wayne, her Mum and Dad's driver.

"Yes Mrs De Montford" He replied.

"All of our cars are in the garage Nathan. Why?"

"Well, there was a white Toyota on the driveway when we came back and only one police car. I want to know who drive that Toyota."

Calls of "Clear, all clear" were being called round the house. A polite knock on the main reception room door indicated their search of the house at least was complete.

"We found no-one ma'am." Advised one of the police officers. Rory walked in shaking his head and slid onto the sofa next to Ana. Nathan pushed past the police officers, detective and Mike, rushing down the hallway and opened the front door to look out onto the driveway. The White Toyota was gone.

He ran back inside. "The Toyota, it gone!" he shouted, not quite sure who to. Dominic stood up straight away, alert, waiting for orders. Everyone else looked at him blankly.

"Nate, I didn't even see this car. Cars come and go in this house all the time, I can't say I ever really pay attention to them and you can't even see the driveway from the parts of the house we use, so I don't see house this information is useful." Gwen was shaking her head.

"You don't see how it's useful?!" Nathan was incredulous, throwing his hands in the air and then dropping them to his sides. "A stranger just opened the gate for myself and Dom and has probably since left in the last 30 minutes, possibly with your children! How is that not important!"

"Nate the police thoroughly checked the house when they arrived. I had already checked the house before them, as had Mike, who woke up when I started screaming. We would have known if the kids were still here, we would have found them and at least heard them."

"Has anyone searched the grounds, Gwen?" Nathan persisted

"The garage only has one entrance and is loud when it opens, its's close to the house and if it had opened, someone in the house would have heard; we did not, until Wayne went in earlier to park. The rest of the grounds, yes, the original teams that came first thing today gave a perfunctory check of the grounds. To be honest Nathan, I don't see why someone would take the children, only to keep them so close to home."

Ana looked over at Gwen, wondering how she was managing to keep it together. She was always able to put a front on and cover up her feelings, even when those feelings were extreme like they were today. She guessed it meant she was always able to function under extremely stressful situations. "Guys," She started "Can we please,"

The sergeant popped her head round the door to confirm the landline monitoring had been set up, they just needed to do the same thing to Gwen's mobile. Gwen immediately left the room to get this done, leaving Ana tongue tied. She didn't want to make a big scene and announce her suspicions about her Father and make it seem like she was trying to get sympathy in the middle of these events, but she also didn't want to not mention it in case it was her Fathers enemies who were responsible. She wished Maryam were here as she was the perfect non-judgemental ear to listen and give advice. She took a deep breath, "Rory, Nate, can I speak with you outside please."

The three friends sat on the settee in the hallway. Ana began explaining about her father's recent change in behaviour and the conversations she'd overheard lately. She wished she had pressed her father for more details on who his enemies were and what exactly he had done as she wasn't giving her friends the full picture, but she also didn't have the full picture.

"So, you're saying that because your dad is taking secret phone calls in private, speaking Russian more than he has done recently and you think you've overheard snippets of conversations, in Russian I might add, that potentially infer he is in trouble, you now believe that the Russian mafia has taken our friends children?" Rory summarised.

"OK, you forget that I am Russian." Ana announced proudly. "But yes, I haven't spoken it much for a while."

"Since you were three years old hun." Added Nathan.

"Yes, yes, fine, well I know what I heard and my Father has always taught me to watch my back. I worry the Russian forces have finally caught up with him and they are hurting his friends and family to get to him. He is too proud to admit to me that he needs help."

"I think that's a bit far-fetched Ana. I mean they're your friends, not his, so it's more likely to hurt you than him, right?" Rory said kindly

"He's known Gwen since she was a child, she's like a second daughter to him, so if anything happens to her or her family, it does hurt him. Please just give me a chance to reason through this."

"Ana." Piped up Mrs Pinecastle. "What were you just saying about your father? How is Ilya doing? It's been years since I laid eyes on that dashing Russian gentleman." Her eyes twinkling at Mr Pinecastle, who muttered. "So inappropriate, given the circumstances."

"Oh, he's very well thankyou Helena. I've not spent a huge amount of time with him either recently, he's been rather busy with, well, I'm not quite sure what. That's what I was talking about actually,", Ana moved in closer to voice her suspicions over the children's kidnapping, but was swiftly intercepted by Rory.

"I'm sure Mr and Mrs Pinecastle have enough on their plate supporting Gwen, without us worrying her over Ilya's business ventures, Ana." Rory looked pointedly at Ana with a "we'll-talk-about-this-later-I-promise" look.

Ana looked away in frustration.

"Right." Announced Nathan. "We have a trip to Beaudesert in order. I suggest you both come with us," he added looking at Ana and Rory. "Gwen has her parents here, Rupert's flying home this afternoon, as far as emotional support goes, she's good. We need to look into this ourselves. If it is linked to Linkertons, we need to find out who and notify the police, but we need more information before we send the police off on a wild goose chase; they wouldn't know where to start."

"But we do?" Asked Rory, following Nathan towards the front door. "Beaudesert?"

"Gwen didn't say? I'll explain in the car." Answered Nathan. "Mike, where is Gwen?"

"She's in with DC Banks, sir, he had a few more questions."

"Can you please tell her we have a lead and are looking into. We'll be in touch later?"

"Of course, sir. And thank you for coming, really, it will have meant so much to her."

"What are friends for right, to lend a shoulder to cry on when their kids have been kidnapped." Responded Nathan grimly. "Where is Ana?"

"she's saying goodbye to Mr and Mrs Pinecastle. She nodded to me that she was coming." Said Dominic.

Leaving the house, Nathan, Rory and Dom walked towards Nathans rental car, Dom getting into the driver's seat. Ana came running out a minute later. "Guys, guys. Explain please. Our friends' children have been kidnapped; we need to be here for her. What is more important than this? And Beaudesert? Ruth isn't back yet, is she?"

"Just get in, I'll explain on the way."

Chapter 34

"Beaudesert is 10 minutes away from here, you've got 10 minutes to tell us why we're blindly following you and Dom to Beaudesert."

"Ana, thank you for coming with me," Nathan gave her a look of genuine gratitude. "And Rory, both of you. I know you have work to get back to."

"I don't think we can work, knowing Gwen's children are out there." Interrupted Rory.

"Yes." Nathan paused. "So, how much has Gwen told you?"

"To be honest, we didn't get much of a chance to speak with her, she was busy speaking to the police and her staff, so we just know basically what you told us when you called us on the way to hers this morning; kids have gone."

"And the bit about the email to the Smith and Bart's guy from the same account." Added Rory.

"Do the others know?" asked Ana?

"Gwen only called me, well technically Dom, and I have only called you guys and Luke to get over there and be with her as I knew Rupert is still overseas. Luke was staying overnight in London last night, which is why he isn't here."

"What do you mean technically Dom?" questioned Ana.

"Yes, we got back from travelling last night and I was tired, I couldn't see, I didn't have my contacts in, I missed Gwen's call, so she called Dom and he's obviously a better adaptive traveller than me and he answered." Nathan spluttered out in one breath. "Anyway. We can get in touch with Nessa and Maryam soon, but right now, this is more pressing. I'll try to get through this before we get to Ruth's.

The email Gwen received said "We will take your children and everything you love dear." Pretty horrific right? We hacked the account this morning and found the email to Gregory, the Smith and Barts guys, who we told you about this morning. I'm pretty certain he isn't involved; I think he's just collateral damage in this person's goal to hurt Rory. There were other emails sent from this email account. They were sent to Ruth. You know the emails she told us about, that she started getting as soon as she came out of hospital last year in December?"

Rory and Ana just stared.

"Well, they're all there, she did indeed receive some awful emails and they contained enough personal information to make them intimidating, not just a random email to a random email. There was another email to an email address, sugarandspice95@allthingsnice.co.uk Don't suppose you guys recognise it by any chance?"

"Nope."

"No, sounds like a teenagers first email address. Mine was something like that," said Ana

"OK, well Gwen is asking around to find out. We'll hack that one too soon, can't do it in the car as internet signal keeps dropping out. So that's mainly what I needed to fill you in on, but guys, I need to tell you, Linkertons badges were left on the children's beds."

Ana and Rory looked at each other.

"Do you think this is related to what we did at Linkertons?" Ana asked tentatively.

"Well, there's a little more to it I'm afraid. Gwen and I, we…you know, let me get to that in a minute. I'm almost certain its related to what we did, why else would they leave our old school badge on the beds of two children they just took.

"Right, so I'm hearing hacking of email addresses and possible break-in and entering. Totally legal detective work. Really something I want to be involved in as a responsible small business owner." Said Rory sarcastically.

"Gwen's children are missing, ok?" Reminded Nathan. "This isn't my normal Thursday morning either you know. I've just come back from Germany last night, I was there for 3 days, working with a new Medi-tech firm specialising in nano technology that can collect, transmit and analyse data from a human body, allowing for early warnings for serious illness to be detected. Before that, I was in Japan, working with a guy helping me with the finishing touches of the app, specifically working on the link between the human data and the labs if you want to know. I have had so many charity galas to attend as everyone and anyone is begging for money from me and I can't say no as all these charities seem to be worthwhile and I have to prepare a speech for tonight as I'm supposed to be doing an awards presentation at a local college where the head apparently wants to push more students to go down the IT career path and hopes I can say something inspiring to them. And now our past is coming back to haunt us. Rory, I am so so tired right now, please don't lecture me on what is right and wrong. I have no problems in recognising this. I'm just trying to get Gwen's children back, and then get retribution for Ruth."

"OK mate, I get it, I get it. It was a flippant remark. Carry on;"

Nathan took a deep breath. "The emails that was sent last night was sent from Beaudesert, which is why we're driving there now."

"Oh Christ!" said Rory. Ana just shook her head in disbelief.

"Let me carry on, I'm almost finished. Yes, Ruth was not lying about the emails and this makes me think that everything else she was telling us was true - possibly she did have someone following her. Unplugging the car, the snakes in the bedroom, spray paint on Sylvia's furs, was her drink spiked at your opening night Rory? I don't know, it just explains events over the last few months a little better and makes me think a third party is involved somewhere, not just with Gwen's children."

"Poor Ruth. She was being stalked this whole time and no-one believed her." Ana looked down, looking ashamed.

"There'll be time to feel bad later, I hate to be harsh but not now Ana. So, I don't know how to play this at Beaudesert. Do we think Sylvia and Steven are involved somehow or do we think the staff are? What information do we give them? Do we sneak in and have a look around?"

"I doubt Steven and Sylvia would do such a thing to Ruth." Rory asserted. I think we should trust them and tell them the truth, what has happened and what you've found. Anyway, you'd never be able to sneak into Beaudesert, they have so many people working there and what would we be looking for anyway?"

"OK, Ana? You happy with that?"

Yes," she replied. "I completely trust Steven and Sylvia.

"Sorted, so Ill lead and you guys' chip in where necessary."

"Nate, this is a conversation with our friends parents that we have known for our whole lives, not a presentation with an investment partner that you need to plan." Reminded Rory.

"I like to be prepared, and have at least the outlines of a plan, that's all," Replied Nathan.

"Here we are." Announced Dom, as they reached Beaudesert and drove up to the house, parking outside. Alastair came outside to greet them.

"Ruth is still not at home, have you come to visit Steven and Sylvia? If so, I'm afraid they are in meetings all day"

"Yes, we have." Said Nathan. "I'm afraid it's really urgent, we need to speak with them now."

"OK sir, I will make it known that you are here. Please come in and make yourselves comfortable, you know your way around. What can we get you to drink?"

"Thank you Alastair no drinks thanks, just Mr and Mrs Dillon."

As soon as xxx had disappeared, Sylvia came running out of the office.

"I thought you would figure it out sooner or later" she said.

Nathan looked at Dom, Rory and Ana in surprise. This wasn't what he was expecting.

"Let's go into the kitchen and sit." Sylvia said, leading them to the second kitchen and getting out a tin of biscuits on the breakfast bar.

The group stared at her in silence, not sure where to start.

"So, let me first tell you why I did it ok?" Started Sylvia. "Well, as you know, she has been in and out of hospital for so many years now and each time, she comes out vowing she is well, throws herself back into work and the same thing happens again. I knew things had to happen differently this time and she had to have longer to heal."

"Wait, you're talking about Ruth?" Rory interrupted

"Yes, of course, who else would I be talking about?"

"Well, Gwen's children were taken last night. That's why we're here.!"

"What?! Oh, my goodness, how has this happened? Who did this?!" Sylvia jumped up in complete shock, her hands shaking. Nathan believed her shock, her reaction wasn't something you could fake.

"Why did you think we were here to talk about Ruth? What did you think we had figured out?" pressed Rory

"Well, it's probably time I came clean now, it's been tearing me apart keeping this a secret. I did a few things to make Ruth seem slightly more unhinged than she is, so that I could convince her Father and you as her friends that sectioning her at the facility in Wales for a longer period of time was the best thing for her. She came out of hospital so quickly in December, I was worried she still wasn't well."

"So, what did you do?" Asked Rory?

"I, put snakes in her bathroom cabinet, knowing that she fears them beyond anything, and then I removed them as soon as she had run out of the room, so there were no snakes when you went up and checked."

"There is something she fears beyond anything else." Interjected Ana. "We all know this. She fears being sectioned when there is nothing wrong with her. Exactly what has just happened to her."

"Well, it was a voluntary admission Ana." Sylvia was trying to justify sending her daughter away, but she knew Ana was right. Ruth had always been quite open about her biggest fear of being locked away in some sort of facility for no reason whatsoever and her family and friends, the people who cared about her most, had fulfilled that wish.

"And there was something wrong with her," Continued Sylvia, "she tried to kill herself remember? She took an overdose of goodness knows what drugs. And then, she came out of hospital so quickly again, although I know this time, she didn't go back to work, but she started planning an ultramarathon race, rather than resting and focussing on getting better. I'm her mother, I knew she needed to take it easy and not work on silly projects. She needed time at a professional facility."

"Sylvia, yes you are her Mother and you know Ruth, you know she's a social butterfly and enjoys having friends and family around her. Not everyone thrives in a hospital, even if it is one of the best private facilities in the country. Ruth doesn't do well in that sort of environment; we've seen that before." Rory tried to reason with Sylvia, but Ana was angry.

"The ultramarathon race was the perfect project for her to put her mind to. It wasn't an intellectually challenging project, it got her out and about, kept her fit, got her talking to local farmers and business, gave her an excuse to start yoga lessons, I don't understand which part of it you think wasn't a good idea?" seethed Ana. "You just want to keep her locked away at home, so you have more company for when you retire in a few years don't you?!"

"I, that's not true Ana!"

Rory put his hand gently on Sylvia's arm. He didn't want her to shut down entirely, they still needed her. "OK Sylvia, we get that you love Ruth and you only want her to be happy right? We all know that right?" His voice calm and level, he looked round, getting reluctant nods of approval from the others. "Let's not say there is something wrong with Ruth ok? She's had her challenges, but it sounds terrible saying there's something wrong with her. So, Sylvia, did you do anything else?"

Sylvia looked at the group of friends remorsefully and shook her head. "Please know I did it for the right reasons."

"Pretty sure I've heard that explanation more than once today." Muttered Dominic.

Nathan looked at him, squinting. He thought Dominic was on his side!

Ignoring the rifts forming in the group, Sylvia carried on explaining what she thought they had come to question her about. "I spray painted my furs."

"What!" Ana shouted.

"Yes Ana. I spray painted my fur coats that I inherited from my grandmother. I knew that Ruth had previously campaigned against wearing fur, she'd never want to inherit these coats from me, so I thought it would be believable that she did it. OK moving on, sent off for a number of adoption agency leaflets in her name. I was worried that she was going rush into another round of IVF or start the adoption process which I didn't think she was ready for so I needed something to prompt that conversation and make her question her own readiness." Sylvia's voice was getting quieter and quieter. "Nathan, you've not said anything. Speak to me." She pleaded

Nathan looked directly at her and said "I trusted you. You called me asking for advice on how to help her. You gave me the final say on sending her away!"

"I know Nathan, I'm sorry I misled you, but I really did think I was helping Ruth in the long run."

"Did Steven know what you were doing?"

"No," replied Sylvia quietly, "I told him everything once Ruth had been driven to Wales."

"Well, that's something that you owned up to him at least." Nathan sighed.

"We've still not talked about these emails yet guys. The reason we came here in the first place," said Ana.

"Oh those emails, Ruth told me about them, but she was never able to show me any proof of the emails, so I thought it was a figment of her imagination. Why, were the emails real?"

"Yes, the emails were real." Nathan was thinking how best to handle this. Should he tell Sylvia the entire truth about the email account they had managed to hack into. Did he believe she was telling the truth about not sending the emails, given what she had just admitted to? He decided he had to trust her. Children were missing and she was surely not involved in that. "Sylvia, an email was sent last night to Gwen, from the same email account that sent Ruth emails over the last few months. The email Ruth received was telling her that her children were going to get taken. This person either is the..." Nathan tried to think of a better word, but couldn't "...kidnapper, or knew they were going to be kidnapped. I traced the IP address. The email was sent from here at 9.32pm."

"Sent from here? What do you mean?"

"Someone was using your WIFI to send this email, so it was someone in your household." Replied Nathan.

"No, it can't be. "Sylvia was hugging herself tightly. "What do you need me to do Nathan?" She asked quietly.

"I need you to think if there were any visitors yesterday. Perhaps someone hung around in the grounds. Who is still working at 9.30 in the evening? Who goes home, who stays at Beaudesert at night-time? That will do for a start"

"Well Alastair was probably still around, I'm not sure what time he goes to bed. That's terrible of me, isn't it? I'll do better with that in the future. Apart from him, Valerie served us our dinner at 9, and we dismissed her then, so she probably went straight to bed. XXX was here yesterday, he wasn't driving, he wasn't driving, he was redecorating one of the guest rooms. Turns out he's got quite a flair for design and he's hoping to do a part time degree in interior design so is building up his portfolio. Now who was working with him"

Nathan sighed loudly. Being succinct was not an ability Sylvia had.

"Ah yes." She continued, "he wasn't with anyone, he was working alone yesterday. We did have a new client with us all day yesterday." Nathan ears pricked up "They flew in from the US for a few days to finalise the contract. They're not staying at Beaudesert, they're at a hotel down the road and thy had definitely left by 7.30, as I had a call from xxx next door at 7.30, just as we were closing the door on the client. We did have one visitor yesterday, quite late actually, we were just finishing our dinner, but he was terribly apologetic. Lovely man. He was asking after Ruth; said he had just finished teaching a yoga class in the area and popped in on the off chance we were free."

"And what did you update him about Sylvia? We're her close friends and you haven't given us any updates!" Ana said accusingly.

"Nothing Ana darling, I have no updates about Ruth. I know she arrived in Wales safely and I was informed after a week that her progress is good. Other than that, I have nothing. She has to complete these first two weeks with no contact from anyone. It's meant to help completely re-set her and no contact from the outside world is allowed to start with. It's a completely different approach to what we've done before, it's really not a hospital and she is free to come and go as she pleases. The only rule is no phones for the first 2 weeks and no visitors. She will be doing lots of yoga, drinking energising juices, and doing a lot of holistic rejuvenating therapies. She can come home after the 2 weeks if she wants, or she can choose to stay on, its completely up to her. I told him, she was still away and we had no updates and that I would tell her that he had asked after her."

Ana wasn't so sure, she wasn't sure how helpful these retreat places were, but figured it was better than being sectioned in a hospital. "Who is this guy anyway, does anyone know him? I've never met him, Ruth hardly talked about him."

"I've met him a few times Ana," Rory jumped in. "Ruth started yoga lessons with him from the beginning of January when I was still living here, I got the impression they really clicked with each other, so I gave them space whenever he was here, but she had a lot of lessons with him, like multiple times a week."

"OK I suppose. Ruth's free to make new friends of course, that's just very quick to start a friendship. Was there something going on between them?" Ana was dubious about Joshua. Ruth was happy go lucky person and outwardly friendly, but it took her a while to properly allow someone in to become a friend and worried he had ulterior motives.

"No, I got the impression that it was completely platonic. He even did a few fun yoga classes with the kids while we were here, he was just a laidback, positive yogi and probably lent a good listening ear to Ruth when she couldn't get that from her friends." Rory looked down, mortified that he hadn't believed his friend had been getting these awful emails.

"You think she told him about these emails?" Said Ana.

"Who knows," Replied Rory, "I mean she tried telling us all, we basically told her that she was going mad and we can see she received a number of emails later on that she never told us about, so maybe. Anyway, where is this going Ana? You think Ruth's yoga instructor email Gwen from Beaudesert last night and then took her kids, having never met Gwen before, ever and having only met Ruth a few months back? Unlikely surely?"

"It's the only lead we've got though, Rory." Said Nathan. "Random person comes to Beaudesert the same time an email gets sent to Gwen about taking her children."

"Can we please just call it kidnap! Gwen's children have been kidnapped ok?! They've not just been taken somewhere, they've been kidnapped!! Stop playing it down!" Ana shouted

"I'm certainly not playing it down Ana. I'm struggling with the gravity of the situation and actually acknowledging what has happened to my friend's children. Ana, I'm not playing this down I swear." Said Rory.

Nathan was nodding in agreement. "Same here and I know that they may be gone, in part because of me."

"It was all of us." Softened, Ana, seeing her friend's anguish. "We all took the punishment and it didn't do us any harm as we studied really hard during our suspension."

"Are you talking about those silly activities when you were at school?" Asked Sylvia

"Those "Silly activities" Sylvia, were a criminal offence and we were lucky that the police were happy with that a suspension was a good enough punishment. We could have all got criminal records at 15 years old!"

"Ana," Sylvia started gently. "I'm really not trivialising this. No-one is playing any of this down. I get the impression there is something else you aren't telling me." Sylvia spoke slowly and intentionally "If you need my help, now is the time to ask. I'm here, no judgement, just listening."

Nathan took a deep breath. "Guys, there is something I need to tell you, related to what we did at school. Sylvia might as well hear this too, if you're ok with that?"

Not knowing what Nathan was about to reveal, Rory and Ana nodded mutely. Dom kept his head down, not making eye contact with anyone. He already knew what Nathan was going to say, he'd told Dom as soon as he'd employed him, after Dom's insistence on disclosing all skeletons in their closets straight away.

"Let me start from the beginning." Nathan started.

"Let me get the kettle on" Sylvia took the kettle over to the sink to fill it up.

Nathan nodded and carried on. "When we were all in year 10, we thought it would be fun to hack into the school database and steal all the parents and student details stored there. Names, addresses, bank details, how the school fees where paid, whether they were paid on time, who had scholarship, bursaries, additional funding, who had free school meals, so much information. I know we were all involved somehow, but it was mainly me. I did the actual hacking and put all the information on a floppy disk, you guys provided lookouts, you distracted the receptionist so I could use her computer, stole the cctv video tapes from the security office, you guys, Ruth, Nessa, Maryam, Luke, Gwen, the whole gang was there, but I was the one who did the crime. You all stood by me after we were caught and didn't let me take the fall alone, I can't believe how lucky I was and still am, to have a group of friends stand by me like that."

"Mate, we all know this happened, what's your point?" Rory was getting frustrated.

"Well, you all thought we were doing it for a bit of fun right? We were just a group of silly teenagers showing off to each other, showing off right? Wrong. I needed to get that information. I made it seem like a game, like a fun challenge for some bored kids that should have been studying for their mock GCSE's."

"You needed that information Nate? I'm confused, why? Who needs a list of parents and students addresses at a school?" Ana asked, taking a handful of biscuits.

"You all know I went to Linkertons on a full scholarship, right? All my fees were paid for, my parents had to pay for nothing. Despite this, they started getting behind on mortgage payments and fell in with some bad people. They started driving things between places and got paid for it. These people, I still don't know who they were, kept asking for more and more from my parents, asking them to take more risks, until eventually they said no more. These people agreed and said my parents could pay their way out."

"Oh, Nate that's awful that you got caught up in this! What where they driving? Where?" Asked Ana

"Oh, they were careful to not allow me to get caught up in it at all. They pushed me to focus on my studies, but I saw them getting into random cars outside the house and get out clutching packages. They all varied in size, but I'm guessing they were carrying some form of drugs. Then they'd drive off late at night, saying they were going for a drive together to have a chat and let me have some "alone time". I of course guessed what they were doing, but I didn't know what to do about it. After about a year and a half of my parents being drug mules, I heard them arguing downstairs about whether or not they should re-mortgage the house to pay their get-out fee. These people were demanding £10,000 to forget who my parents are and leave them alone and Mum and Dad didn't have that sort of money."

"Oh Nathan, why didn't you come to us?" Asked Sylvia

"I only joined the school in year 7 and I didn't know you well enough or at least as well the rest of the gang and my parents hadn't made an effort to get to know you, so we couldn't. Anyway, these people came to the house one evening, demanding a delivery somewhere and my Mum was refusing. Dad was out; he'd got a second job working nights at a pallet storage warehouse. My Mum sounded like she was starting to panic, so I came downstairs and asked them to leave, in my nicest polite, please-don't-hurt my-Mum voice. They laughed at me of course, a skinny teenager reeking of hesitation, awkwardness and fear, trying to stand up to two adults who probably had knives in their back pockets. They pushed me up against a wall, not enough to hurt me, but enough to let me know they were in charge said they had a job for me and left."

"Was that when you started training with the rugby team?" Asked Rory

"Yes, I decided I never wanted to feel that weak and out of control again. So anyway, a week later they caught up with me. I'd just got off the bus from school and was walking home. They pulled up in a car next to me and told me to get in."

"Did you?" Said Ana, surprised. Nathan was always lecturing them on their own personal and cyber security.

"No of course not! Do you know how dangerous it is to get in cars with strangers?! No, I bent down and leant through the window. Made me feel slightly less intimidated too as I was taller than them and also not trapped in a car. They did indeed have a job for me. To hack into the school's database and release all the details onto Locos, you know, that social media platform that lasted like 2 years? If I did this, they would assume my parents fee to be paid and leave us alone. As you know, I did put everything on Locos, although it was only there for 2 days before it was taken down. My parents and I were then left alone. Mum and Dad died never knowing what I did, which I'm glad for. They thought these people stopped coming round because of how forceful they'd been when they told them enough is enough and that these bad guys were scared of such heavily principled people. Bless them, they definitely weren't scarily forceful people and they definitely weren't overly morally conscientious to have become involved with these people in the first place, but I do know that they loved me fiercely and everything they did was for me. So that's about the gist of it. No more secrets. Oh yeah, Gwen knew, she promised not to tell."

Ana delicately put her mug on the counter top. "Nate, I don't know whether I'm angry that you kept this a secret for so many years, or sad that you kept this a secret for so many years. Either way, thank you for telling us and I am sorry for what you went through. And I agree, it's a good thing your parents didn't ever know the reason behind what we did, its better they thought it was a silly teenage prank. But how is this relevant to finding the kidnappers?"

"Well, I'm not quite sure what these guys my parents worked for wanted with the school database information. I didn't ask and to be honest, I didn't want to know. I assumed they got everything they needed before it was taken down from Loco as I never heard from them again. It just feels like someone from Linkertons has unfinished business or was unfairly treated somehow, I mean why else would they leave a Linkertons badge for us to see?"

"So, plan of action, we give Joshua a visit and find out if it was him that sent the email to Gwen and if so, erm I guess he has taken, I mean kidnapped the children?" said Rory spurring everyone into action. "I think he has a yoga studio near here, so it shouldn't be difficult to find him."

"Yeah," agreed Nathan, "but I think just you and Ana should go to Joshua. I'll stay here with Dom and Sylvia, if that's ok with you Sylvia?" He looked up at Sylvia who gave a quick nod. "We need to dig out the list of parents and students who had their details leaked onto social media Sylvia, I'd appreciate your input please, you knew a lot of the parents and still have some interaction with some of them, so you might be able to give a little context to their lives so we might be able to narrow down anyone that has a revenge agenda. Sylvia, do you have a car we can borrow please?"

"Of course. I'll call Frank and let him know his services are required. He'll drive the car round to the front and you can him to drive you anywhere. Let me speak to Steven and let him know I won't be joining him back in the meeting. He can continue without me." Sylvia hurried off to the office.

Rory and Ana stood up to go, Ana had already found Joshua's yoga studio on google maps. "Is this him?" She showed a photo from his website to Rory.

"That's our guy!"

"Guys?" Nathan paused, "You can't be overly soft with him, ok? He has potentially kidnapped our friend's children, you've got to be at least a little bit, how do I put this..."

"Threatening?" suggested Ana

"Yes, I'm mean don't get yourselves thrown in jail, but you know don't be Mr and Mrs Nice guys."

"Nate, I'm pissed, I'm not playing Mrs Nice Guy today." Nate saw her icy stare as she nodded a goodbye to him and walked out to meet Frank on the driveway.

Rory said his goodbyes to Nathan and him and Ana headed off to Joshua's yoga studio.

Chapter 35

Dom had already opened up his laptop and was ready and waiting.

"So, I'm guessing you know exactly where to find this list of names Nate?"

"Correct, I kept them just in case something like this ever came up again, or in the unlikely case I was blackmailed. I'll send them over to you. Can you start looking into the names from the top, I'll start at the bottom?"

"How many people are on this list?"

"Well, it was just our year group thankfully, so not that many people. 67 names, addresses and other bits of information."

"That's still a lot Nate. 67 people who could possibly be looking for revenge."

"Don't I know it. Let's make a start then."

Sylvia bustled back into the kitchen 10 minutes later with an address book and her mobile phone. "Right," she said, tapping the address book, "this has all the addresses of all the parents I have stayed in touch with from Linkertons. And on this we'll be able to find my messages and emails between them recently, although I've got to admit, none of them are in my close friendship circle, they're more acquaintances."

"Great, thanks Sylvia, it's a start." Nathan looked over at Dom, who was already busy searching through someone's LinkedIn profile. "Let's aim to get this done in 2 hours. Hopefully by then we'll have a lead. Dom, who are you looking into?"

"Mr and Mrs Archwell, Kit Archwell was the student. Fees paid on time, parents are both doctors, both have recently published articles in medical journals and seem to be at the peak of their careers in relatively senior positions. Kit is running a medical sales business, judging from his posts on social media seems to be doing pretty well for himself, married 1 daughter, holidays on yachts, and lots of sunny places. Happy families."

"Sylvia, do you remember them?" Asked Nate

"Yes, Kit was always doing clarinet solos in school concerts, quite a high achiever if I remember rightly. Not in touch with his parents, never was, but I know they live in the Midlands as I've seen their names on a few fundraisers I've been to. I wouldn't recognise them if I saw them."

"So, they seem fairly stable, are we happy to eliminate this family for now and move on?" Dom queried.

Sylvia nodded.

"Yes, I think so." Said Nathan. "OK I have Mrs Westlake here and David Westlake. No LinkedIn, no social media. David was in my maths class and possibly a few others, I can't specifically remember. He was adopted. Quiet but happy guy."

"Yes, I knew his Mum." Piped up Sylvia. "She died of lung cancer a few years ago. Heavy smoker. I stayed in touch with her vaguely over the few decades, but then we got closer before she died. She asked if she could come to the stables when she got ill. Seems like a strange request, but she used to come over a couple of times a week and spend time with the horses, just helping to feed them, groom them, sometimes shed just sit with. Oh Dominic, is that Angie Aktar?" Sylvia called over to Dominic who was scrolling through her Facebook profile.

"Yes Sylvia. She goes by Angela on her social medias. It's amazing the amount of information these boomers put on their social media, very few of them seem to have private profiles. This lady's whole life is on here. Please tell me your social media situation is better than that Sylvia?"

"Oh Dominic, I don't have any social media. It's hard enough keeping the Dillon Hire website up to date. Yes, yes, I remember Angie, she was one of the governors of the school when Ruthie was there."

"Guys guys, please!" Interrupted Nathan. "Can we please do this methodically otherwise were never going to get through everyone. Let's go back to the Westlakes. Can we see anything in their lives since Linkertons that would suggest that they have soe sort of vendetta against us?"

"I don't think so dear." Decided Sylvia. "David became a teacher, can't remember what he taught but Sharon talked about him a lot when she came over and was very proud of him. They seemed a happy family unit."

"OK, so the Westlakes are eliminated. Let's keep going methodically please. The Aktars. Mr and Mrs, along with Louise the daughter. Dom, what's the deal with them?"

"I'm still looking Nate, give me 5 minutes."

"5 minutes!! Winona and Alfie might not be able to wait 5 minutes!! Look faster!"

Dominic and Sylvia looked at Nathan.

"I'm sorry I'm sorry. I just feel so helpless at the moment and the only thing I know that I, we can do right now is research these families. And even that might not give us any leads. I'm clutching at straws here."

"We'll get there Nate, we will. I'm not going to tell you do have patience as I know better than that, but I also know that you know how long this will take so you gotta give me some space." Dom reached across the breakfast bar and put his hand gently on Nathans arm.

"Shall I also run through the list at the same time and make notes?" Sylvia suggested. "I'll just jot down any contact details I have, and what I know about the family, if I know them."

"Yes, "breathed Nathan. "Why don't you carry on with names from the top, so the Aktars, Mum was the governor, please rack your brains for anything else. Here, use this laptop to make notes." Nathan slid another laptop across the counter. "The list of names are here and there's a new word document open here. Happy?"

"Yes. So Angie Aktar was a governor, she was also, ooh was it a bank? She was always dressed quite corporately. OK I'll come back to that. Mr Aktar, hmm, not sure of his first name or even what he did for a job, but he was never around, so why would I remember him." Sylvia paused and saw Nathan and Dominic both staring at her. "OK ok, in my head, yes yes, I know!"

Chapter 36

They were halfway through the list and Nathan was getting frustrated again.

"This is ridiculous! So far we've got 12 families eliminated and 21 families with possible motives to want revenge on our group and only 2 with direct links. How are we going to narrow this down?"

"We start with those 2 families with direct links," Dominic decided "Ill carry on with the basic research of the list, you and Sylvia carry on with the deep dive. So that would be the Charles's and the Sykes. Specifically find out all you can on Omar Sykes, and Rachel Charles."

"Yes, I definitely remember Luke saying that he had been approached by Omar to represent him as a bit of pro bono work, but he couldn't do it, he had no capacity at all, so knowing what we do now, that he just got out of prison, I'd put him as a prime suspect. Rachel, yeah looks like she's been searching for a job ever since Rory's company let her go, so I guess a good place to start. I bet their paths didn't even cross whilst they worked there, they were in completely different departments, cities and she changed her name when she got married, so he probably never even knew she worked there."

"Still worth a try. Unless Gwen receives a ransom note asking for money, I think we can safely assume the reasons behind Winona and Alfie's kidnap are the same as the reasons behind the actions leading up to Ruth's stint in rehab, the break in of the farm and attack on you Nate and the sabotage of Rory and Amelia's restaurant."

"Which is what?" Asked Sylvia

"Well probably some sort of revenge, payback I guess." Dominic shook his head looking at the screen of his laptop. "This family is unbelievable. The O'Neil's. They are serial entrepreneurs and serial failures. Over the past 35 years, this family has opened and wound up no less than 14 companies! Their latest company last filed accounts in September last year according to companies house and the balance sheet is not looking too healthy. Danielle O'Neil, the daughter is listed as a company director for the current and last 8 companies, so looks like she has gone into the family business."

"Which is?" Asked Nathan.

"Current business is a workplace consultancy business, essentially restructuring office space, before that its always been some sort of facilities management business. They're not doing very well professionally, but I can't see any reason for them to have a vendetta against them. Happy for them to be eliminated?"

"Yes, move on. I'm downloading Omar's criminal record. Let's see what he got put away for."

"Are you sure you want to be doing that Nate you know, hacking the police's database? If you're in for long enough, they'll be able to trace you." Warned Dom.

"Yes, I know, I'm not hanging about. Sylvia, close your ears."

"Not listening boys!" called Sylvia over the top of her laptop. "Got something here though. I recognise one of the girls in a photo on Louise's Facebook profile."

"Louise next door?"

"Yes, Louise Hartley, next door, she was in your year remember?"

"Oh yes." Nathan rolled his eyes. "I'll never forget it, she followed Rory round like a puppy dog for years, but was awful to the rest of us. She's happily married right? Doesn't work?"

"Yes, she's happily married, never worked a day in her life. Her husband works for her dad and they live at the family home."

"She still lives with her parents?"

"She does, yes, she still lives next door. I guess they never gave her motivation to move out. Plenty of space for them to live without getting on top of each other, no bills, work is a 5 minute walk away for her husband; he works in the family business, I mean it's a perfect set up, why would she move on. So, anyway, there's a photo from Bonfire night last year, and I'm pretty sure that girl in the photo there, on the end, is Rory and Amelia's front of house girl at Renshaw's."

"What? No surely not. Louise would never hang out with a waitress. She'd always go on about the staff in her parents' house and would talk about how she was so glad she was born into the class she was born in, blindly discuss her privilege. Completely ignorant to the world around her. She was so obnoxious!"

"Not a fan then Nate?" Dominic raised an eyebrow.

"Not at all, awful girl. She was one of the few people at school who looked down her nose at me because I didn't have designer everything, even though I definitely wasn't the only one."

"There's always a few token poor people at a private school." Dominic smirked. "I'm pulling your leg mate; I know what you're saying."

"So, lets pay her a visit." Nathan jumped up.

"Who, Louise or the front of house girl? Can anyone remember her name?" Asked Sylvia sheepishly. "I had a long conversation with her about the locally made wine, she had a lot of knowledge and enthusiasm for it and held my attention well, but I'm ashamed to say her name has eluded me."

"It was Corinne, Sylvia. I think we go next door to speak to Louise first as she's so close." Nate was already putting his coat on, his mind made up. "I'll go by myself, can you two please stay here and carry on with your research?"

"Of course." Said Sylvia. "Its best you drive, it's a 20 minute walk otherwise."

Dominic threw the car keys over to Nathan.

"20 minute walk to the neighbours, I probably wouldn't call them neighbours!" chuckled Nathan.

"Well, it is the countryside and they are the closest humans to us. The effort on keeping this neighbourly relationship alive though is definitely more from their side. Are you happy you know the way?"

"Yes thanks, I know where the entrance to their driveway is at least, Ruth's pointed it out to me before. Right, see you both soon. I've got my phone on me if you need me."

Dominic's phone received a notification. He picked up his phone and frowned, starting to scroll.

"Wait, Nate. I think you need to see this before you go. I just received a notification, the article has only just come out." Dominic handed the phone over.

Nathan started reading. He felt sweat prickling on his forehead and his heart started to race. He looked over at Dominic, who was beavering away at his laptop again. "It's on all the tech media outlets Nate, I can't stop it. It's only a matter of minutes before it's on the BBC and mainstream news outlets."

"Who would do this? I mean you know it's not true right?" Nathan spluttered.

"Of course, Nate. Look you just head off, I'll see if I can trace this story and perhaps, Sylvia, you wouldn't mind continuing our research? Ill set you up and show you what to do."

A bewildered Sylvia nodded and turned her laptop towards Dominic for him to show her what to do.

Nathan wiped his forehead and ran down the hallway, jumped into the rental car and drove the 2 minutes' drive to Louise's house, trying to forget the news headline he had just read and focus on the task in hand. He wasn't sure what tact to try, suddenly feeling exposed, insecure, and nervous. He realised the only things he ever did by himself were work related. That was the area of his life that was nearly always slick and completely in control, he was confident whenever he had to deal with work, but anything that wasn't remotely work related, Dom dealt with. Grocery shopping, done by Dom. Travel, down to the tiniest detail of getting his clothes dry cleaned before flying home to getting him to the correct hotel and airport on time, organised by Dom. Bills, paid by Dom. Remuneration of his personal staff, although few, was always done by Dom, Via Nate's bank account of course. Dom's days off were few and far between and Nate noticed that he always organised his days off around Nathan, making sure he wasn't going to be travelling anywhere, or running any important meetings that required his support. Nate needed Dom and Dom knew this. Was it healthy to be this dependent one someone? Is that what a relationship felt like? He'd heard Rory say he couldn't live without Amelia if she died; did he mean that emotionally he'd struggle, or that practically she did so much for him, that he wouldn't know how to function. Nate knew he wouldn't be able to function without Dom for sure. He wished he was here.

"You can do this" he told himself. "You are a strong erm a strong…oh what was the rest of that bloody positive affirmation crap I was meant to repeat to myself?! OK let's do this." He shook himself out before noticing someone walking towards his car. He realised he'd been sat on the driveway for a little longer than he'd planned, which obviously looked very conspicuous, especially when your house had a quiet private driveway like this.

It was Louise.

"Fuck Fuck Fuck Fuckity Fuck!" Thought Nathan as he breezily climbed out of the car, trying to quash his escalating hyperventilating with a big wave and overly friendly smile.

"Is that Nathan?!" Squeaked Louise. "Nathan Render!! Oh, my goodness, what a wonderful surprise."

Her voice really did carry. Nathan's breath was catching in his throat. Thankfully he'd pulled up close to the farthest point away from the door of the house, so he still had about 15 seconds before she reached him.

"Think of a plan." He thought.

His chest was tightening.

"Pull yourself together". He thought

Louise was getting closer.

"Good guy, bad guy. Which? I need Dom" He thought.

His palms were sweating.

"It's just a panic attack, look at a tree, count to 10. 1...2." He thought.

Hi chest was hurting. The world was spinning in front of him.

"Poison! I've been poisoned! Must have laced the steering wheel whilst I was inside! My hands have absorbed the poison!" He thought.

He held the car to steady himself.

"Oh God! I've been poisoned! I can't stop it now. We'll never get those kids back!" He thought.

"Nathan? Mum, call an ambulance! Nathan?"

Nathan opened his eyes to see a beautiful face staring down at him. He could smell Chanel Chance. One of his favourites. He focused on the face in front of him. Wow that was a lot of makeup for a beautiful face. Louise. He started remembering and his breathing got faster and shallower again. He hadn't been poisoned. Forcing himself to breathe slower, he sat up slowly.

"I need Dom." He managed to get out. His hands were tight fists, unable to unbind them, he tried to point at his pocket, motioning for Louise to get his phone out. She didn't understand, too caught up with the fact that an old school friend had just turned up at her house for seemingly no reason and just had a panic attack and collapsed.

"Nathan, I don't know who Dom is, but shall we get you off the floor? Those Balenciaga trainers are far too nice to be scraping on the driveway darling."

Nathan ignored her and stayed on the floor. Struggling to slow down his heart rate and his breathing. He was here now. He had to confront her. Bad cop he decided.

"Louise, we know." He took a few breaths. "About Corinne, about the emails, about everything." Pausing, he looked up at Louise for her reaction, but couldn't gauge much as her mother came outside.

"Did you say something about an ambulance Louise dear?!" She called.

"Hello Mum! No thanks, we're all good."

"Pardon?" Came the shout back from the house.

Louise faced her Mum and gave her a double thumbs up and a wave to end the conversation. Her Mum, apparently satisfied turned around and went back inside the house. Louise turned back to Nathan and looked at him, apparently wanting more information before she spoke further. It was a battle of wills; who would break the silence first.

Louise broke first.

"OK, so, yes, fine, but she needed to go to rehab to recover properly, so all we did was help with that, is that what my you came here for? Not to gloat about how well you're doing with your app company?"

"What do you mean recover properly? Gloat?! What the? I mean, give me a break here. You were all smiles and concern a minute ago. Who is we?" Nathan's confidence was fading. He looked up at Louise standing over him, one hand on the car, the other hand on her hip, looking like she was about to berate Nathan for brushing past her Ralph Laurent jacket. He felt like he was at school again, taking the full force of her meanness. "Not now, not now, not now." He thought.

Nathan sat up straighter, still not feeling good enough to stand.

"Ruth, if that's who you mean by "she," did not need to go to rehab, she was getting better. She was doing really well actually until someone started sending her those awful emails and making her question herself. In fact, her friends and family started questioning her judgement, but that's what you wanted right? She went away to rehab, but this time, it was a different one, on a volunteer basis, it's basically a spa, so you didn't fulfil her nightmare of getting sectioned when she is absolutely fine. Why do you hate her so much? Why do you hate us all so much? What we did never affected you. If it did, tell me so I can make it right!"

Nathan looked questioningly at Louise, who had been stunned into silence. Nathan took her silence as, "No, what you did, never affected me." And carried on.

"I did not come here to gloat Louise. I don't ever gloat about how successful I am, because you what, I'm not a dick, but if I was, *you* would not be the person I care about enough to gloat to. I came here to find out where the kids are and get them back. You need to tell me where they are now."

"Oh no he, did it?!" Louise stared blankly ahead.

"What do you mean he did it? You mean, *you*, did it? You and Corrinne."

"No Nathan. You've got it all wrong. Can we drive and talk?"

"Yes, we can drive next door and talk." Nathan slowly picked himself up off the floor.

"To Beaudesert? I can't go next door. I can't let Sylvia know. She'll tell my parents and they can't know."

"Jesus Louise! The police and everyone are going to find out soon, as soon as we get those kids back, so you can swallow your pride and come next door."

"Fine. At least let me drive then." Louise held out her hand asking for the keys.

"Not a chance you psychopath." Nathan opened the driver's door and lowered himself into the seat.

Louise looked over at him, completely seriously. "I'm not the psychopath here Nathan."

Chapter 37

5 Minutes later, Nathan and Louise were walking through the reception area at Beaudesert towards the kitchen where Dom and Sylvia had since been joined by Steven. They all looked up as they came in, Nathan slightly

out of breath and Louise not her usual poised self. Sylvia knew something had happened.

"Nathan, you look pale."

"I'm fine Sylvia." He looked at Steven and nodded.

Sylvia looked at Louise "Hello Louise." She said flatly. "I'm guessing Nathan has filled you in on what happened. Hopefully you have something to add, which is why you're here?"

"Firstly," Louise started grandly. "I need to…"

"No, no, no." Interrupted Steven. Everyone looked up at Steven, a man who spoke very little and kept it succinct when he did. Louise stopped and lost her trail of thought, surprised by Steven's interruption. " Louise, this is what is going to happen, Nathan and Dominic are going to ask you some questions. Perhaps myself and Sylvia may do too. You will answer these questions and only these questions. When finished, you will elaborate and tell us anything else we need to know. Understood?"

Louise mutely nodded.

"Now sit down."

Louise made a dignified attempt to get onto one of the bar stools, which was rather difficult wearing a pencil skirt, but after a few grunts, she made it.

"Tea?" Asked Sylvia?

"Me?" Louise looked surprised.

"Yes, you Louise, we're not monsters!"

"Please. Milk no sugar."

"Over to you Nathan." Prompted Steven.

"Right, ok." Everything was starting to swim in front of him again. Nathan grabbed hold of the breakfast bar in front of him to steady himself.

"Nathan, what's wrong?" Sylvia bustled round and herded him to a lower kitchen chair. "You're not OK!"

"I am, really, I'm fine, I just had a minor panic attack at Louise's and, I just need to take a moment."

"From what I saw, it wasn't minor, Nathan." Louise had recovered her composure and jumped off the stool and took over from Sylvia making the tea. "He fainted, Sylvia and was hyperventilating for quite a while."

"Yep, correct, I'll be fine." Nathan brushed off Louise. "Tea three sugars please Louise."

"Nathan, I would question you more if we didn't have two missing children out there. Right now, I'm trusting you to not be lying to me. Have a biscuit" Sylvia thrust the biscuit tin at him.

Dominic stood up and went to the head of the table. Everyone shuffled round the breakfast bar, understanding that Dominic was taking Nathan's place. Louise took her spot again in the hot seat on the bar stool, her neck flushing red as she waited to be questioned by Dominic.

Dominic looked over at Nathan, hoping to get just a starter sliver of information about what Louise had told him, but his eyes were closed, he was exhaling through his mouth and definitely not able to give Dominic anything, so he started.

"Gwen's children are missing, Louise. They were taken last night or this morning. We know Ruth has been getting emails, awful emails that then disappear from her email account so she couldn't prove it. We know this same person blackmailed Gregory Barts at Smith and Barts to drop the lease to Rory and Amelia for their restaurant." Dominic paused to let this sink in, looking at Louise the whole time. She didn't seem surprised. None of this was new information.

Dominic continued. "We know you and Corinne are friends." That was a push, they'd only seen one photo with the two of them in, but he took a chance. Louise looked a little surprised by this one.

Dominic continued, this time talking louder. "You targeted Ruth as soon as she came out of hospital, when she was weak and vulnerable, making her feel like her friends and family had turned against her, making her question her own sanity. She is now living her worst nightmare; she was sectioned and there was nothing wrong with her because of you!" Dominic was clutching at straws now; Ruth hadn't been sectioned, but close to it and she hadn't gone to rehab purely because of the emails and they also didn't know that the emails were actually sent by Louise, but he wasn't getting much of a reaction from her, so he needed to get more extreme.

Dominic was about to start round four of his interrogation, lecturing or whatever this was, when Steven stopped him.

"Dominic, ask her a question. Louise, assume we know everything. Dominic, what do you need to know first?"

"Where are the children?" Dominic asked without hesitation.

"Hello, nice to meet you." Louise replied cockily. Steven glared at her and she retreated into herself like a little girl. With a slightly apologetic look, she replied, "I don't know Dominic. But I think I know who took them."

"Who?"

"Joshua, he's a yoga instructor, he got quite close to Ruth and started teaching her yoga too."

Nathan opened his eyes. "When you said "Oh no he did it." Is that what you meant?"

"Yes." Replied Louise, suddenly very interested in the handle of her mug.

"Joshua has Gwen's children?" Nathan jumped up, "So Ana and Rory should be at his studio by now, they'll get them back, I'm sure of it! I'll call them!"

"Nathan! No! Wait! You can't do that! You have to understand something." Louise held Nathan's gaze until he realised, she was serious and not being a brat.

"What?" He snapped.

"Joshua is a psychopath. Like seriously. He's talked about kidnapping children for a while now, how he'd do it, what he'd do and." Louise trailed off, looking around the room for something to change the subject, but failed. "He killed his dog. He said he was practising. For what, I'm not sure. He only does something if it benefits him." She'd stood up now, her hand was rubbing her temple. "You have to warn them before they get there." Louise looked frightened.

"They'll be fine, Louise. Rory and Ana are pretty capable. How do you know Joshua?" Nathan was looking better with a little colour in his cheeks.

"What is it about Joshua being a psychopath that you don't understand?! You need to call Ana and Rory and warn them!" Louise's shrill voice pierced the room.

Nathan picked up his phone and called Rory.

No answer.

"Maybe they're still driving," he reasoned. "You need to tell us more. How do you know Joshua?"

"He was my yoga instructor. I started going to yoga classes at his studio a few years ago. We had chemistry and I started having an affair with him. He's quite easy on the eyes, you know. It was great to start with. I mean, as much as having an affair can be. I felt awful being unfaithful, but Bobby's always in the office with Dad, the kids are at school, I don't have any hobbies or friends really, I'm. Nothing. He made me feel good about myself. Until he didn't. He started suggesting I leave Bobby and then started demanding it. That was never going to happen, so I stopped the affair, stopped going to his yoga classes, cut all ties with him. Well, I tried."

Nathan was surprised. All of this was just not what the exterior Louise ever showed. Questioning her self-worth, unhappiness in her marriage, an affair, this was not the same girl he knew at school.

"Joshua started coming to the house, with a new feng shui business that Mum got sucked into. He completely charmed her and she let him stay around, gave him some sort of small job most weeks, so he was always always there. He threatened to tell Bobby about us, he threatened to hurt my kids, he pushed me up against a wall so many times with his hands around my neck. To start with, I thought it was just a show of strength and that he would never actually hurt me, but later on, I wasn't so sure. He beat up the gardener because I spent some time chatting to him one summer and he got jealous. We were working on our sensory garden and always just discussing garden things, but he didn't believe me so found out where he lived and broke in and beat him up. Clive thought he was unlucky and armed robbers broke into his place in a random attack. There was nothing to be jealous about, but it was like he felt like he owned me and was allowed to feel jealous. Joshua wouldn't let me leave my parents. Bobby had been talking about us getting our own place up the road, but Joshua said he would burn it to the ground if we did. I believed him, so I put Bobby off the idea. Just said my parents needed me, they'd miss seeing their Grandchildren, easier to get to the office, not exactly categorical deal breakers, but generic excuses that he bought."

"I feel bad for you. I really do, Louise, no-one should have to go through that, but, Gwen's kids?"

"I'm getting to it. You need to understand how evil he really is. So, I introduced Joshua to greyhounds. A friend of mine owns what used to be a greyhound racing track. They no longer race dogs there as a spectator sport, but he built a lovely kennels and keeps a load of his own rescue dogs there that he cares for, people pay to use the track to exercise their dogs and he runs a day care for dogs there too, so it's well used. Anyway, he needed another income stream as he wasn't quite making enough to survive, so I thought perhaps Joshua could use some of the space there to run a greyhound yoga class. You know like they do goat yoga, well same thing, just with greyhounds mooching round the room. Joshua would pay to rent the room out, so a bit more cash for my friend and it would keep Joshua away from me for a bit longer. It worked well for a while. But then greyhounds started going missing. 5 went missing in total and the last one that went missing turned up a week later, on the grass in the middle of the greyhound stadium, with its head neatly chopped off and placed next to its paws, which had also been removed from its body."

"Christ! That's some games of thrones disgusting sickness. What makes you think it was Joshua?" Nathan asked, picking up his phone to call Rory again.

"I just knew. I'd already seen his true personality and had my suspicions of what he was capable of, and that just proved it. My friend had his suspicions, as he'd watched how Joshua was with his clients, overly charming and friendly, and then he'd seen him by himself, setting up the room with or without the dogs, he said it was like a dark cloud had engulfed the room and that someone else had taken over Joshua. It scared him and he didn't want Joshua around after the second dog went missing, but I asked him to give him the benefit of the doubt. I said Joshua had had a hard life and just needed a break. Not true at all, his yoga business is doing brilliantly and I know nothing about his life before that. I shouldn't have vouched for him, but I wanted him away from my family. Anyway, as soon as the fifth dog was found in that awful state, my friend called me and said he'd asked Joshua to leave. We both knew it was Joshua that did it – police were involved of course, but nothing could be proved. Joshua blamed me of course and he hurt me afterwards. He said as recompense for him losing business. I think he was more upset that he couldn't play out his sadistic fantasies anymore. He I should have fought his corner harder to allow him to stay with the dogs. I knew then, I mean really knew then, that he was a psychopath, that doing whatever he did to those dogs gave him an outlet for his dreadful urges. Now he no longer had access to the stadium and thus the dogs, he had a hunger that had to be quashed somehow. I didn't know what he was capable of, so I since then, I've just agreed to most of his requests."

"Winona and Alfie?" Nathan reminded, putting down his phone in frustration. He still couldn't get through to Rory or Ana, their phones weren't even ringing, they were just going through to voicemail.

"Yes. So, when I was having an affair with him, I told him about what you guys did at school."

"What? Why? How did this affect you?"

"Well, it didn't really, I mean, I knew some people whose lives have been affected, but not me personally. Nate, you and the gang had such a tight friendship for so many years, you all have such perfect lives and, what an amazing support system you give each other. I mean, you always had sleepovers here throughout school, you know each other's families, go to their birthdays, weddings. Whenever Ruth was ill, you guys were always there for her. I never had that." Nathan felt a twinge of sympathy for Louise. She was right, they were lucky to have the support group that they did, but he knew it was a rarity, not many people had a tight friendship group of 8 people, most people only had a few close friends, so she was comparing herself to an exceptional case.

"I grew up next door to Ruth, remember. I've seen her develop these friendships and have these relationships her whole life. My parents have always compared me to her and I now always compare myself to her. I was never going to do anything about it, I mean my, my." She took a deep breath and forced herself to say it. "My jealousy, but I just wanted to offload. Bobby thinks I'm being silly when I mention your friendships and won't allow me to talk about it, but Joshua listened, so I told him everything. He thought it could be fun if I did something to get back at you guys, like give me a one up and that would help me stop comparing my lack of friendships, to your abundance of them. I thought he meant like a few prank calls, flour in your umbrella, frogs in your wellies, something childish like that, so I gave him your names and we didn't speak about it again for years."

"You gave our names to a psychopath?!" Shouted Nathan.

"I didn't know then, Nate, I swear! I thought he was charming, kind, funny. If I'd known he was going to kidnap Gwen's children, I wouldn't have told him anything, I swear, please believe me. The first I found out that he'd been working on something was when Ruth came back home last Christmas. Mum, Dad and I came over the day after Ruth got out of hospital; just before we came over Joshua had also heard that she was back."

"How?" asked Nathan

"The gardeners." Offered Sylvia. "Our Gardner and the xxx gardener are husband and wife and the biggest gossips around, but brilliant at their jobs, which is why we keep them."

"Correct. So, Joshua told me to get Ruth's phone if I could and if not, to find a way to get Joshua into Beaudesert somehow. I managed both. I swiped Ruth's phone and offered Joshua up as a yoga instructor to help with her recovery after running."

"Why the bloody hell did you need her phone? You know what, it's not important right now. Where are the kids Louise?"

"I have a few ideas." Louise faltered. "He said if I didn't do what he said, he would hurt my children."

"So, what did he say to do?" Dom had stood up and was already packing away the laptop, knowing Louise was about to give them some places they could try to find Winona and Alfie.

"Well, nothing for now, I have no idea what he's done."

"So technically, you're not disobeying him?" Added Dom.

"True. Can I just phone the school and tell them to keep extra eyes on my children today?"

"Gwen's kids first. Where are we driving to?" Asserted Nathan.

"OK, we're going to Renshaw's." Louise submitted.

Before they left Beaudesert, Dominic pulled Nathan aside. "Nate, its all over BBC news. Do you want to release a statement?"

"Ugh. Do you think not releasing a statement makes me seem guilty?"

"I'm afraid so Nate. I think you should say something."

"Fine, do you think we should say something along the lines of "Nathan Render vehemently denies these acrimonious claims and looks forward to addressing them when more details are released." Sound alright?"

"Perfect. I'll get onto it now. Are you happy to drive?"

Chapter 38

Dominic, Nathan and Louise jumped into the rental car and drove to Renshaw's. Nathan knew they wouldn't be open to the public for lunch yet, but the building at least might be open as the chef would start prepping for the lunch service soon.

"What do you think we're going to find there? She's not told us why we're going there" Dom asked quietly, whilst Louise was on the phone.

"Dom, I am hoping we find two happy children, but goodness knows. I mean why would they even be there? I still can't get through to Rory or Ana." Nathan tapped his phone in his hand desperately.

"All good." Said Louise from the back, putting her phone away. "I've told the school that we are worried that a disgruntled customer might turn up at the school to try and frighten the children, so all the teachers are on high alert and will be double checking id's of everyone on site and will be double checking parents and nannies at pick up time."

"Good, good." Said Nathan. "The last thing we want is two more missing children. So, carry on then, why did you need Ruth's phone, what was Joshua's ulterior motive for getting access to Beaudesert and why Renshaw's?"

"HIs main motive I don't really know, but I guess he gets thrills out of psychological and physical torture. Ruth felt the full force of his psychological torture. I don't know about the physical torture, but I know he has needs or urges. He hurt me a few weeks ago, so that might have got it out of his system for a while."

"He hurts you? So does he rough you up a bit, push you against a wall, that sort of thing?" Nathan wanted details to better understand this man's sordid mind.

"Yes and more. When everyone is working in the office, he makes me take my top off. He gets a lighter out and burns me. Always in the same place, the top part of my ribcage, but on the outside, so it's sort of hidden by my arm. It's never noticeable with clothes on, even in the summer and even Bobby hardly notices it. I told him it was an old horse-riding injury that flares up when I've had a hot bath. He believes me, never questioned it. Anyway, it is what it is."

"What! What do you mean it is what it is? Louise, you can't just take that! You need to get him put in prison for that!" Nathan was horrified.

"And how do I do that? I've no proof and if there was an investigation, I've no idea what he could do to my family. I need to protect them, and this is the best way I know how. To be submissive and acquiesce to absolutely everything he asks. You asked why he needed to get invited into Beaudesert, I don't specifically know why, but it was part of his plan to torture Ruth. The phone he wanted because, look guys, I'm really sorry about this, but he cloned Ruth's phone and that one I did know about as he's done it to my phone. Over the last 5 years or so, he's learnt a lot about technology, not sure who from, but he went from being a complete technophobe when I first met him, to being able to clone phones himself, hack into all sorts of online places that shouldn't be hacked and loves talking about new technology. It's mostly completely lost on me, but I can see he has built his knowledge up from somewhere. Perhaps he is blackmailing someone really clued up on this sort of stuff to tell him all about it, or at least the bits he needs to know."

"So that's why the messages on Ruth's phone disappeared!" Said Nathan.

"What do you mean?" Louise asked

"Whenever Ruth received an email from, I'm assuming Joshua, it always got deleted before she could show anyone, even screenshots were deleted from her phone. She was adamant she had taken screenshots a number of times and the just disappeared. He was able to see when she had read the message and was then able to delete it straight away, along with any screen shots she had taken and could stop any emails from going out if she tried to forward it. Genius really"

"Oh gosh, that's manipulation on another level. Yes, I know the emails were from Joshua. He gave me updates over the last few months telling me what he had sent to her. It was awful, I know it was"

"If he had access to all Ruth's phone data, he could probably track her location." Said Dominic

"Crikey, you're right," said Nathan. "And read all her messages, know where she was going to be before she went."

"Yes, he did follow her. He told me a number of times, like I would be pleased about it."

"Weren't you?" asked Nathan.

"Well to start with, I was a little bit. I thought the emails were cruel, but a 30 years of jealousy made me feel like she deserved it too. But then his torment went on for too long and it made it worse that I know she felt like she was getting close to him and had made a new friend. It definitely got too much, but I can't stop him, I'm too scared. I have no control over him at all."

Nathan just shook his head. Struggling between feeling sympathy for Ruth and hatred for what she had facilitated. "So why Renshaw's?"

"I think Rory may been the next person on his list to target."

"But you'd already got the lease on his original restaurant cancelled at the last minute. He lost a fair amount when that happened. The chef had to be paid to keep him, even though he wasn't working, he paid a number of the local farmers a goodwill payment just to stop them from terminating contracts with him for early cancellation, a few suppliers refused to do business with him in the future, the reputational damage was still pretty bad. Why would you want to harm him again?"

"I didn't do all of that! I wouldn't want to ever hurt Rory. I've always had a soft spot for him."

"Bullshit. You probably got wind of their new business and set out to sabotage it. The lease was cancelled just before Christmas. You blackmailed Gregory at the lease hold company."

"I don't know who Gregory is and I haven't blackmailed anyone!"

"The same person that blackmailed Gregory was the same person emailing Ruth over the last few months. So, Joshua. You must have known. He must have mentioned something." Reasoned Nathan.

"I have committed no crime here!" Cried Louise indignantly. "No crime punishable by law that is. I had an affair, yes. I told Joshua things I shouldn't have. I stole Ruth's phone for a few hours, but I gave it back. I have done what Joshua has asked of me, but I'm no criminal!"

"You're complicit Louise!" Shouted Nathan. "You knew what Joshua was capable of when you were doing his bidding. You are guilty of allowing these children to go missing, you were complicit in allowing Ruth to question her sanity, Rory almost lost his business because of your loose lips. What else has he done? Was it Joshua who broke into and trashed my flat in LA and knocked me out at the farm down the road at Christmas?"

"You're right, you're right. I'm complicit, but you know why. He owns me now. Please help me."

"I'll park over there, by the red Honda." Nathan said aloud for no reason other than to stop this conversation with Louise. "Louise, we'll carry on this conversation later. Dom, do you think we should have a plan before we go in?"

"I guess so. So, stating the obvious, shall we try the front door first?" Suggested Dom.

"I meant,"

Nathan's phone rang. It was Gwen.

"Gwen?"

"Nathan, I've found out who that other email was sent to, sugarandspice95@allthingsnice.co.uk. It was Adie, our nanny. I trusted her! My whole family trusted her! We, I, the kids loved her!"

"Gwen, what did she do?" pushed Nathan.

"Well, not a huge amount really, she just didn't turn on the monitor linked to the camera in Alfie's room for the last week, so she wouldn't have heard anything. She said she received a letter in January at our house, showing a photo of the Ofsted reporting requirements when a child in your care has an injury. Turns out the last child she was a nanny for, an 8-

year-old girl, fell out of a tree and broke her leg in multiple places. She didn't report this to Ofsted, although as a registered nanny, apparently she should have and she thought I would fire her if I found out. I don't even care about that sort of stuff! It sounded like a complete accident, it's not like she abused the child. Anyway, she got another letter through the post yesterday, hand delivered, addressed to her, telling her to turn the monitor off in the evenings for the whole week. She said she thought someone was going to use the window in the kids room to break in and steal my handbags and jewellery as my closet is opposite the kids room. Absolute rubbish! She must have had an inkling!"

"Have you told the police Gwen?"

"Of course, I have! They're fully involved Nate. They've taken the letter she got yesterday for testing and they're looking into that email account too. Still no sign of my babies. Mum and Dad have contacted a private investigator they've used before, he'll be over shortly. Any luck your end?"

"Gwen, its Joshua, Ruth's yoga instructor. It's all him. Everything, the emails, the phone cloning, the, well, Louise thinks he kidnapped Winona and Alfie."

"Phone cloning? Louise? Who is Louise?"

"You know, lived next door to Ruth when we were younger? She was in our year at school."

"Oh yes, I remember, how's she involved?"

"She knows Joshua and anyway, we're at Renshaw's and we're hoping they're here."

"Renshaw's, why would Rory take you there?" Gwen was so confused.

"Rory isn't actually here, he's at the yoga studio with Ana, looking for Joshua who is apparently a psychopath. I'm not quite sure why we're here. Talk later?"

"What yoga studio? Jesus Nate," Gwen sighed "Should I send a detective over to work with you?" Gwen knew Nathan's expertise in tech was phenomenal, but doing anything that wasn't technology related wasn't his strong point, his mind was scatty. "At least tell me Dom is with you?" Dominic always seemed to help Nathan to focus and think better, or at least have confidence in his thoughts and actions.

"He is. And Louise."

"Fine. I'll go. Find my kids, please Nathan, try to focus."

Nathan turned to Louise, "Why are we here?"

"I'm only guessing Nate, but Joshua talked about taking Gwen's children quite frequently. He thought it would make me happy and I just smiled and nodded whenever he spoke about it, just humouring him. I never thought he'd do it. He also talked about bringing down Rory's restaurant. I don't know how he was going to do it, he never talked about that in much detail, but if some kidnapped children were found at his restaurant, that's surely a good way to bring down the owner and their business?"

"Jeez, who thinks like that?" Nathan turned away disgusted.

Louise ignored him, clearly feeling better now Joshua was no longer a secret. "We check here first, if they're not here, we check Joshua's yoga studio,"

"That's where Ana and Rory are meant to be right now." Reminded Nathan. "Dom, can you try calling them again please? I'm getting worried."

"Is Corinne going to be in there too, Louise? How do you know her" Asked Nathan.

"I don't know. Joshua introduced me to her a year or so ago. He told me I had to be her friend and if she ever asked me anything, that I had to do it. Fortunately, she never asked me to do anything for her and we just went out for dinner and drinks a few times to convince Joshua that we are now friends. Ugh." She shivered at the memory. "Dinner with a waitress, just so inappropriate for a lady of my standing to be accompanying someone in such a position, but I did what I had to."

"Not changed a bit." Thought Nathan.

Dom got out the car, phone to his ear, trying Rory and Ana again. The three of them walked across the road to the restaurant. The front door was open. Nathan put his hand up in a fist to signal the other two to stand still in silence. They listened and heard movement upstairs.

Walking as quietly as they could, they walked through the restaurant to the door leading to the kitchen and the stairs. They opened the door and walked into the small hallway at the bottom of the stairs and stood and listened again. There were definitely voices coming from upstairs.

"How do we do this, shall I go upstairs slowly, or barge in, or what?" Nathan looked around and Dominic was already walking slowly up the stairs, decision made for him. He reached the top, where there was a small landing and a closed door to the left, a closed door to the right and a bathroom directly in front. The voices were coming from the door on the left. He motioned for Nathan to come up the stairs behind him.

"OK, on my count of three, we open the door and dart into the middle of the room, to startle them." Dominic whispered. `

"One, two." Dominic and Nathan looked at each other, confirming trust that the other was not going to back out.

"Three!"

Dominic opened the door and ran into the middle of the room, closely followed by Nathan.

They looked round the room. It normally fit three tables and accompanying chairs, one 4-seater and two 2-seater tables, but they had been pushed aside and were dumped in one corner of the room. In the middle of the room was a rug. On the rug was a box, and playing with the box and its contents were Winona and Alfie.

"Hey Uncle Nate" Smiled Winona, looking up from the box, not the slightest bit phased that 2 grown men had just loudly barged into the room.

Nathan and Dominic didn't move, they just stared at the children. Nathan was at least expecting them to be tied up, aged even, but not sat up here of their own free will, playing.

"Winona, Alfie!" He recovered himself, running over to hug them. "Are you ok? Did he hurt you? Are you hungry? Thirsty?"

"I think Alfie might want some milk, he only left us with hot cross buns and juice and Alfie doesn't like juice. And he said we could play with this game, but it's boring." Answered Winona "We were a bit scared because we were on our own for so long Uncle Nathan. Is Mummy with you?"

"I bet you were, you guys are so brave. No Mummy is not with me, but shall we call her? Dom, could you call downstairs to Louise and ask her to get some milk? There's bound to be some in the kitchen.

Nathan didn't want to ask too many questions about their ordeal in case they were traumatised, although they seemed to be coping pretty well.

"So, what's this game?" He asked, phone in one hand calling Gwen, the other hand turning the box over.

"Nate?" Gwen answered.

"Gwendoline, let me hand you over to someone." Nathan announced before handing the phone over to Winona.

Their chatter blurred into the background; Gwen's relieved shrills travelling across the room. The box Nathan turned over had Linkertons written on the top. There were eight small wooden figurines, each with a name on. There was a board on which presumably the game was played, showing local places. Nathan got chills down his spine. The names on the wooden figurines were Ruth, Nathan, Rory, Luke, Vanessa, Ana, Gwen and Maryam. The places on the board were all of their places of work, or home addresses. There was a box of cards, most of which were now sprawled across the floor and bent, probably in boredom by Winona and Alfie. Nathan turned over one of the cards. It said, 'Rory, at Beaudesert with the shotgun'. Joshua had created in essence whodunnit game and had left it there for the kids to play with. He wanted it to be seen, he wanted to scare everyone. Nathan quickly put all the contents back into the box, prising one last card out of Alfie's hands.

Dom came back into the room with some milk for grateful Alfie. Winona came back to Nathan, "Mummy wants to speak to you again." She said

"Nate, Thank you, you found my babies. Tell me, are they really ok?"

"They're absolutely fine Gwen, Alfie's drinking some milk as we speak, Winona has been eating hot cross buns and they're just a bit bored and scared from being alone."

"My poor darlings. I'll be there soon ok."

"See you soon Gwen" Nathan could only think about the game that Joshua had created. Why. What was its meaning?

Chapter 39

Nathan, Dominic and Louise had headed back to Beaudesert, Louise meekly requesting a lift home from Dominic, insisting she had no more information to give them, whilst Nathan went into the house.

Rory, Ana and Luke were already sat in the kitchen with Sylvia, Luke having got a train back from London as soon as he heard Winona and Alfie had been kidnapped. Maryam was on her way over from Birmingham and was due to arrive at the house any minute, but was listening in on the conversation on a phone call through Rory's phone in the middle of the breakfast bar. Vanessa was still in London, unable to drop everything as she had a meeting with a top West End theatre producer, showcasing the musical she had just written.

Nathan was filling them in on the events of the morning. "So, Gwen whisked them off home 20 minutes later and Rupert should be landing around about now, so she won't be alone."

"She's not alone Nathan." Said Ana rolling her eyes. "The whole staff of the house are there, minus the nanny of course, plus the security team that she's employed will be arriving at the house in," She looked at her watch, "an hour. It's a high-end security team that my Father has used before, if they say a time, they'll be there, extremely reliable."

"You know what I mean, a shoulder to cry on, someone to drink a g and t with. Anyway, Ana, Rory, fill us in on what happened with you guys."

Ana started describing what they found when they got to Joshua's yoga studio. "We couldn't find it to start with, we were driving round the countryside for a good 20 minutes, until Rory saw a small dirt track and suggested we go down it and lo and behold, the studio was in a field at the bottom of the dirt track, over a stile. We had to walk most of the way and leave the car at the top. Goodness knows where his clients park when they go there for a yoga class, there's space for maybe 2 cars at the mouth of the track and that's it. It's a gorgeous little studio though, in a small field, with glass walls around most of it, so the main studio looks out onto the countryside."

"He wasn't there guys." Said Rory "All the lights were on, and it looked like there was a log burner on too, in a separate part of the building. We could see the door from the outside and it had a security coded door, probably the office, but we couldn't see in. I mean it looked like the studio was prepared to run a class, with the lights and heating on, but when we tried googling a timetable, we had no reception. We were both running up and down the field to try to get reception, but nothing."

"Yea, it was so weird, wasn't it Rory, as soon as we crossed the stile, which, by the way had a massive orange box attached to it, we both got reception again. We tested it out, when out phones were on the studio side of the stile, no signal, on the road side, we had signal. We really were in the sticks! I thought the box might have been some sort of reception blocker, but Rory said that was a ridiculous idea."

"Did it have pictures of bees over the box? Did you see a brand name at all?" Asked Nathan.

"Yes there were bees over it. No brand name, just some numbers and letters, I can't remember what they were though."

"Sounds like a reception blocker to me. I've got one in the door of my condo in LA. You can only get signal if you're on my WIFI. The company is an online tech company TEW68F. Weird right? Maybe the letters are the initials of the founders? I've never really questioned the name to be honest. But that's strange, why would he have a reception blocker at his yoga studio?"

"Perhaps to ensure that his clientele are purely focused and digital free?" Offered Sylvia.

"Or perhaps so that nobody can call for help if they need it." Suggested Ana.

"OK, well we never need to go back. Well done Ana, on identifying the signal blocker; sorry for not believing you." Submitted Rory.

"So, let's look at this game then. I can't visualise it from what you were describing Nate." He pulled the box into the middle of the breakfast bar and started taking out the contents. "So, creepy characters with all of our names on, check, stalker board with our addresses and places of work on. Vanessa's address of place of work isn't on here though, how did she manage to escape so lightly?"

"Hello Sylvia. Hey guys." Maryam was led in by Alastair and gave Sylvia a kiss and waved to everyone else, taking her place at the breakfast bar and hanging up her phone. "So maybe Vanessa isn't on the board because she moves house quite a lot and changes work fairly frequently, so it might be harder for this guy to track down?"

"Actually, yes Maryam!, That makes sense." Agreed Luke. "OK, so this board is quite scary in itself, Beaudesert is on there, my place, God, even my Mums house is on there, Ana's gallery, your work Maryam, Gorcotts Comp, is that your kids school Rory?"

"Yes. And that red square is where they have swimming lessons. Do you think they're next?!" Rory jumped up

"Look, this is just a power play at the moment, showing us how much information he has, how much he knows about us." Reassured Luke. "That courthouse there, is the one I've been working at recently with the gang London gang I'm representing. No-one should know that information. OK, enough of the board, he's proven he knows where we live, where we work, where our kids will be most of the time, and what we do for fun, so one up to him. These cards, let's look at them." Luke spread some of the cards out in front of him and picked one up. "'*Pay a fine to the architect, alcoholic Mum loses the family home*'. What's that supposed to mean? OK, next one, '*Stay at home, do not leave the house for 2 months, see how* it feels to have crippling agoraphobia now'. I mean, what does that even mean? This next one says 'Oh dear, the adoptions no longer a secret, pay a fine to the local newspaper to stop the story' I thought you said it was like a game of Cluedo Nate?"

"The one card that I picked up and read, it was very much like Cluedo, the card said 'Rory at Beaudesert with the shotgun." So yeah, it did sound like a murder mystery game, but these cards are a bit like monopoly. There were no instructions."

"I don't think it's a game that's meant to be played." Said Luke, looking at the board and a few more of the cards. "I think it's meant to just scare us. He knows a lot about us, but these cards are meaningless right? He's just messing about."

"Ahem, not meaningless for me." Rory piped up. "Me, at Beaudesert with the shotgun. So, ahem." Rory looked nervously at Sylvia, who had never heard this story. "Sylvia, remember Milly Molly, the American saddle bred horse you had? Well, Ruth and I went out for a ride one Saturday, she took Milly Molly and I took Eldorado. Well, we rode a little too fast without warming up and Milly Molly got injured. Well, it was a little more than injured, as we were almost back at the stables, her front left leg just went and she fell down. Ruth tumbled off the horse, but was fine, Milly Molly's leg was broken. Eloise, the stable girl at the time was so worried that it was her fault for not coming out with us and managing our speed and taking care of the horses. She checked the horse over and said she'd be lame and the best thing for her was to shoot her. So, we did. We got one of the shotguns from the gun cabinet and shot her in the heart. We told you she'd had a cardiac arrest because we didn't want to upset you. Remember when you came to say goodbye to her, she was covered in a blanket? That was to cover up the gunshot wound. I'm sorry Sylvia, we should have told you the truth."

Sylvia stared at Rory speechless for a moment. "Thank you Rory. I know how much you love horses and you have passed that love on to your children. I'm sure you will have done what was best for the horse. No more secrets yes?" Sylvia looked around the room to nodding heads.

"So, thanks for that revelation Ror." Luke continued. "Well then there's a possibility that each of these cards here contain something relevant to each of us. We should go through each one I think. Guys, just managing expectations here, I'm here for the rest of the day, but I can't stay too late, I have court tomorrow and I need to prepare."

"Of course, Luke, thanks for dropping everything and coming in the first place. Any help is appreciated." Nate said. "This may be the end of this guy's torment, you know Ruth got sent to rehab, Rory had a fairly major setback to his restaurant plans, my pad was broken into and I was knocked out and Gwen's children were taken. He didn't go to Linkertons did he?"

"I don't remember him being there." Said Ana confidently. "I knew most people, being head girl and I'm good with faces, I don't remember him."

"So maybe it really was what Louise said, that he targeted us because she gave him a reason to. He knew about what we did, although it's not like it was a secret, but I mean we don't broadcast it do we? He researched us, stalked us, and probably got enjoyment out of what he did. We just need to find him now so he doesn't carry on." Nathan looked over at Dominic, wondering if he'd been able to trace Joshua's phone.

As if he had an instinct to tell when Nathan was looking at him and knew what he was asking without even asking it, Dominic said, "I haven't actually started tracking Joshua's phone yet. I was trying to find the link between Corinne and Louise. I don't think she was going to give us any more information about that relationship. She blamed it on Joshua didn't she, said he forced her to be friends with this girl, but why? Renshaw's also had not been broken into by Joshua, the lock was still intact, the door wasn't damaged, so did Corinne leave the restaurant open for Joshua?"

"Corinne didn't close last night, it was myself and Amelia, but she does have a key." Said Rory

"So, Corinne could have come back later on and opened up the front door to the restaurant." Dominic continued. "So, I started looking into her background. She doesn't have a huge social media presence, but I was able to find out where she went to school and also some previous workplaces, following her national insurance number. So, I popped these workplaces into some software I have, that stores data we have researched for all persons currently linked to yourselves and Linkertons. Guess what, there was a match. She worked at a yoga retreat company at the same time as a Mrs Francis, from 2009, to 2013. Mrs Francis looks to have been one of the teachers at your school. Now, I can't tell you what the link is, but their submitted accounts for 2010, when they were both working there, list that there was an average of 18 people working at the company that year, so they definitely will have known each other."

"I remember Mrs Francis. She taught me GCSE Biology" Said Ana "Can't say I remember much about her though. I think she was in her fifties when we were there, so she's probably in her seventies now."

"Guys, I represented her son in court, remember?" Luke paused, clearly thinking back over the case. "We lost the case and he ended up with prison time. It was one of my earlier pro bono cases and I was desperately trying to get experience with the youth side of criminal law and trying to bring in clients, but I really did try my hardest. I told him I had the backing of a big city law firm, which I did, I mean I did have my company's backing, but they were one of the best companies in the UK for employment law and sports law, not youth crime. I thought I could develop my own client pool and open a new department purely for youth crime."

"Which you did mate." Reminded Rory.

"I did, but when I represented Mrs Francis' son, I was no expert and he could have done with someone with more expertise than me. I asked my boss for support, but she said I was on my own as this was additional pro bono work that I had taken on of my own volition, on top of what was expected of me, and they just didn't have the resources to help with extra cases. He got three years in prison, but really shouldn't have got anything, it was really unfair. Case of wrong place, wrong time, wrong crowd."

"Don't be too hard on yourself Luke. He was lucky to get someone like you. As a pro bono case, he definitely could have got a lot worse." Maryam put an arm round Luke's shoulder and gave him a reassuring squeeze.

"Thank you Luke." Dominic nodded towards Luke and continued telling the group what he had managed to dig up on Corinne. "Mrs Francis lives in Coventry still, I can't find the whereabouts of Ryan, her son though. I propose that Rory asks Corinne if she had any involvement with the break-in today, if she says yes, obviously get as much information from her, why, who, when, etcetera. If she says no, take her at her word and carry on as normal."

"No-one else has a key! It must have been her! Especially now we have link between her and Linkertons, tenuous though it may be, with her vaguely knowing Louise, I can't let her continue working for us! My children, Amelia, the business, I can't let her get any closer to us."

"Hear me out Rory. It's just for a short amount of time. I can track her movements. If she denies any involvement, but she is guilty, she'll want to contact someone to tell them of her success or at least the fact she hasn't been caught. We can follow her, track her texts, phone calls and emails, assuming you have her number and email address. She may lead us to Joshua."

"Fine. A week. A week to track her, then if we've still got nothing, then I can confront her right? You do know that under the Protection from Harassment Act 1997, you... "

"Yes, we know Rory, we know." Nathan interrupted.

"Ryan actually works in a sandwich shop in Birmingham city centre." Said Maryam "I recognised Mrs Francis in there once last summer. Once id reminded her who I was, we got talking. I've been in on my lunchbreak a few times since. He knows we're friends." She said, looking at Luke, "Mrs Francis said in probably the first five minutes that we'd met, that he'd been the victim of a miscarriage of justice. She asked if I knew you, Luke, which I of course said yes. She said you had done your best and left it at that. I've never sensed any awkwardness or animosity from Ryan since. I'll head over next week on my lunchbreak and ask if he know Corinne."

"Oh wow, what a small world!" Said Luke.

"Yeah! OK, so, you get what you can out of Ryan. In the meantime, I think we need to go back to Joshua's studio and get into that office. I suggest we go tonight. If he knew we were there earlier, he'll likely have let his guard down a little now, I mean why would we visit twice in a day right?. He might even be hiding out there, if we're lucky!"

"Nate, I'm not sure we should be playing James Bond here. Shall we just get the police to go over?" Suggested Maryam.

"We can't do that. They need a warrant to do that sort of thing. Plus, it would take too long to explain to them why we think Joshua was to blame for the kidnap, so why bother with the police when we can just it ourselves. Whose with me?"

"Nope, not me, Nate, I need to speak to Amelia and I don't want to leave her and the kids alone tonight. I vote to get the police involved." Said Rory.

"Me neither, I really need to get back to work, sorry guys. I'll have a bit more capacity to help towards the end of next week." Luke bowed out.

"Ana? Nathan asked his friend hopefully.

"Fine." She said "Just don't get me arrested Nathan."

"Yay!" Nathan gave a little dance of triumph. "Dom, are you happy to do some late night espionage?"

"Absolutely." Confirmed Dominic.

"I think we've asked Sylvia and Steven to do enough. Maryam, perhaps you could be our driver? Stay in the car by the top of the track leading to the yoga studio?"

"Sure guys." Said Maryam a little uncertainly, but glad she wasn't being volunteered to actually break in.

Chapter 40

Later that evening the three friends were parking at the top of the track that Ana and Rory had found earlier that day. Leaving Maryam in the car, Ana, Nathan and Dominic jumped over the stile with the signal blocker and headed down the track into the pitch blackness of the signal free field. Ana led the way down the track, which opened out when it reached the field after a short walk. The yoga studio was no longer lit up and there was no smoke coming out of the chimney, suggesting Joshua probably wasn't there.

Emboldened by this knowledge, they walked up to the main doors. Ana gave them a push.

"Locked. There's another door round the side, I think it goes into the office, follow me." Said Ana.

The found the side door that Ana thought was the office door. It was also locked.

Dominic had a backpack on, normally filled with all things technology, laptop, charger, various phone chargers, external hard drive, anything that might be useful for Nathan's work. This time, he had other "useful" items. He put his backpack on the ground and pulled out a crowbar.

"Wow, wouldn't want to cross you, Dominic. You are prepared for every eventuality!" Exclaimed Ana.

They used the crow bar to break into Joshua's office space, as quietly as 3 amateur burglars could. They turned on the lights in the office, expecting to see a desk, filing cabinets, but this was no office set up. This was a bed sit. A sofa-bed against one wall, there was a clothes rail, even toothbrush an toothpaste on the sink. Standing to the side of the sofa-bed was Joshua. Poised to run.

"Joshua?" Asked Ana.

"Anastasia. How nice to meet you in person replied Joshua.

"Yes, you know my name, good for you. You know all of our names, well done." Said Ana drily.

"Aha, but you don't know how much I know about you all."

"Obviously." The Russian stoic in Ana coming out as she was clearly not rising to Joshua's baiting.

"Well, you should be scared of how much I know. You have no idea what is coming."

"OK sure. We know you about what we did at Linkertons because Louise told you as she hates us. Fine. You decided to target us as we were a fun group to harass. Fine, whatever, you sad, lonely man. The kids are fine, Ruth will be fine, the restaurant is fine, Nathan is fine, this harassment stops now. We are making a citizen's arrest now. You need to take responsibility for at least kidnapping Winona and Alfie and the years of abuse of Louise."

Nathan and Dominic were moving closer to Joshua.

"Now just hold it there boys." Joshua cackled, pulling out a knife from somewhere. "I'm not finished yet. I'm only just getting started. I've been planning this for years. You know, there's a lot of people out there that you have made enemies of."

"Like who?" Snapped Nathan.

"You really have no idea?!" Spat Joshua, before pushing Ana backwards and running through the office door into the yoga studio. The office door slammed behind him and locked. Ana banged on the door in frustration and then turned to run out of the side office door and follow Joshua.

"Don't" Said Nathan. "He's dangerous."

"There's three of us! We can stop him!"

"Please, it's not worth it, we have his hideout. It looks like this is where he lives. He wont have anywhere to run to, so the police will catch him soon. Let's look around this place."

"Fine." Said Ana. Obviously not fine.

"He has a load of wigs here. So weird. He's probably been impersonating people or at least using a disguise." Said Dominic

"Is there a red wig there?" Called Nathan, looking through some paperwork on Joshua's desk, trying to find something, anything on him.

"Yep. A short red one, a long black one a short blo…"

"Ruth said that she thought Fergus had visited her in hospital. Do you remember Fergus Ana?"

"Her ex from a few years ago? Army boy?"

"Yes, that's the one. He had red hair and a unique moustache. Anyway, Ruth checked with him and he didn't visit her. He was working abroad. I reckon Joshua dressed up as him and visited her."

"Christ, why?" Said Ana.

"All sorts of reasons. To get the names of doctors that were treating her, find out the medication she was on, possibly just intimidate her, make her question herself." Suggested Dominic.

Ana looked at him wearily, then sniffed. "I can smell smoke guys."

"The yoga studio's on fire! Oh gosh, the office door is locked! We'll never get out! We're going to be burnt alive!" Nathan was banging on the office door that led into the Yoga studio.

"Nathan, mate, the office has 2 doors. Behind you. Its open still. Opens out onto the field. We're good. Let's go." Dominic patted Nathan's shoulder.

Arriving back at Maryam's car, a hot sweaty mess, Nathan, Ana and Dominic slammed the car doors shut, full of adrenaline. Excitedly retelling Maryam what had happened as she tried to drive them home as calmly as possible.

"He must have run into the woods, I didn't see anyone run past me." She said. "And why would he burn down his own yoga studio. It sounded beautiful."

"Evidence. Burning evidence," Panted Nathan

"We lost him." Said Ana, staring straight ahead. "And it sounded like he wasn't finished with us."

Chapter 41

Three days had passed since Gwen had been separated from and re-united with her children. Winona and Alfie were fine, they had returned to school with an exciting story to tell and hadn't had nightmares in the evening about it. She marvelled at the resilience of children. Gwen had employed a private security company on a contract basis to work on her estate. She had three security around her and the children at all times of the day at home and if she left the house, one of them would go with her.. The school was deemed a safe place, so no additional security was employed there. They knew that Joshua was still at large, but they had to get on with their lives. I mean what else could Joshua do to them really? It was a very impersonal vendetta he was fulfilling on behalf of someone else. He committed a crime serious enough to be imprisoned, he surely wouldn't continue any more abuse knowing his sentence would only get worse, the more he did.

Frustratingly, the police said that there was no usable evidence left at the house or the restaurant where the children were taken, so they probably wouldn't be able to tie Joshua to the kidnapping, and even if the kids could identify him, they would probably need something more. Nathan couldn't help thinking that now they knew Joshua had been planning something for years, not much was going to stop him from doing whatever he was going to do.

Nathan was thinking about the app he had been getting closer to launching. It had gone through the final test phases with an outsourced software company based in Silicon Valley with no major issues. The next phase was getting the software correctly installed and users trained up at the GP end, for all those doctors that had already signed up. Nathan was then heavily reliant on an English social media marketing company that was going to market the product and get users signed up. These next two months were going to be full on, but so worth it. If this initial roll out phase was a success, he could roll the app out internationally and do a huge amount of good. He just had to silence this smear campaign that someone, or more correctly, Joshua, had started, trying to tar his image.

Nathan was grateful that his investors believed him, that he didn't rape these women, but he still had to convince the marketing companies that he was innocent. "So much for innocent until proven guilty," he thought.

Nathan and Maryam had just met outside Maryam's offices. Nathan had insisted that Maryam not meet Ryan alone, so they walked in together. Ryan looked up to serve them and Maryam introduced herself again.

"Ryan, hi, I'm Maryam."

"Hi!" he smiled "Yes, I remember you. Can't remember your order though. One of my Mum's students from Linkertons right?"

"Yes. This is my friend Nathan. We were hoping to have a quick chat to you about Corinne?" Asked Maryam gently.

"Corinne? Blimey, OK. What do you need to know?"

"Well, what is your relationship with her and what is her relationship with your Mum?"

"Easy. Her relationship with me was girlfriend for 2 years. Can I just serve this lady behind you please."

Maryam and Nathan stepped out the way for a moment, patiently waiting for Ryan to finish serving his customer. They moved back over when Ryan motioned for them to come back. "Yeah, she was my girlfriend during my trial and then I broke up with her when I did my time. Bit of a loose cannon back then, really clingy and didn't take it too well when we broke up. I don't see much of her now; she's a meth head and I don't want to be around that. I hang around a good group of people these days, I'm in a good place."

"Corinne is a crystal meth addict?!" Asked Nathan, shocked.

"Yes, that and heroin. She hides it well doesn't she? Always has been, on and off. None of her teeth are her own, they all fell out."

"Wow. She's the front of house at my friend's restaurant and she seems so well put together." Maryam was shocked too, although wasn't really sure what a drug addict should look like.

"Yeah, she's a great actress. Be careful around her, she'll do anything for a chunk of cash. So, her relationship to my Mum, they worked at the yoga retreat company. Mum worked there for a few years after she retired from teaching and they just hit it off, got on really well together. The age gap didn't seem to be a thing and they just became great friends."

"Thanks Ryan." Maryam turned to go, "Ryan, can I ask, how does your Mum feel about you having to do a prison sentence?"

"Oh, she hates it. Any opportunity she gets, she lectures me on how I should have taken it to the court appeal, sued my solicitor, who was Luke as you know, write to the newspapers. She even suggested I try to bring down Luke's career, extreme I know, but I guess, I was her only child and she just wanted what was best for me and she can't let it go. Prison was shitty, but you know I did help to beat someone up so badly that they permanently lost the feeling on one side of their face, so it's not like I was completely innocent. Luke did a great job."

"Thanks for your help Ryan." Nathan and Maryam walked towards the door.

"Maryam, Luke inspired me to become a solicitor. I'm studying part-time. Tell him that when you next see him?"

She nodded.

Chapter 42

Rory's phone buzzed. It was a Nathan starting a group call. He left the room and answered quickly. Nathan's face popped up on the screen, followed by Luke, Vanessa, and Gwen.

"Hey mate. Look, this is a really bad time for me, we're about to start lunch service, we're fully booked."

Rory was at the restaurant, looking around the room, checking everything was ready.

"Don't worry, we'll keep it quick – Maryam's with me too. Luke, Nessa, Gwen, you guys ok?"

They all gave a thumbs up, not wanting to keep Nathan from his news.

"Rory are you alone in the room?" Nate asked.

"Just me and Amelia, Corinne is working the dinner service today." Replied Rory, understanding what Nathan was asking.

"Great. So, Maryam and I just met up with Ryan at his sandwich shop. Corinne was his girlfriend just before he went to prison. I'm surprised you never met her Luke. He said she's bad news, meth and heroin addict and took it badly when they broke up."

"A drug addict?! I really never suspected. Amelia, come over here and listen to Nate. Corinne's a drug addict!"

"Anyway, Ryan said she would do anything for a bit of cash for her drug habit, so be careful."

"Crikey, I'm shocked. She can't work here now though. Let's do spot drugs tests for Corinne and the chef Leia. I know a local company that can do them, I'll see if I can get them in tomorrow. She's signed a contract agreeing to a zero-tolerance policy so if it came back positive, that's grounds for dismissal."

"I think that's the best plan. Sorry to be the bearer of bad news. One sec, I'm just handing the phone over to Maryam."

"Hey guys." Maryam jumped on the call. *"Luke, Ryan told me he is studying to become a solicitor now because you inspired him. He wanted you to know."*

Luke paused and smiled. *"Thanks Maryam, that means a lot."*

"No worries. So, Nate or myself will message the group chat to update Ruth and Ana when they get to their phones. See you guys soon."

They all hung up the call and Rory stood staring at Amelia, shaking his head. "I knew we should have used an agency. What were we thinking employing someone who just walked in off the street asking for a job? No references, just stupid. Stupid!"

"Hey, hey! She's done a good job though hasn't she. We liked her assertiveness didn't we? To be out prowling the streets, knocking on doors to find a job, that's so proactive, she's a go-getter. And on the face of it, we chose the right person, she works hard, the customers like her, she promotes Renshaw's values and is happy to chat with the customers in more detail about our ethos. It can't be helped that she's a drug addict, it's not the kind of thing you look for when you're interviewing someone."

"That's not the main reason I'm annoyed. Yes, we shouldn't have employed a drug addict, but I'm more annoyed by the fact that we employed someone that Joshua wanted us to employ. He must have told Corinne to go and get a job here, so he could 'handle' us. We need to be careful Amelia. He's still out there and we don't know what he's capable of."

Chapter 43

"Maryam!"

"Nessa! What's wrong?"

"My car, it's on fire! Noooooo!" She sobbed.

"What? Have you had a crash? Where are you?"

"No, no crash. Never mind, Can I come to your please?"

"Yes, of course. Where are you? I'll come and get you?"

"Its fine, I'll get a train. See you later"

Maryam hung up on her friend. Vanessa's car was on fire? If she hadn't had a crash, how was it on fire? She knew Venessa parked her car in some questionable places in London, but cars are not generally vandalised in the middle of the day.

Maryam had so much on her mind at the moment, what with accepting the job with Sylvia and Steven, and Nathan telling her yesterday that he thought her dad was involved with Joshua as he'd seen some paperwork with Keith's company name on it. He said they'd run out of the office too quickly for him to pick up the paperwork or take a photo of it. Parking the issue with her Dad, she decided to deal with one issue at a time.

Maryam went back to reading through the third version of the contract sent over by Steven and Sylvia's lawyers. She'd looked through the books of their business and decided to accept their offer that they made last year, helping to get the company floated, but she wanted to stay on as CFO. Sylvia and Steven had agreed and they had spent the last 2 weeks going backwards and forwards trying to finalise a contract. This was the one she thought as she read through it.

She took a deep breath and picked up letter of resignation and made her way to her bosses office.

An hour later, she came back to her office. Maryam's boss had graciously, but reluctantly accepted her letter of resignation. With no upcoming new contracts in place and growth of the company continuing at a smaller rate, there was no room for promotion for her, so she said she was expecting that they would lose her. They agreed that Maryam would work her three month notice period, with the hopes that a replacement could be found before the three months were up.

Her phone had seven missed calls from Vanessa when she eventually picked it up. Calling Vanessa back straight away, she answered immediately.

"Maryam?"

"Yes, what's wrong?"

"Maryam, I'm in a police station, can you come and get me please?"

Maryam walked into a police station in Hemel Hempstead, not quite sure to expect. With only the brief, garbled conversation she'd had with Vanessa to go off, she didn't really know what she was walking into.

She walked up to the desk.

"Hi, I'm here for Vanessa Mayfield."

"And you are?" A police officer behind the desk barely even looked up from his computer.

"Her friend. Does she need a lawyer because he can be on video call if needed." Maryam had asked Luke to be on standby if she needed him.

"She's been let off with a warning. She's in the waiting room through there. We just didn't want to leave her alone, she seemed. Unhinged."

"Right." Nodded Maryam and headed through to the waiting room. Vanessa jumped up as soon as she saw her friend and ran over, giving her a big hug.

"Let's go." Said Maryam. Looking her friend up and down, she looked distinctly grubby and thin. "Let's get a McDonalds on the road."

A 2-hour car journey later and a McDonalds pit stop, and Maryam had got to the bottom of what had happened to Vanessa. She had been living in her car on and off since January this year. She was evicted from her flat just after Christmas last year and had been saving up for another place and staying in a youth hostel for a night here and there. Working in the bar most evenings, they had a shower there, which she was using and in the daytime, she would generally be at the library working on her musical.

She was parked near the library today as she hadn't had work last night and wasn't due in tonight either, and although she had now finished her musical, she'd started to see this library in St John's Wood like home. It was big enough for no-one to notice her coming in every day, but small enough to feel cosy, quiet and safe. Plus, it was in a nice area, so was lovely and clean too. She heard a commotion outside and saw a car on fire near fire, walked a little closer and realised there were two cars on fire – hers and the one next to it had just caught alight.

All of her belongings were in that car, she had nothing in storage, nothing at her parents' house, nothing at a friend's house, nothing left. She was homeless, had £120 in her bank account and had no clothes or belongings. She called Maryam in hysterics and then realised she had to let it all go. This was her chance to start afresh. She wanted to be a musician and she wanted stability, but first of all she needed a hug from her friend. So, she jumped on a train to Birmingham. Without a ticket. The transport police picked her up and she uncharacteristically lashed out and punched one of the officers escorting her off the train, which is when she got taken to a police station and given a written warning. She felt lucky to just have a written warning.

"I had no idea things were so bad Ness. You should have come to me!"

"I know, but I had my pride still. Ha, that's all gone now. I've got nothing to be proud of." She looked down miserably.

"You have plenty to be proud of!" Maryam insisted. "Aside from being an utterly wonderful human being, you are a gifted musician, you have written a musical for god's sake! Which, by the way, have you heard any more about it?"

"No, I played the main melody that repeats all the way through to the theatre producer, it was Mason Lord by the way, and then talked him through the story. He wasn't easy to read through. I even designed the sets in little shoe boxes, but when I stood up from the table to point out a feature on the closing set, I wobbled the table and knocked 3 of the sets off the table. They went everywhere, it was a mess. I'm pretty sure he's not going to want to progress it."

Maryam patiently waited for Vanessa to finish before showing her excitement. "Mason Lord! Wow, even I know him! Didn't he produce Cats and Annie?"

"Yes, that's the guy."

"Well, to have even secured a meeting with him is an achievement."

Maryam drove down into the car park underneath her flat and parked up.

"Hey, do you have security cameras here? You know, in the car park?"

"Yes, we do. Annoyingly though they're not pointed at the bins, which is what we really need as someone keeps on dumping their rubbish in front of the bins, they can't seem to bring themselves to open up the bin and put the rubbish in it!" She rolled her eyes. "Why?"

"Oh no reason. I guess just checking that we're safe you know from that guy."

"This apartment building is so secure. No-one who lives here holds the door open for anyone they don't know. You need a fob and a security code to get in and there are security cameras in the foyer. It's really safe, I promise."

"OK thanks. Maryam. I think the fire was done on purpose."

"Shall we call the others Ness?"

"I think I might need to put on my big girl pants and tell everyone yes."

"Do you want a bath or shower first?"

"Can we just call the others first please?"

"Of course."

They entered Maryam's immaculate apartment. Vanessa turned all the lights on as soon as they walked in, even in the two bedrooms. Maryam was certain she heard her even opening the wardrobe doors. They settled down on stools around the breakfast bar in the kitchen. Maryam called the group while Vanessa poured them both a large glass of wine.

"Hey guys. Hope you're all having a good day? 2 more days until Ruth gets out by the way wahoo!"

"Hey! Yes, don't we know it. Not sure how our first conversation with Ruth is going to go down, but I'm definitely looking forward to seeing her." Said Ana. "Anyway, to what do we owe this pleasure? You OK?"

Making sure that everyone had answered so that Vanessa didn't have to retell her story, Maryam decided it was time to hand the floor over to Vanessa. "I have someone with me everyone." She tilted the phone so Vanessa came into view.

"Oh, hey girl"

"Heyy"

"Nessa!"

"Hey you how you doing?"

"Yay, Ness is in town!"

Came the chorus back from her friends.

"So, I'm just going to jump straight into it. Please, no judgements, questions or comments till the end."

Vanessa finished telling her ordeal to her friends gaping faces.

"Why didn't you tell us?! We could have helped you!" Said Ana.

"Well, it's kind of embarrassing. You guys are all so successful in your careers, you all own your own places, you're all winning in life. My pride just took over. I'm sorry, I should have come to you earlier and then I wouldn't be in this mess." Vanessa stifled tears, realising what a great group of friends she had and genuinely wishing she had spoken to them earlier "Oh yeah and if I don't turn up for tonight's shift at the bar, I probably won't have a job either." She added miserably.

"First of all, Ness" started Luke,, "you know not to compare yourself to anyone right? We all have such different careers, you just can't compare them, I mean you probably have the toughest but most rewarding career. Musicians and composers always struggle to make money. It doesn't make you less than anyone. Secondly, I wouldn't assume that we are all really happy right now, take a look at Ruth for a starter. Rory and Amelia have been working on the restaurant for a while now and that must have been hard on them."

"Too right mate. We still love each other but we can't stand being around each other too at the moment. I know well get through it, but it's been tough." agreed Rory.

"My latest app release has been almost scuppered because of those defamatory accusations, so I'm not exactly happy with life right now." Added Nathan.

"Mine and Laura's marriage is strained at the moment because we can't seem to find time for each other" admitted Luke.

"My career isn't going quite the way I had planned" said Maryam elusively.

"Ness, remember my kids just got kidnapped, so I'm questioning all my life choices." Added Gwen "Ana? What's not great with your life at the moment?"

"Well, my life is pretty great and I have no complaints, but I feel for you guys, I do."

Everyone laughed at Ana's brusqueness. If you wanted a straight answer, Ana would always give you one and not sugar coat it.

"By the way, is anyone meeting Ruth tomorrow? Is she even coming home, or is she staying for longer, you know two weeks is hardly a life changing amount of time? Should we call her as soon as she gets hers phone back? When will she get it back?" Asked Ana

"Sylvia has been in touch with the retreat and Ruth has indeed made the decision to come home tomorrow." Informed Nathan, who had been in contact with Sylvia almost every day over the last two weeks.
"Apparently she has had a life changing experience whilst she's been there and she is a new person. She doesn't want anyone to meet her apart from xxx, who will drive her back to Beaudesert and she will contact us from there. I'm sure shell call us as soon as she gets home, so let's just make sure we have our phones on loud so we can be there for her. I'd suggest we don't tell her anything about what's happened to start with. What do you all think?"

Everyone agreed with him.

Vanessa nodded in agreement with Nathan and also acceptance of her friends brief comments about their lives, that not everyone's lives were as perfect on the inside as they seemed on the outside.

Maryam gently prompted Vanessa. "You said you thought the fire wasn't an accident, hun."

"Yes. So, since Christmas last year, I think I've been followed by someone. When I was up here in the hotel, there was a white car that just always seemed to be around. I think it may have been some sort of Toyota, I mean maybe, I'm not sure. Anyway, since the start of the year, I've been seeing a white car wherever I am. I know that sounds vague, but whenever I come out of the library, the car's there, whenever I come out of work, the car's there. Different times of the day and different places, it's always there. I know you're going to say I'm being paranoid; I live in a big city and there a lot of cars and it's probably a coincidence, but I really feel like I'm being watched all the time. When I started sleeping in the car, I knew there were risks involved, so I always chose safer areas with lower crime rates, but that never shifted the feeling that I was being watched."

"We definitely won't say you're being paranoid will we guys?" Said Gwen. "We did that to Ruth, said she was being paranoid, didn't believe her and look what awful things have happened this year. We believe you Ness. The question is, what should we do about it?"

"We need Ruth." Said Nathan. She always guided them and provided a focus. He knew they were going to spend the next 30 minutes talking around what they might do, could do, should do, but not actually decide on anything.

Nathan was right. They ended the call 30 minutes later, no closer to a plan to figure out who Vanessa's stalker was, and a lot more on edge.

Chapter 44

Vanessa woke up in a cold sweat. She picked up her phone. Checked her emails. Nothing. She breathed a sigh of relief and fell back into a fitful sleep.

She woke up again. Checked her phone, still nothing. Reminding herself that she was turning over a new leaf, starting again, she knew that in order to start over with a completely new slate, she needed to tell someone about these emails that she'd been getting. She couldn't live her life on edge all the time, always watching her back. The emails were similar to the ones that it sounded like Ruth was getting earlier in the year. She wished she'd said something at the time. She was getting emails too. To start with, she'd just ignored them, assuming it was some sort of virus causing her to be targeting, but when Ruth had said she'd got these emails too and no-one believed her, she thought she definitely wouldn't be believed, as the 'arty, whimsical' one of the group. They all thought she had her head stuck in the clouds and just thought of happy little melodies for her imaginary musical, the eponymous composer.

Looking round Maryam's guest bedroom, she gazed at the photos on the wall of Maryam's holidays. Cambodia, New York, Iceland, South Africa road trip along the garden route, scuba diving off the great barrier reef, there was a photo of herself and Maryam when she'd taken her along to France for a cycling holiday in the Loire valley. That was a beautiful trip, lots of good wine, delicious food, beautiful scenery and they turned their phones off the whole time, it was a great way to reset. Maryam tended to go away by herself a lot of the time, so didn't have to agree on a time and place with someone and just did whatever she wanted, no compromise. Vanessa envied that in Maryam. Although a reserved introvert, Vanessa always preferred holidays with at least one other person, telling herself she enjoyed the company. She didn't, she just didn't have the confidence to do it. She resolved there and then to go away by herself when she was financially stable to do so. Probably one night camping somewhere; not glamorous, or epic, but that wasn't the point.

A siren outside brought her back to the present. Her heart skipped a beat, she checked her room just still had her in it and fearfully checked her phone. Realising how much this stalker had taken over her life, she decided wasn't going to shake this stalker or at least the feeling of having a stalker without telling her friends, so she got up, tiptoed into the kitchen, and started making Maryam breakfast in bed.

"So, can you remember when was the first of these emails?" asked Maryam kindly, 20 minutes later, before eating a mouthful of overcooked, half disintegrated poached eggs.

"Probably around the first week of January. I started deleting them at first because I thought they were a virus. Sorry about breakfast by the way, it's been a while since I cooked." Vanessa laughed awkwardly, leaning back on Maryam's bed. "Then when I lost the flat, I seemed to have more time on my hands and, sleeping in my car, I was more aware of what and who was around me, so I kept track a bit more. The emails came a couple of times a week generally. The last one was yesterday just after the fire. Let me show you." She opened her emails on her phone and handed it over to Maryam.

"'**Linkertons spoilt brats. Now you know how it feels to lose everything'**." That's pretty harsh. So, he knew about the fire. Or started the fire. We need to show the others. Nathan and Dom started making a list of people at Linkertons, or linked to Linkertons who may want some sort of revenge. Don't worry, well get to the bottom of this. And thanks for breakfast it was lovely to have it made for me." Maryam smiled at her friend.

"Thanks. And thanks for letting me stay here for a while. I really appreciate it. Right, I'll go and tidy up the kitchen and let you chill for a while."

"Give me half an hour and I'll be up and ready to take you clothes shopping. Sound like a plan?"

"Sounds like a plan." Vanessa didn't normally like accepting charity, but right now, she had no home, not much money and no job, so she had no choice but to accept.

Chapter 45

"So, if you all download this app onto your phone, I'll be able to see what messages and emails you receive. I'll get the notification the same time as you, it basically clones your phone, so no privacy for a while if you're ok with that?"

Maryam hesitated, but then agreed like the rest of her friends to download this app and let Nathan have access to her phone. She hadn't told her friends yet that she'd accepted Steven and Sylvia's offer of employment and didn't want Nathan to find out inadvertently through seeing an email from them, but then she knew if Nathan did see an email giving it away, he was at least discreet.

"Anyone hear from Ruth yesterday by the way?" Asked Rory

"Sylvia text me to say she arrived at Beaudesert safely. I'm a little worried that Sylvia will let everything slip, knowing her, but it's out of our control. Hopefully we'll hear from her soon."

"Guys I've got to shoot off, Laura and I are going out for brunch. We'll all message the group if we hear from Ruth yes?" Said Luke.

"Agreed." Said Ana. "I'm off to church."

"Church?!" exclaimed her friends at once.

"Yes, with Dad. Long story, but the Russian mafia are not after him, neither is the Russian government. Goodbye."

Nathan hung up the call and watched on his laptop as his friends all downloaded the app onto their phones. It was a true display of their trust in him, allowing him access to their phones, and he had no intention of breaking their trust and reading any historic emails or messages. He was only interested in everything that came through from now. He wished that Vanessa had gotten over her self-doubt and mentioned these emails earlier in the year. Not only would it have helped them to better support Ruth when she was getting these emails, but Vanessa's life would have also been less tormented. Perhaps they could have discovered who it was earlier and stopped Joshua at the beginning. "Hindsight, ah hindsight." He thought.

He walked to the dining room of the farm house, where Dominic was working at his laptop.

"Any luck tracing who these people are Dom?" Nathan asked miserably.

"Not yet. I really don't think they exist."

"Of course, they don't bloody exist! It's because I didn't do it!"

"No, what I mean is, we think Joshua has managed to get some girls to make these claims, but I don't think he even has that. I think he has fabricated some emails and managed to persuade a few media channels that he has got girls willing to come forward and testify this. One a few media channels have published this, all the others are happy to follow suit and what was once an idea in Joshua's repugnant mind, becomes a rumour, which becomes a "report of", which becomes a story, which, once published by the major news outlets becomes fact."

"So, you're saying that as pretty much everyone who could publish the story, has published it, it is now fact?"

"I think the public believe it is fact right now, yes. But, what I mean is that we just need to find these falsified emails, publish them and then your credibility is on fire again. Tech news daily, the first to publish the story, must have been shown something that they thought was credible in order to publish the story in the first place. A head line of Tech millionaire, Nathan Render, accused of rape by 3 different women is pretty defamatory and they'd only print that with decent evidence. Now, their article describes them having seen communications from the women. So, Joshua probably falsified some communication from 3 women accusing you of this. We just need to find this. The journalist who wrote this is Jules Leopold. I think I need to hack into his emails and find out exactly where they were sent from. You happy for me to do that?"

"I understand. Yeah, I think we've hacked into enough databases to get into big trouble already. One more isn't going to harm us if we get found out. I've got your back.. Do it."

Nathan had to disprove this story. One of his investors had started planting the seed of doubt, suggesting he was going to pull out, not wanting his own reputation to be tarnished by working with an accused serial rapist. The UK social media marketing company he was working with to promote the app had put all work on hold, pending a review by the court, which could take years. Joshua had possibly just destroyed years of work with a few simple emails.

Nathan's phone rang. It was a number he didn't recognise, so he answered warily.

"Nathan Render speaking."

"Nate, it's me, Ruth."

"Ruth! Ruth, How are you? I mean where are you, I don't know this number you're calling me from!"

"It's called a landline number Nate. We have one at Mum and Dads." She said drily.

"Oh. Right. Yeah, of course, sorry."

"I didn't want to use my mobile because it's been cloned, as you know."

"Ah, so your Mum told you, even though we asked her not to."

"Yes."

"Exactly how much did she tell you?"

"Everything, I think. Including the snakes and the furs. Although I'd already guessed the furs was her, when I was in rehab. You know what gave her away? She spray painted all but one, a sandy coloured one, goodness know what animal, but I know it had always been her favourite, she said she used to dress up in it when she was younger, why would anyone else choose to not spray paint that specific coat."

"The furs?! She didn't mention that to us!" Said Nathan, incredulous that his friends mum would go to such lengths as spray painting her own fur coats, just to get her daughter into Rehab.

"The snakes though, that was low. Anyway, a spot of relaxation in the Welsh countryside was exactly what I needed and I feel great. I'm inviting everyone over this afternoon, kids and partners too, for a little catch up, you free? I hear you're having a tough time."

"Great deduction skills Miss Holmes! Yeah, what time?" Nathan ignored Ruth's comment, obviously prompting him to give up more information about the news stories. He felt like his whole world was crumbling around him and couldn't put into words how tough things had actually been though, so ignored it. He knew Ruth wouldn't take it personally.

"3pm."

"Can Dom come?"

"Of course. I feel like he's almost family anyway. Is he family Nate?"

Nathan ignored that too.

"See you at 3."

Chapter 46

Ruth called round all of her friends on her parent's landline and everyone turned up at 3, eager to see their friend and apologise to her. They all felt so guilty for not believing her. Ruth wouldn't have any apologising at all though. She said she understood that it was hard to believe her when she had no evidence and given her previous paranoia, she understood why they all thought it best she went to rehab.

"You know, we keep calling it rehab, it really was a beautiful retreat. There were people there who were burnt out from work, even a Mum there who was burnt out from looking after her kids. We were given healthy meals, went for hikes in the mountains, there was a spa and a gym, we did yoga every day." She paused. "Ah yes, so this yoga instructor that cloned my phone, that came into my home, that taught me yoga almost every day for months, that I spilt my heart and feelings to is a psychopath. Can we discuss?"

Gwen and Rory looked over to the kids, checking they were out of earshot. They were in the pool house at Beaudesert, the four kids having a whale of a time with Amelia, Steven and Sylvia in the heated pool. Valerie had brought them a cream tea with all the trimmings, and even made low-sugar scones for the kids.

"Let's not be awkward about this guys." Ruth continued, "I made a mistake by bringing him into my life so easily and you made a mistake for not believing me about being stalked. So, I've not turned my phone on since I've had it back. I wanted to enjoy the journey home, just with my thoughts and lots of coffee – I haven't had caffeine in two weeks. Then when Mum told me my phone had been cloned, I obviously didn't want to use it."

"Ruth I can probably just remove the technology from your phone quite easily. It's probably just a small app that he downloaded, simple enough to remove." Reassured Nathan.

"Thanks, but I've got a plan." Said Ruth conspiratorially. "Unless he's been watching the house, which I doubt as he's probably too scared to get close to us now, as he knows that you all know he kidnapped Winona and Alfie, he doesn't know I'm back yet. So, I was thinking that I turn my phone on and message the group that I'm home and ask for a meet up, see if he bites and follows us."

"Good idea said Luke. "He's not running any classes at his studio right now, his website says they are all cancelled due to unforeseen circumstances, I guess you could call burning down your own home and workplace unforeseen circumstances. He's bound to be on edge and will be keeping an eye out for your phone."

"Yeah. I also told him I was going away for around two weeks just before I left too, so he'll be expecting me to turn the phone back on."

"I think we can do one step further than just asking for a meet up. We should dangle a carrot in-front of him. He wants to destroy us all right? For no other reason than Louise told him she disliked us, we stole lots of data that we shouldn't have and he sees us as a perfect group of people that he can easily torment. He gets satisfaction from psychological and physical torture right? So, what if we hand him one of us on a plate?" Rory was getting excited.

"Ana, I would think you are the hardest to get to and bring down. You have so many walls up around you in every sense of the world, I think he probably doesn't have a plan for you. What if we make up a story about your art gallery losing business and you needing to borrow money. Banks won't lend to you anymore, so you are asking an under the table loan shark type of person for a short-term cash influx to keep the business afloat." Rory looked up excited.

"Yes Rory, I'm happy to lie and sell my soul for the right cause and this of course is the right cause, but how will this lure in Joshua?" Asked Ana, reaching for a scone.

"Jam before cream!" Squealed Gwen horrified, watching Ana slowly smear jam over her scone.

"OK," Continued Rory. "Hear me out. So, Ruth messages the group saying she is home. We all message back with the usual niceties, then we cut to the chase and tell her that some awful things have happened these last two weeks and tell her not to contact Joshua no matter what. Joshua will love reading that as it will feed his psychopathic desire to destroy, corrupt and destabilise the group. We'll agree to meet up and tell her all about it, but only in person because Ana needs to borrow some money from us.."

"Maybe we should leave out the part about Ana needing to borrow money. Surely she'd go to her Dad if she needed to borrow money?" Reasoned Maryam.

"I would, yes." Clarified Ana.

"So, perhaps we target Nathan then?" Vanessa paused, thinking. "He's desperate. Years worth of work have been for nothing. His reputation is in tatters."

"Cheers Ness, I mean that's all pretty close to the truth." Said Nathan sarcastically, feeling sorry for himself.

"Fixing your media problem is another task Nate, right now, we're trying to lure in Joshua right? So, how about we say Nathan is ready to sell the grunt work of his app to some silicon valley company that will use it to build the same app, just without Nathan's name. We can float some figures about, suggesting you're going to sell the work for a few million, a lot less than you value the work at, but hey ho. Mention that the work is now all on your laptop at the farmhouse. Say you're not there at the moment, but will be there in an hour. Joshua will break into the farmhouse to steal Nate's laptop and we will all be there waiting to catch him red handed."

"Yes!" Shouted Nathan. "He's already broken into the farmhouse once before, at least I'm pretty sure it was him and I reckon he orchestrated the break in at my condo in LA too, so I'm pretty sure that's what he's after."

"So, when shall we do this?" Said Vanessa, keen to get started

"Well Ruth's only just got back so perhaps next weekend?" suggested Maryam, well aware that Monday to Friday was busy for most of her friends.

"I cannot live on edge for another week." Vanessa stood up. "Gwen, the person that kidnapped your children is still out there! Ruth, look what he did to you? Nate? He's ruined everything. Today. Now. Please."

Maryam smiled at Vanessa's sudden assertiveness. "Fine with me." She said.

"Thanks, hun, but you don't need to be my advocate. I'm seeing everything clearer than ever. I'm well rested and really, I'm good to go now."

"Fine by me I think, if you let me just check with Laura. Shall I Amelia to come over?" said Luke.

"Its ok thanks, Ill go over there and speak to her in private if that's ok, so she doesn't feel put on the spot in front of everyone. But probably a yes from me." Said Rory walking over to the pool.

"Fine." Said Ana

"Me too, but I'm staying here with the kids and security." Confirmed Ana.

"Luke and Rory just gave me a thumbs up from the pool side, so let me grab my phone from my room and we can get started."

Chapter 47

Gwen stayed at Beaudesert and they moved back to the house with the kids, Amelia, Dominic and Gwen's security. Sylvia asked Valerie to make the kids some dinner and they made themselves comfortable in the games room. Dominic was assigned to stay at Beaudesert to be form of base communications and he was to do any quick research or hacking if necessary.

The seven remaining friends headed over to the farmhouse and were there by 5pm and started the WhatsApp communication. Dominic had

Ruth's phone as the location tracker was still on it, so they had pre-agreed how the conversation was going to play out before they left. They tried not to get through the conversation too quickly, so that it didn't seem staged. More difficult than they thought when they were sat next to each other, knowing exactly what they were going to say. How long would it normally take to think about how to respond and then actually type it and send it. Most people were probably going about their everyday tasks during a group message conversation, like making cups of tea, going to the loo, having conversations, so they had to leave pauses for all of that. By 5.45, they had agreed that they were going to meet at the farmhouse by 7, hoping that would give Joshua enough time to consider his options and choose the option of the farm house break in.

Maryam and Vanessa positioned themselves in one of the outhouses that faced the barn. it was usually off limits, as per the contract that Nathan signed whenever he stayed there, as it contained farm equipment that was actually used, but the farmer was out in the fields spraying fertiliser on the potatoes, and it looked like he was only halfway through, so would be back late at night, so he'd never know.

Nathan, Ruth and Luke were hidden in different positions in the house. Rory and Ana were sat in the Model Y Tesla they'd driven there in, parked round the back of the house.

Joshua predictably turned up half an hour after their final text, giving himself 45 minutes to search the house for Nathan's laptop, before everyone was due to arrive.

Maryam and Vanessa started the group call as he drove down the driveway to the farmhouse. He parked outside and looked around briefly. He must have known it was a working farm, so the lights on in the main farmhouse a few hundred metres away and the lights of the tractor in the field behind the smaller farmhouse didn't faze him. He went up to the door and let himself in.

"He's got a bloody key!" Whispered Maryam!

"That must be how he broke in last time!" whispered Nathan. "I knew it was him!"

"What do you mean you knew it was him...we've never even met him Nate!" whispered Ana back.

"I'll look into it, I don't understand how he has a key." said Dominic, also on the call.

"OK, we're coming into the house." Whispered Rory. "More man power."

Nathan was hidden behind heavy curtains in the lounge. Not the most original hiding place, but a good one, given how heavy the curtains were. Joshua knew exactly where Nathan and Dominic did their work as he was heading straight through to the dining room. Nathan gave it a few seconds before coming out of his hiding place and quietly following him into the dining room. Knowing Ruth and Luke were also hidden in the dining room gave Nathan more confidence to get closer to Joshua, ready to confront him. But his confidence was short lived. Sensing someone was behind him, Joshua spun round to see Nathan staring at him, like a rabbit caught in headlights. Realising he'd been set up, he looked for a way out. But he looked around for a second too long, as Ruth and Rory flung themselves out of their respective hiding places in the dining room and went to tackle him. Seeing Nathan as the easier target, he threw all of his weight at him and managed to knock him over. "Run!" Shouted Nathan. Signalling to Ruth and Rory that he was fine and they should go after to him and hopefully prompting Luke and Ana to get back into the car and catch up with him.

Luke and Ana saw Joshua running out of the house to his car. Deciding they wouldn't catch him on foot, they ran back to their car.

"What's going on guys? Update." Shouted Dominic desperately.

Ruth and Rory ran out of the farm house just as Joshua had started the car. He reversed away from them quickly, but Ruth was a fast runner. She printed towards Joshua's car, staring him straight in the eyes. No-one noticed Vanessa behind the car.

Running out of the outbuilding, she ran towards Joshua's car, screaming. Joshua knocked her over and carried on reversing straight into the doors of the outbuilding. Maryam screamed, but managed to jump out of the way just in time.

"Joshua stared at what he had just done. The scene in front of him unfolding over the space of 2 seconds. Nathan staggering out of the farm house, Ruth staring at him, pure venom in her eyes, Maryam on her knees, cradling Vanessa's limp body, Rory standing next to her holding his head. The Tesla screaming round from the back of the house. Joshua snarled and sped forwards away from the outbuilding doors, back down the driveway.

Vanessa opened her eyes and started moaning.

"Lay her flat Maryam, lay her flat." Said Ruth calmly. "OK, he drove over her middle half. She could have a broken pelvis and serious internal bleeding. Someone call an ambulance."

"Already done." Said a voice from someone's phone. "ETA 7 minutes."

"Thanks Dom." Said Ruth, not knowing whose phone she was talking to.

"You guys need to follow him. Please go, I'll be fine. I'm not going through this much pain for nothing. GO!"

"I'll stay with her." Nodded Maryam. "You should go,"

Rory, Luke and Nathan jumped in to the car and Ana screeched down the driveway following Joshua.

Chapter 48

"Right, turn right, that's him going down there!" pointed Luke

"Seatbelts?" Ana asked

They all quickly put their seatbelts on, very aware that Ana had done an evasive driving course and they should be fairly safe in her hands, but her love of speed fearlessness wasn't exactly shared by everyone else.

"Do we have a plan?" Asked Luke

"Citizen's arrest when we stop?" Suggested Ana

"That's very civilised of you" Said Ruth. "I was thinking we run him off the road and then we tie him up and pull every hair off that insane head of his and then hand him over to the police, completely naked and devoid of any dignity."

"Thought about this a lot haven't you?" Nathan squeezed her hand.

"He's going towards Linkertons. Yes, he's pulled in, over there in the staff car park." Said Rory.

"Following." Ana said, focused. "Flinging the car behind Joshua, boxing him."

"He's up there, on Stanley's turret!" Shouted Luke, running towards the stairs to get up one of the old Georgian towers. Ruth, Nathan, Ana and Rory following closely behind.

"I've called the police," panted Ana, as they sprinted up the spiral staircase.

They burst through the doors at the top, automatically fanning out to stop him from getting away, although they all knew there was only one way up and down this tower. By the time they got there, Joshua had climbed onto the L of the large Linkertons sign which was placed proudly on top of this tower. He started walking precariously backwards and forwards along the foot long piece of metal.

Ruth walked slowly towards him.

"Joshua. Come down." Ruth spoke calmly, but purposefully.

"GET HER AWAY FROM ME!" Joshua screamed. His walls were down. They were seeing the real Joshua. "I despise you Ruth, I hate you. Don't come near me!"

Shocked at his outburst, Ruth quickly retreated to where the rest of her friends were standing by the door.

Nathan walked forwards with his hand out.

"Joshua, come down, we can talk about this."

"I think we're long past talking Nate!"

"Just come down Joshua and we can talk, or not talk. Either way, it's not safe up there mate."

"MATE?! MATE?! We are not mates. At least not anymore."

"What do you mean not anymore?" Nathan was confused.

"I lived next door to you Nathan, for 18 years. We played together in my flat. We had a great time, until you got a scholarship to that school and you changed. You stopped coming over to play. You stopped inviting me over to play, but you had Ruth over to your place. You stopped talking to me, until eventually, you never even looked at me, never acknowledged me, I was chewing gum under your shoe. I was nothing to you. Our friendship meant nothing and Ruth took over"

"JJ? You're JJ from next door? I didn't know it was you!" Nathan was astonished

"Of course, you didn't, why would you? You probably don't even remember what I looked like!"

"I remember you had fiery red hair."

"Yeah, well my hair is dyed brown now, people always seem to take me more seriously with brown hair."

"Why do all of this JJ"

"DON'T CALL ME THAT! I'm Joshua now. JJ was a pathetic, pitiful wretch of a boy, controlled by his poor excuse for a Mother. He's long gone."

"OK, Joshua." Said Nathan slowly. "Tell me why. I'm sorry I stopped talking to you, but you know I was a child. Didn't we just naturally grow apart? I had homework.to do after school, I needed to do well for my parents."

Two police officers burst through the door to the top of the tower. Assessing the situation, they started to walk slowly towards Joshua.

"I wanted to do well for my Mum too, but as soon as you went to that school, she started comparing me to you. "Nathan's joined orchestra, Nathan plays chess, Nathan's studying so hard with Ruth" Your Mum was always gossiping with my Mum on the landing. She'd always talk about how amazing you and Ruth were, but my Mum never had the same feelings about me. It was always, "Oh JJ never listens in class, JJ doesn't care, I wish JJ was more like Nathan." Do you know how much that hurts?"

"We can't imagine Joshua." Said Ana sympathetically.

"SHUT UP!" Joshua screamed. "You stupid rich bitch! This is about Nathan and Ruth, you were just all happy collateral damage, providing me with an immense amount of entertainment."

"You did all of this because you were jealous of Ruth and I became friends?"

"No, I did this because you ditched me completely. You couldn't see how bad my life was and just left me to be alone and Ruth took you away from me."

"Joshua, I didn't realise how bad your life had become."

"No, of course you couldn't see, you were too involved in your own new life, with sleepovers at Beaudesert, riding on your friends horses, going on holidays skiing with your friends, learning to sail, I mean, why would you notice what was going on across the hallway, when you've got all that in your life."

"I was lucky, yeah, I had rich friends that were happy to include me in their lifestyles, but I still always lived in that same council flat as you and my parents died when I was 18 you know.".

"Oh yes, I did know, I wasn't allowed to forget; the whole block of flats held months' worth of memorial services, memory walks and vigils for them, even did a collection for you at university."

"Which I paid back plus more."

"Oh, look at you, such a saint." Joshua edged towards the edge of the building.

"Joshua, look, we can talk about this." Shouted one of the police officers, a feeble attempt at building up a rapport before the long negotiation of bringing a jumper back inside.

Joshua ignored them.

Nathan ignored them.

"Look, I know I'm not a saint, but I haven't forgotten where I came from. I appreciate everything I have. I give back in so many ways. Please step away from the edge." Nathan pleaded

"Au contraire Nate. You fly around in a private jet, rent out entire homes to live in when you're away from your multi-million-pound condo in LA, shall I go on?"

"What do you want from me Joshua? You knew Ruth's biggest nightmare was being put in an institution when she wasn't crazy and you managed to do that, you have destroyed my reputation to the point that I probably won't get this app up and running and the trauma you have inflicted on the rest of my friends is unforgiveable. What do you want? An apology"

"I don't want an apology. I didn't battle through my teens and wait through my twenties and half my thirties for a mere apology! I want exactly this. I want to see the despair in your eyes. I want to see the hatred of you in your friends eyes. This happened to them because of you, they need to understand that. If you had only been considerate of your old friends from next door, none of this would have happened."

"What happened to you Joshua?" Nathan probed

"Well apart from the fact that I didn't grow up with rich friends? Well, my Mum started verbally abusing me for years. She had to stop work as she had no childcare for me. Yes, your Mum used to look after me whilst she was at work, but because she had to ferry you around everywhere to all your school activities, she wasn't around to look after me. We were so poor, both Mum and I stole from the co-op down the road just to eat. She couldn't get her act together to get any form of benefits until I was 13 and filled in the forms for her. She hated me. She saw me as a parasite that used up her energy. Her resources. Her time. Her money. She put cigarettes out on my skin and told me it was to motivate me to be better at school. She made me get drugs for her, from when I was 12 years old, when she started needing to numb her pain, her boredom, her realisation that had achieved nothing in her worthless life, apart from create a woeful excuse for a son."

Nathan didn't know what to say.

"Ha! You think that stopping me is going to give you peace in your lives?! The game has only just begun!" Joshua called out as he stepped over the edge, falling to his death.

Nathan screamed and screamed and screamed.

Ruth watched the two police officers run to the edge of the tower, gormlessly gaping and wondered what they thought they were going to see. They radioed for back up and ran downstairs, no acknowledgement that the group of friends had just witnessed someone commit suicide.

Nathan had stopped screaming. Ruth, Rory, Ana and Luke scooped him up off the floor and fumbled their way downstairs without saying anything.

Two police cars turned up within 4 minutes and a white tent was erected around Joshua's body. The school caretaker emerged from his house on site, alerted by motion sensors linked to his house. The police filled him in on what had happened and he was hovering about, not sure what he should be doing. The friends all gave their statements to the police and were too, hovering about in silence, not sure what they should be doing.

"'The game has only just begun'…What are we supposed to take from that?!" Luke asked his friends breaking the silence.

"He's just messing with us." Ruth sounded a lot more certain than she felt. "He's lost and he wanted to die thinking that we thought we had lost."

Luke nodded uncertainly.

"He's gone guys. We can all have peace now." Ana said.

Their phones all beeped. They all picked up their phones to see who it was.

"New from the hospital perhaps." Said Luke, unlocking his phone.

"**'The game has only just begun'** But he's dead! I saw his brains spilled out onto the pavement!" Said Ana.

"Do you think he set a text to get sent on a timer?" Asked Rory.

"I'm sure it's possible, but I reckon someone else sent this." Said Nathan

"I thought we were done with this!" Luke looked around. "Someone must be watching us to know when to send this!"

They all looked around, but there were so many emergency services around them, as well as members of the public trying their best to look like they weren't watching, it could have anyone. A white Toyota drove by slowly, as did a number of other cars, taking in the scene, again, trying to look like they weren't being nosy. Dominic called Nathan, who updated him on what had happened. Told him Joshua was gone and they were all safe.

"Nate, I found out how Joshua got that key to the farm." Dominic said.

"Oh great, thanks. How? Let me put you on speakerphone"

"The person that we deal with via the rental website is not the owner, just the housekeeper. The actual property is owned by a business. Kingsley commercial properties Limited."

"Beverley Kingsley's family owns it?!"

"Yes, they bought it about 6 months ago. We've been using that same farm house for years and years. She's been working with Joshua?" Nathan was incredulous. They all were.

Ruth knew now, that the game really had just begun. She had lost months of her life to this man and his games; he had almost broken her. But now she was strong, she was feeling confident and she was pissed off. All Ruth could think of now was vengeance.

Printed in Great Britain
by Amazon

31149832R00119